The Evil People

Being thirteen strange and terrible accounts of Witchcraft, Black Magic and Voodoo

Edited by
Peter Haining

ENSIGN BOOK

AN ENSIGN HORROR

Ensign edition published in MCMLXXIV by
World Distributors (Manchester) Ltd
12 Lever Street, Manchester M60 1TS

First published in Great Britain by
Leslie Frewin Publishers Limited

Copyright © MCMLXVIII by Leslie Frewin
Publishers Limited

Made and printed in Great Britain by
C. Nicholls & Company Ltd
The Philips Park Press, Manchester

SBN 7235 5197 9

For my son
RICHARD
in the hope
that the dark
will hold no
fears for him

Contents

Introduction

I burn the Devil-cake, proclaim
These adorations of Thy name.
Behold this bleeding breast of mine
Gashed with the sacramental sign!
I stanch the blood; the wafer soaks
It up, and the high priest invokes!
This Bread I eat. This oath I swear
As I enflame myself with prayer:
'There is no grace: there is no guilt:
This is the Law: DO WHAT THOU WILT!'

So WROTE ALEISTER Crowley, the self-confessed devotee of Black Magic who was called 'The Great Beast' and 'The Wickedest Man in the World'. He devoted his life to probing the secrets of the Dark Powers and through drugs, sex orgies, blood sacrifices and sacrilegious rituals learned as much of the ways of evil as any man in recent times.

The subject of Black Magic – and Witchcraft and Voodoo come to that – is endlessly fascinating to many people, though very few of them would choose to investigate it as deeply as Aleister Crowley did. Their interest stems from the curiosity in all of us about the constant struggle between the powers of good and evil – but it is a curiosity that does not allow for actual experimenting or involvement.

So they – and we – do the next best thing: read stories of the rites. Like those which form this collection. For here you can meet witches and warlocks, satanists and the disciples of Voodoo without running any actual risks – apart from a certain shaking of the nerves.

Together these stories – most of which have never been anthologised before – form a Black Book of the secrets of evil. If you have ever wanted to know what it needs to be a warlock let the most famous macabre writers in the world give you some instructions . . . in thirteen unholy lessons.

P H

Broxbourne, Hertfordshire
November 1967

I

The Nocturnal Meeting

W Harrison Ainsworth

Although the literature of Witchcraft and Black Magic — in the form of records and ancient manuscripts — goes back almost to the dawn of history, it is only in comparatively recent times that it has been used extensively as the subject matter for fiction. One of the first people to write novels of Witchcraft and the lore of the supernatural was William Harrison Ainsworth (1805–82) who produced a great book, The Lancashire Witches, in 1849. Ainsworth, a writer of considerable talent, published much of his work initially in weekly episodes and consequently built up a tremendous popular following. Contemporary critics, however, condemned most of his writing as gruesome and pandering to the lowest tastes — and this may well have played a major part in his work being virtually unknown today. It is my pleasure in beginning this anthology to reintroduce him to readers with a story of the dark arts which, though it contains numerous elements of fantasy, has still lost none of its power over the years.

THE MERRYMAKING WAS at its height when Mistress Nutter and her daughter slipped quietly away and climbed up the staircase to their room. On gaining the head of the stairs they paused for a moment to listen to the sounds arising from below. Suddenly was heard a loud cry, and the music, which had waxed fast and furious in order to keep pace with the dancers, ceased at once, showing some interruption had occurred, while from the confused noise that ensued, it was evident the sudden stoppage had been the result of an accident. With blanched cheek Alizon listened, scarcely daring to look at her mother, whose stern expression of countenance, revealed by the lamp she held in her hand, almost frightened her; and it was a great relief to hear the voices and laughter of people begin again in a few moments.

Mistress Nutter moved on; but a new feeling of uneasiness came over Alizon as she followed her down the long dusky corridor, in the direction of the mysterious chamber where they were to pass the night. The fitful flame of the lamp fell upon many a grim painting depicting the sufferings of the early martyrs: and these ghastly representations did not serve to reassure her. The grotesque carvings on the panels and ribs of the vaulted roof likewise impressed her with vague terror, and there was one large piece of sculpture – Saint Theodora subjected to diabolical temptation, as described in the Golden Legend – that absolutely scared her. Their footsteps echoed hollowly overhead, and more than once, deceived by the sound, Alizon turned to see if anyone was behind them. At the end of the corridor lay the room once occupied by the superior of a religious establishment, and still known from that circumstance as the 'Abbot's Chamber'. Connected with this apartment was a beautiful oratory, and though now no longer applied to purposes of worship, it still contained sculptured ornaments and painted glass in its casements.

The abbot's room was allotted to Alizon's friend, Dorothy Assheton; and from its sombre magnificence, as well as the ghostly tales connected with it, had impressed her with so much superstitious misgiving, that she besought Alizon to share her couch with her, but the young girl did not dare to assent. Just, however, as Mistress Nutter was about to enter her own room, Dorothy appeared in the corridor, and, calling to Alizon to stay a moment, flew quickly towards her, and renewed the proposition. Alizon looked at her mother, but the latter decidedly, and somewhat sternly, negatived it.

The young girls then said good-night, kissing each other affectionately, after which Alizon entered the room with Mistress Nutter, and the door was closed. Two tapers were burning on the dressing-table, and their light fell upon the carved figures of the wardrobe, which still exercised the same weird influence over her. Mistress Nutter neither seemed disposed to retire to rest immediately, nor willing to talk, but sat down, and was soon lost in thought. After a while, an impulse of curiosity which she could not resist prompted Alizon to peep into the closet, and pushing aside the tapestry, partly drawn over the entrance, she held the lamp forward, so as to throw its light into the little chamber. Mistress Nutter had noticed the movement, and instantly and somewhat sharply recalled her.

As Alizon obeyed, a slight tap was heard at the door. The young girl turned pale, for in her present frame of mind any little matter affected her. Nor were her apprehensions materially allayed by the entrance of Dorothy who, looking white as a sheet, said she did not dare to remain in her own room, having been terribly frightened, by seeing a monkish figure in mouldering white garments, exactly resembling one of the carved images on the wardrobe, issue from behind the hangings on the wall, and glide into the oratory, and she entreated Mistress Nutter to let Alizon go back with her. The request was peremptorily refused, and the lady, ridiculing Dorothy for her fears, bade her return; but she still lingered.

Unable otherwise to get rid of the terrified intruder, whose presence was an evident restraint to her, Mistress Nutter, at length, consented to accompany her to her room, and convince her of the folly of her fears, by an examination of the oratory. Alizon went with them, her mother not choosing to leave her behind, and indeed she herself was most anxious to go.

The abbot's chamber was large and gloomy, nearly twice the size of the room occupied by Mistress Nutter, but resembling it in many respects, as well as in the dusky hue of its hangings and furniture, most of which had been undisturbed since the days of Paslew. The very bed, of carved oak, was that on which he had slept, and his arms were still displayed upon it, and on the painted glass of the windows. As Alizon entered she looked round with apprehension, but nothing occurred to justify her uneasiness. Having raised the arras, from behind which Dorothy averred the figure had issued, and discovering nothing but a panel of oak; with a smile of incredulity, Mistress Nutter walked boldly towards the oratory, the two girls, hand in hand, following tremblingly after her; but no fearful object met their view. A dressing-table, with a large mirror upon it, occupied the spot where the altar had formerly stood; but, in spite of this, and of the other furniture, the little place of prayer, as has previously been observed, retained much of its original character, and seemed more calculated to inspire sentiments of devotional awe than any other.

After remaining for a short time in the oratory, during which she pointed out the impossibility of any one being concealed there, Mistress Nutter assured Dorothy she might rest quite easy that nothing further would occur to alarm her, and recommending her to lose the sense of her fears as speedily as she could in sleep, took her departure with Alizon.

But the recommendation was of little avail. The poor girl's heart died within her, and all her former terrors returned and with additional force. Sitting down, she looked fixedly at the hangings till her eyes ached, then covering her face with her hands and scarcely daring to breathe, she listened intently for the slightest sound. A rustle would have made her scream – but all was still as death, so profoundly quiet, that the very hush and silence became a new cause of disquietude and, longing for some cheerful sound to break it, she would have spoken aloud but from a fear of hearing her own voice. A book lay before her and she essayed to read it, but in vain. She was ever glancing fearfully round – ever listening intently. This state could not endure for ever, and feeling a drowsiness steal over her she yielded to it, and at length dropped asleep in her chair. Her dreams, however, were influenced by her mental condition, and slumber was no refuge, as promised by Mistress Nutter, from the hauntings of terror.

At last a jarring sound aroused her, and she found she had been awakened by the clock striking twelve. Her lamp required trimming and burnt dimly, but by its imperfect light she saw the arras move. This could be no fancy, for the next moment the hangings were raised, and a figure looked from behind them; and this time it was not the monk, but a female robed in white. A glimpse of the figure was all Dorothy caught, for it instantly retreated, and the tapestry fell back to its place against the wall.

Scared by this apparition, Dorothy rushed out of the room so hurriedly that she forget to take her lamp, and made her way, she scarcely knew how, to the adjoining chamber. She did not tap at the door, but trying it, and finding it unfastened, opened it softly, and closed it after her, resolved if the occupants of the room were asleep not to disturb them, but to pass the night in a chair, the presence of some living beings beside her sufficing, in some degree, to dispel her terrors. The room was buried in darkness, the tapers being extinguished.

Advancing on tiptoe she soon discovered a seat, when what was her surprise to find Alizon asleep within it. She was sure it was Alizon — for she had touched her hair and face, and she felt surprised that the contact had not awakened her. Still more surprised did she feel that the young girl had not retired to rest. Again she stepped forward in search of another chair when a gleam of light suddenly shot from one side of the bed and the tapestry, masking the entrance to the closet, was slowly drawn aside. From behind it, the next moment, appeared the same female figure, robed in white, that she had previously beheld in the abbot's chamber. The figure held a lamp in one hand, and a small box in the other; and, to her unspeakable horror, disclosed the livid and contorted countenance of Mistress Nutter.

Dreadful though undefined suspicions crossed her mind, and she feared, if discovered, she would be sacrificed to the fury of this strange and terrible woman. Luckily, where she stood, though Mistress Nutter was revealed to her, she herself was screened from view by the hangings of the bed, and looking around for a hiding-place, she observed that the mysterious wardrobe, close behind her, was open, and without a moment's hesitation, she slipped into the covert and drew the door to, noiselessly. But her curiosity over-mastered her fear and, firmly believing some magical rite was about to be performed, she sought for means of seeing it; nor was she long in discovering a small eyelet-hole in the carving which commanded the room.

Unconscious of any other presence than that of Alizon, whose stupor appeared to occasion her no uneasiness, Mistress Nutter placed the lamp upon the table, made fast the door and, muttering some unintelligible words, unlocked the box. It contained two singularly shaped glass vessels, the one filled with a bright sparkling liquid, and the other with a greenish-coloured unguent. Pouring forth a few drops of the liquid into a glass near her, Mistress Nutter swallowed them, and then taking some of the unguent upon her hands, proceeded to anoint her face and neck with it, exclaiming as she did so, 'Emen hetan! Emen hetan!' — words that fixed themselves upon the listener's memory.

Wondering what would follow, Dorothy gazed on, when she suddenly lost sight of Mistress Nutter, and after looking for her as far as her range of vision, limited by the aperture, would extend, she became convinced that she had left the room. All remaining quiet, she ventured, after a while, to quit her hiding-place and, flying to Alizon, tried to awaken her, but in vain. The poor girl retained the same moveless attitude and appeared plunged in a deathly stupor.

Much frightened, Dorothy resolved to alarm the house, but some fears of Mistress Nutter restrained her, and she crept towards the closet to see whether that dread lady could be there. All was perfectly still; and somewhat emboldened, she returned to the table, where the box, which was left open and its contents unguarded, attracted her attention.

What was the liquid in the phial? What could it do? These

embers. Around the fire were ranged, in a wide circle, an assemblage of men and women, but chiefly the latter, and of these almost all old, hideous, and of malignant aspect, their grim and sinister features looking ghastly in the lurid light. Above them, amid the smoke and steam, wheeled bat and flitter-mouse, horned-owl and screech-owl, in mazy circles. The weird assemblage chattered together in some wild jargon, mumbling and muttering spells and incantations, chanting fearfully with hoarse cracked voices a wild chorus and, anon, breaking into a loud and long continued peal of laughter. Then there was more mumbling, chattering, and singing, and one of the troop producing a wallet, hobbled forward.

She was a fearful old crone; hunchbacked, toothless, bleareyed, bearded, halt, with huge gouty feet swathed in flannel. As she cast in the ingredients one by one, she chanted thus:

> *Head of monkey, brain of cat,*
> *Eye of weasel, tail of rat,*
> *Juice of mugwort, mastic, myrrh —*
> *All within the pot I stir.*

'Well sung, Mother Mould-heels,' cried a little old man, whose doublet and hose were of rusty black, with a short cloak of the same hue, over his shoulders. 'Well sung, Mother Mould-heels,' he cried, advancing as the old witch retired, amidst a roar of laughter from the others, and chanting as he filled the cauldron:

> *Here is the foam from a mad dog's lips,*
> *Gather'd beneath the moon's eclipse,*
> *Ashes of a shroud consumed,*
> *And with deadly vapour fumed,*
> *These within the mess I cast —*
> *Stir the cauldron — stir it fast.*

A red-haired witch then advanced, and, taking from her wallet a small clay image, tricked out in attire intended to resemble that of a man, plunged several pins deeply into its breast, singing as she did so, thus:

> *In his likeness it is moulded,*
> *In his vestments 'tis enfolded*
> *Ye may know it, as I show it!*
> *In its breast sharp pins I stick,*
> *And I drive them to the quick*
> *They are in – they are in –*
> *And the wretch's pangs begin*
> *Now his heart*
> *Feels the smart;*
> *Through his marrow,*
> *Sharp as arrow,*
> *Torments quiver.*
> *He shall shiver,*
> *He shall burn,*
> *He shall toss, and he shall turn,*
> *Unavailingly.*
> *Aches shall rack him,*
> *Cramps attack him;*
> *He shall wail,*
> *Strength shall fail,*
> *Till he die*
> *Miserably!*

As the crone retired, another witch advanced, and sung thus:

> *Over mountain, over valley, over woodland, over waste,*
> *On our gallant broomsticks riding, we have come with frantic*
> *haste,*
> *And the reason of our coming, as ye wot well, is to see*
> *Who this night, as new-made witch, to our ranks shall added be.*

A wild burst of laughter followed this address, and another wizard succeeded, chanting thus:

> *Beat the water, Demdike's daughter!*
> *Till the tempest gather o'er us;*
> *Till the thunder strike with wonder*
> *And the lightnings flash before us!*
> *Beat the water, Demdike's daughter!*
> *Ruin seize our foes, and slaughter!*

As the words were uttered, a woman stepped from out the circle, and throwing back the grey-hooded cloak in which she was enveloped, disclosed the features of Elizabeth Device, one of Mistress Nutter's servants and a woman of evil repute. Her presence in that fearful assemblage occasioned no surprise to Alizon, though it increased her horror.

As the man concluded his chant, clouds gathered thickly overhead, obscuring the stars that had hitherto shone down from the heavens. The wind suddenly arose, but in lieu of dispersing the vapours, it seemed only to condense them. A flash of forked lightning cut through the air, and a loud peal of thunder rolled overhead.

Then the whole troop sang together:

> *Beat the water, Demdike's daughter!*
> *See the tempest gathers o'er us;*
> *Lightning flashes – thunder crashes,*
> *Wild winds sing in lusty chorus!*

For a brief space the storm raged fearfully. The wind raved around the ruined pile, but its breath was not felt within it, and the rain was heard descending in deluging showers without, though no drop came through the open roof. The thunder shook the walls and pillars of the old fabric, and threatened to topple them down from their foundations, but they resisted the shocks. The lightning played around the tall spire springing from this part of the fane, and ran down from its shattered summit to its base, without doing any damage. The red bolts struck the ground innocuously, though they fell at the very feet of the weird assemblage, who laughed wildly at the awful tumult.

Whilst the storm was at its worst, while the lightning was flashing fiercely, and the thunder rattling loudly, another witch, with a chafing-dish in her hand, advanced towards the fire and placing the pan upon it, threw certain herbs and roots into it, chanting:

> *Here is juice of poppy bruised,*
> *With black hellebore infused;*
> *Here is mandrake's bleeding root,*
> *Mixed with moonshade's deadly fruit;*
> *Viper's bag, with venom fill'd*
> *Taken ere the beast was kill'd;*
> *Adder's skin, and raven's feather,*
> *With shell of beetle blent together:*
> *Dragonwort and barbatus,*
> *Hemlock black and poisonous;*
> *Horn of hart, and storax red,*
> *Lapwing's blood, at midnight shed*
> *In the heated pan they burn,*
> *And to pungent vapours turn,*
> *By this strong suffumigation,*
> *By this potent invocation,*
> *Spirits! I compel you here!*
> *All who list my call appear!*

After a moment's pause, she resumed as follows:

> *White-robed brethren, who of old,*
> *Nightly paced yon cloisters cold,*
> *Sleeping now beneath the mould,*
>   *I bid ye rise.*
> *Abbots! by the weakling fear'd,*
> *By the credulous revered,*
> *Who this mighty fabric rear'd!*
>   *I bid ye rise!*
> *And thou last and guilty one!*
> *By thy lust of power undone,*
> *Whom in death thy fellows shun!*
>   *I bid thee come!*
> *And thou, fair one, who disdain'd*
> *To keep the vows thy lips had feign'd;*
> *And thy snowy garments stain'd!*
>   *I bid thee come!*

During this invocation, the glee of the assemblage ceased, and they looked around in hushed expectation of the result. Slowly then did a long procession of monkish forms, robed in white, glide along the aisles, and gather round the altar. The brass-covered stones within the presbytery were lifted up, as if they moved on hinges, and from the yawning graves beneath them arose solemn shapes, sixteen in number, each with mitre on head and crosier in hand, which likewise proceeded to the altar. Then a loud cry was heard, and from a side chapel burst the monkish form, in mouldering garments, which Dorothy had seen enter the oratory, and which would have mingled with its brethren at the altar, but they waved it off menacingly. Another piercing shriek followed, and a female shape, habited like a nun, and of surpassing loveliness, issued from the opposite chapel, and hovered near the fire. Content with this proof of her power, the witch waved her hand, and the long shadowy train glided off as they came. The ghostly abbots returned to their tombs, and the stones closed over them.

The storm had well-nigh ceased, the thunder rolled hollowly at intervals, and a flash of lightning now and then licked the walls. The weird crew had resumed their rites, when the door of the Lacy Chapel flew open, and a tall female figure came forward.

Alizon doubted if she beheld aright. Could that terrific woman in the strangely-fashioned robe of white, girt by a brazen zone graven with mystic characters, with a long glittering blade in her hand, infernal fury in her wildly-rolling orbs, the livid hue of death on her cheeks, and the red brand upon her brow – could that fearful woman, with the black, dishevelled tresses floating over her bare shoulders, and whose gestures were so imperious, be Mistress Nutter? Mother no longer, if it indeed were she! How came she there amid that weird assemblage? Why did they so humbly salute her, and fall prostrate before her, kissing the hem of her garment? Why did she stand proudly in the midst of them, and extend her hand, armed with the knife, over them? Was she their sovereign mistress, that they bent so lowly at her coming, and rose so reverentially at her bidding? Was this terrible woman, now seated on a dilapidated tomb, and regarding the dark conclave with the eye of a queen who held their lives in her hands – was she her mother? Oh, no! no! – it could not be! It must be some fiend that usurped her likeness.

Still, though Alizon thus strove to discredit the evidence of her senses, and to hold all she saw to be delusion, and the work of darkness, she could not entirely convince herself, but imperfectly recalling the fearful vision she had witnessed during her former stupor, began to connect it with the scene now passing before her. The storm had wholly ceased, and the stars again twinkled down through the shattered roof. Deep silence prevailed, broken only by the hissing and bubbling of the cauldron.

Alizon's gaze was riveted upon her mother, whose slightest gestures she watched. After numbering the assemblage thrice, Mistress Nutter majestically arose, and motioning the old crone who had conducted the ceremony towards her, some words passed between them, the import of which did not reach the listener's ear. In conclusion, however, Mistress Nutter exclaimed aloud, in accents of command – 'Go, bring it at once, the sacrifice must be made.' And on this the other woman hobbled off to one of the side chapels.

A mortal terror seized Alizon, and she could scarcely draw breath. Dark tales had been told her that unbaptised infants were sometimes sacrificed by witches, and their flesh boiled and devoured at their impious banquets, and dreading lest some such atrocity was now about to be practised, she mustered all her resolution, determined, at any risk, to interfere and, if possible, prevent its accomplishment.

In another moment, the witch returned, bearing something living, wrapped in a white cloth, which struggled feebly for liberation, apparently confirming Alizon's suspicions, and she was about to rush forward, when Mistress Nutter, snatching the bundle from the old witch, opened it, and disclosed a beautiful bird, with plumage white as driven snow, whose legs were tied together, so that it could not escape. Conjecturing what was to follow, Alizon averted her eyes and, when she looked round again, the bird had been slain. Mistress Nutter held the ensanguined knife aloft, and casting some ruddy drops upon the glowing embers, pronounced, as they hissed and smoked, the following adjuration:

> *Thy aid I seek, infernal Power!*
> *Be thy word sent to Malkin Tower,*
> *That the beldame old may know*
> *Where I will, thou'dst have her go –*
> *What I will, thou'dst have her do!*

27

An immediate response was made by an awful voice issuing apparently from the bowels of the earth.

> *Thou who seek'st the Demon's aid,*
> *Know'st the price that must be paid.*

The queen witch rejoined:

> *I do. But grant the aid I crave,*
> *And that thou wishest thou shalt have.*
> *Another worshipper is won,*
> *Thine to be when all is done.*

After a moment's pause, the voice added,

> *I have done as thou hast will'd —*
> *Now be thy path straight fulfill'd.*

'It shall be,' replied Mistress Nutter, whose features gleamed with fierce exultation. 'Bring forth the proselyte!' she shouted. And at the words, her swarthy serving-man, Black-adder, came forth from the Lacy Chapel, leading a young girl by the hand.

At the sight of the girl, a loud cry of rage and astonishment burst from Elizabeth Device, and she rushed forward.

'This is my chilt!' screamed Elizabeth. 'She canna be bap-teesed without my consent, an' ey refuse it. Ey dunna want her to be a witch — at least not yet awhile. What may yo here, yo little plague?'

'Ey wur brought here, Mother,' replied the girl, who was named Jennet.

'Then get whoam at once, and stop there,' rejoined Elizabeth, furiously.

'Nay, eyst nah go just yet,' replied Jennet. 'Ey'd fain be a witch as well as yo.'

'Ho! ho! ho!' laughed the voice from below.

'Nah, nah – ey forbid it!' shrieked Elizabeth; 'ye shanna be bapteesed. Whoy ha' he brought her here, Madam?' she added to Mistress Nutter. 'Yo ha' stolen her fro' me. Boy ey protest agen it.'

'Your consent is not required,' replied Mistress Nutter, waving her off. 'Your daughter is anxious to become a witch. That is enough.'

'She is not owd enough to act for herself,' said Elizabeth.

'Age matters not,' replied Mistress Nutter.

'What mun ey do to become a witch?' asked Jennet.

'You must renounce all hopes of heaven,' replied Mistress Nutter, 'and devote yourself to Satan. You will then be baptised in his name, and become one of his worshippers. You will have power to afflict all persons with bodily ailments – to destroy cattle – blight corn – burn dwellings – and, if you be so minded, kill those who hate, or who molest you. Do you desire to do all this?'

'Eigh, that ey do,' replied Jennet. 'Ey ha' more pleasure in evil than in good, an' wad rather see folk weep than laugh; an' if ey had the power, ey wad so punish them os jeer at me, that they should rue it to their deein' day.'

'All this you shall do, and more,' rejoined Mistress Nutter. 'You renounce all hopes of salvation, then, and devote yourself, soul and body, to the Powers of Darkness?'

Elizabeth, who was still kept at bay by one of the witches, shaking her arms, and gnashing her teeth in impotent rage, now groaned aloud; but ere Jennet could answer, a piercing cry was heard, which thrilled through Mistress Nutter's bosom, and Alizon, rushing from her place of concealment, passed through the weird circle, and stood beside the group in the midst of it.

'Forbear, Jennet!' she cried; 'forbear! Pronounce not those

impious words, or you are lost for ever. Come with me, and I will save you.'

'Sister Alizon!' cried Jennet, staring at her in surprise, 'what makes you here?'

'Do not ask – but come,' cried Alizon, trying to take her hand.

'Oh! what is this?' cried Mistress Nutter, now partly recovered from the consternation and astonishment into which she had been thrown by Alizon's unexpected appearance. 'Why are you here? How have you broken the chains of slumber in which I bound you? Fly – fly – at once, this girl is past your help. You cannot save her. She is already devoted. Fly. I am powerless to protect you here.'

'Ho! ho! ho!' laughed the voice.

'Do you not hear that laughter?' cried Mistress Nutter, with a haggard look. 'Go!'

'Never without Jennet,' replied Alizon, firmly.

'My child – my child – on my knees I implore you to depart,' cried Mistress Nutter, throwing herself before her – 'You know not your danger – oh, fly – fly!'

But Alizon continued inflexible.

'Yo are caught i' your own snare, Madam,' cried Elizabeth Device, with a taunting laugh. 'Sin Jennet mun be a witch, Alizon con be bapteesed os well. Your consent is not required – and age matters not – ha! ha!'

'Curses upon thy malice,' cried Mistress Nutter, her voice trembling. 'What can be done in this extremity?'

'Nothing,' replied the voice. 'Jennet is mine already. If not brought hither by thee, or by her mother, she would have come of her own accord. I have watched her, and marked her for my own. She is fated!'

As the words were uttered, the shade of the abbot glided forwards, and touching the shuddering child upon the brow with its finger, vanished with a lamentable cry.

'Kneel, Jennet,' cried Alizon; 'kneel, and pray!'

'To me,' replied the voice; 'she can bend to no other power. Alice Nutter, thou hast sought to deceive me, but in vain. I bade thee bring thy daughter here, and in place of her thou offerest me the child of another, who is mine already. I am not to be thus trifled with. Thou knowest my will. Sprinkle water over her head, and devote her to me.'

With a terrible scream Mistress Nutter sank to the ground and beat her hands on the earth. And all hope fled from her heart.

2

The Peabody Heritage

H P Lovecraft

———◆———

2

Despite the fact that his work was almost completely un-known during his lifetime, the reputation of H P Lovecraft has grown steadily over the past thirty years and he is now frequently mentioned in the same breath as such famous fellow Americans as Poe, Bierce and Hawthorne. A strange retiring man, Lovecraft lived in Rhode Island and absorbed himself completely in the study of history and the Occult. His work was mainly published in small amateur publica-tions and consequently he lived in penury for much of the time. He died in 1937 and it was only then, thanks to the publicising of his talent by young enthusiasts like August Derleth and Donald Wandrei, that the general public slowly became aware of his strange and fantastic talent. This story, a grisly tale of Witchcraft in a rural American community, was left unfinished by Lovecraft at his death and has been brilliantly completed by August Derleth. It is yet another splendid epitaph to this neglected writer who has at last found his true place in the annals of macabre literature.

I NEVER KNEW my great-grandfather Asaph Peabody, though I was five years old when he died on his great old estate north-east of the town of Wilbraham, Massachusetts. There is a childhood memory of once visiting there, at a time when the old man was lying ill; my father and mother mounted to his bed-room, but I remained below with my nurse, and never saw him. He was reputed to be wealthy, but time whittles away at wealth as at all things, for even stone is mortal, and surely mere money could not be expected to withstand the ravages of the ever-increas-ing taxation, dwindling a little with each death. And there were many deaths in our family, following my great-grandfather's in 1907. Two of my uncles died after – one was killed on the Western front, and another went down on the *Lusitania*. Since a third uncle had died before them, and none of them had ever married, the estate fell to my father on my grandfather's death in 1919.

My father was not a provincial, though most of his forbears had been. He was little inclined to life in the country, and made no effort to take an interest in the estate he had inherited, beyond spending my great-grandfather's money on various investments in Boston and New York. Nor did my mother share any of my own interest in rural Massachusetts. Yet neither of them would consent to sell it, though on one occasion, when I was home from college, my mother did propose that the property be sold, and my father coldly dismissed the subject; I remember his sudden freezing – there is no more fitting word to describe his reaction – and his curious reference to 'the Peabody heritage' – as well as his carefully phrased words: 'Grandfather predicted that one of his blood would recover the heritage.' My mother had asked scornfully: 'What heritage? Didn't your father just about spend it all?' to which my father made no reply, resting his case in his icy inference that there were certain good reasons why the property could not be sold, as if it were entailed beyond any process of law. Yet he never went near the property; the taxes were paid regularly by one Ahab Hopkins, a lawyer in Wilbraham, who made reports on the property to my parents, though they always ignored them, dismissing any suggestion of 'keeping up' the property by saying it would be like 'throwing good money after bad'.

The property was abandoned, to all intent and purpose; and abandoned it remained. The lawyer had once or twice made a half-hearted attempt to rent it, but even a brief boom in Wilbraham had not brought more than transient renters to the old homestead, and the Peabody place yielded inexorably to time and the weather. It was thus in a sad state of disrepair when I came into the property on the sudden death by motor-car accident of both my parents in the autumn of 1929. Nevertheless, what with the decline in property values which took place subsequent to the inauguration of the depression that year, I determined to sell my Boston property and refurbish the house outside of Wilbraham for my own use. I had enough of a competence on my parents' death so that I could afford to retire from the practice of law, which had always demanded of me greater preciseness and attention than I wished to give to it.

Such a plan, however, could not be implemented until at least part of the old house had been got ready for occupation once more. The dwelling itself was the product of many generations. It had been built originally in 1787, at first as a simple colonial house, with severe lines, an unfinished second storey, and four impressive pillars at the front. But, in time, this had become the basic part of the house, the heart, as it were. Subsequent generations had altered and added to it – at first by the addition of a floating stairway and a second storey; then by various ells and wings, so that at the time I was preparing to make it my residence, it was a large, rambling structure, which occupied over an acre of land, adding to the house itself the lawn and gardens, which were in as great a state of disuse as the house.

The severe colonial lines had been softened by age and less regardful builders, and the architecture was no longer pure, for gambrel roof vied with mansard roof, small-paned windows with large, figured and elaborately sculptured cornices with plain, dormers with unbroken roof. Altogether the impression the old house conveyed was not displeasing, but to anyone of architectural sensibilities, it must have appeared a woeful and unhappy conglomeration of architectural styles and kinds of ornament. Any such impression, however, must surely have been softened by the tremendously spreading ancient elms and oaks which crowded upon the house from all sides save the garden, which had been taken over among the roses, so long grown untended, by young poplar and birch trees. The whole effect of the house, therefore, despite the accretions of time and differing tastes, was of faded magnificence, and even its un-painted walls were in harmony with the great-girthed trees all around.

The house had no less than twenty-seven rooms. Of these, I selected a trio in the south-east corner to be rehabilitated, and all that autumn and early winter, I drove up from Boston to keep an eye on the progress of the venture. Cleaning and waxing the old wood brought out its beautiful colour, installing electricity removed the dark gloom of the rooms, and only the waterworks delayed me until late winter; but by February the twenty-fourth, I was able to take up my residence in the ancestral Pea-body home. Then for a month I was occupied with plans for the rest of the house, and, though I had initially thought of having some of the additions torn down and the oldest parts of the structure retained, I soon abandoned this project in favour of the decision to keep the house as it was, for it had a pervasive charm born, no doubt, of the many generations which had lived there, as well as of the essence of the events which had taken place within its walls.

Within that month, I was quite taken with the place, and what had been primarily a temporary move was gladly embraced as a lifelong ideal. But alas, this ideal grew to such proportions that it soon brought about a grandiose departure which subtly altered my direction and threw me off the track on a course I had never wished to take. This scheme was the determination to move to the family vault, which had been cut into a hillside within sight of the house, though away a little from the highway which passed in front of the estate, the remains of my parents, who had been decently interred in a Boston plot. This was in addition to my resolve to make an attempt also to bring back to the United States the bones of my dead uncle, which reposed somewhere in France, and thus re-unite the family, as far as possible, on the ancestral acres near Wilbraham. It was just such a plan as might occur to a bachelor who was also a reclusive solitary, which I had become in the short space of that month, surrounded by the architect's drawings and the lore of the old house which was about to begin a new lease of life in a new era far, far removed from that of its simple beginnings.

It was in pursuit of this plan that I made my way one day in March to the family vault, with the keys the lawyer for the estate had delivered into my hands. The vault was not obtrusive; indeed, no part of it was ordinarily visible except the massive door, for it had been built into a natural slope, and was almost concealed by the trees which had grown without pruning for decades. The door and the vault, as well, had been built to last for centuries; it dated back almost as far as the house, and for many generations every member of the Peabody family from old Jedediah, the first to occupy the house, onward, had been interred here. The door offered me some resistance, since it had not been opened for years, but at length it yielded to my efforts and the vault lay open to me.

The Peabody dead lay in their coffins -- thirty-seven of them, some in cubicles, some outside. Some of the cubicles where the earliest Peabodies had lain held only the remains of coffins, while that reserved for Jedediah was completely empty, with not even the dust to show that coffin and body had once reposed in that place. They were in order, however, save for the casket which bore the body of my great-grandfather Asaph Peabody; this seemed curiously disturbed, standing out of line with the others, among those more recent ones -- my grandfather's and my one uncle's -- which had no cubicles of their own but were simply on a ledge extended outward from the cubicled wall. Moreover, it seemed as if someone had lifted or attempted to lift the cover, for one of the hinges was broken, and the other loosened.

My attempt to straighten my great-grandfather's coffin was instinctive, but in so doing the cover was still further jostled and slipped partially off, revealing to my startled gaze all that remained of Asaph Peabody. I saw that through some hideous error, he had been buried face downward – I did not want to think, even at so long a time after his death, that the old man might have been buried in a cataleptic state and so suffered a painful death in that cramped, airless space. Nothing but bones survived, bones and portions of his garments. Nevertheless, I was constrained to alter mistake or accident, whichever it might be; so I removed the cover of the coffin, and reverently turned skull and bones over so that the skeleton of my great-grand-father lay in its rightful position. This act, which might have seemed grisly in other circumstances, seemed only wholly nat-ural, for the vault was aglow with the sunlight and shadows that speckled the floor through the open door, and it was not at that hour a cheerless place. But I had come, after all, to ascertain how much room remained in the vault, and I was gratified to note that there was ample room for both my parents, my uncle – if his remains could be found and brought thither from France – and, finally, myself.

I prepared, therefore, to carry on with my plans, left the vault well locked behind me, and returned to the house ponder-ing ways and means of bringing my uncle's remains back to the country of his birth. Without delay, I wrote to the authorities in Boston on behalf of the disinterment of my parents, and to those of the county in which I now resided for permission to re-inter my parents in the family vault.

The singular chain of events which seemed to centre about the old Peabody homestead began, as nearly as I can recall, on that very night. True, I had had an oblique kind of warning that something might be amiss with the old house, for old Hopkins, on surrendering his keys, had asked me insistently when I came to take possession whether I was sure I wanted to take this step, and had seemed equally intent upon pointing out that the house was 'a lonely sort of place', that the farming neighbours 'never looked kindly on the Peabodys', and that there had always been a 'kind of difficulty keeping renters there'. It was one of those places, he said, almost with relish at making a distinct point, 'to which nobody ever goes for a picnic. You'll never find paper plates or napkins *there!*' – a plethora of ambiguities which nothing could persuade the old man to reduce to facts, since, evidently, there were no facts, but that the neighbours frowned upon an estate of such magnitude in the midst of what was otherwise good farming land. This, in truth, stretched out on all sides of my property of but forty acres, most of it woods – a land of neat fields, stone walls, rail fences, along which trees grew and shrubbery made adequate cover for birds. An old man's talk, I thought it, given rise by his kinship with the farmers who surrounded me: solid, sturdy Yankee stock, no whit different from the Peabodys, save that they toiled harder and perhaps longer.

But on that night, one on which the winds of March howled and sang among the trees about the house, I became obsessed with the idea that I was not alone in the house. There was a sound not so much of footsteps as of *movement* from somewhere upstairs, one that defies description, save that it was as of someone moving about in a narrow space, forward and back, forward and back. I remember that I went out in the great dark space into which the floating stairway descended, and listened to the darkness above; for the sound seemed to drift down the stairs, sometimes unmistakable, sometimes a mere whisper; and I stood there listening, listening, listening, trying to identify its source, trying to conjure up from my rationalisation some explanation for it, since I had not heard it before, and concluded at last that in some fashion a limb of a tree must be driven by the wind to brush against the house, forward and back. Settled on this, I returned to my quarters, and was no more disturbed by it – not that it ceased, for it did not, but that I had given it a rational excuse for existence.

I was less able to rationalise my dreams that night. Though ordinarily not at all given to dreams, I was literally beset by the most grotesque phantasms of sleep, in which I played a passive role and was subjected to all manner of distortions of time and space, sensory illusions, and several frightening glimpses of a shadowy figure in a conical black hat with an equally shadowy creature at his side. These I saw as through a glass, darkly, and the twilit landscape as through a prism. Indeed, I suffered not so much dreams as fragments of dreams, none of them having either beginning or ending, but inviting me into an utterly bizarre and alien world, as through another dimension of which I was not aware in the mundane world beyond sleep. But I survived that restless night, if somewhat haggardly.

On the very next day I learned a most interesting fact from the architect who came out to discuss my plans for further renovation, a young man not given to the quaint beliefs about old houses common to isolated, rural areas. 'One who came to look at the house would never think,' he said, 'that it had a secret room – well hidden – would you?' he said, spreading his drawings before me.

'And has it?' I asked.

'Perhaps a "priest's hole",' he guessed. 'For runaway slaves.'

'I've never seen it.'

'Nor I. But look here . . .' And he showed me on the plans he had reconstructed from the foundations and the rooms as we knew them, that there was a space unaccounted for along the north wall upstairs, in the oldest part of the house. No priest's hole, certainly; there were no Papists among the Peabodys. But runaway slaves – perhaps. If so, however, how came it there so early, before there were enough slaves to make the run for Canada to justify the room's coming into being? No, not that either.

'Can you find it, do you think?' I asked.

'It has to be there.'

And so indeed it was. Cleverly concealed, though the absence of a window in the north wall of the bedroom ought to have warranted an earlier examination. The door to it was hidden in the finely-wrought carvings which decorated that entire wall, which was of red cedar; had one not known the room must have been there, one would hardly have seen the door which had no knob and worked only by pressure upon one of the carvings, which the architect found, not I, for I have never had an adeptness at things of that kind. However it lay rather within the province of an architect than my own and I paused only long enough to study the rusty mechanism of the door before stepping into the room.

It was a small confining space. Yet it was not as small as a priest's hole; a man could walk upright in it for a distance of ten feet or so, though the slant of the roof would cut off any walking in the direction opposed to it. The long way, yes; across to the wall, no. What was more, the room bore every sign of having been occupied in past time, for it was left undisturbed, there were still books and papers about, as well as chairs which had been used at a small desk against one wall.

The room presented the most singular appearance. Though it was small, its angles seemed to be awry, as if the builder were subtly determined to confound its owner. Moreover, there were curious designs drawn upon the floor, some of them actually cut into the planking in a crudely barbarous fashion, roughly circular in plan, with all manner of oddly repellent drawings around the outer and inner edges. There was a similar repulsiveness about the desk, for it was black, rather than brown, and it had the surprising appearance of having been burned; it looked, indeed, as if it served in more than the capacity of a desk. On it, moreover, was a stack of what looked at first glance to be very ancient books, bound in some sort of leather, as well as a manuscript of some kind, likewise bound.

There was little time for any examination, however, for the

architect was with me and, having seen all he wished, which was just sufficient to verify his suspicion of the room's existence, he was eager to be off.

'Shall we plan to eliminate it, cut in a window?' he asked, and added, 'Of course, you won't want to keep it.'

'I don't know,' I answered. 'I'm not sure. It depends on how old it is.'

If the room were as ancient as I thought it to be, then I would be quite naturally hesitant to destroy it. I wanted a chance to poke around it a little, to examine the old books. Besides, there was no haste; this decision did not need to be made at once; there were other things the architect could do before either of us need think about the hidden room upstairs. It was there that the matter rested.

I had fully intended to return to the room next day, but certain events intervened. In the first place, I spent another very troubled night, the victim of recurrent dreams of a most disturbing nature, for which I could not account, since I had never been given to dreams except as a concomitant of illness. These dreams were, perhaps not unnaturally, of my ancestors, particularly of one long-bearded old fellow, wearing a conical black hat of strange design, whose face, unfamiliar to me in dream, was in actuality that of my great-grandfather Asaph, as a row of family portraits in the lower hall verified next morning. This ancestor seemed to be involved in an extraordinary progression through the air, quite as if he were flying. I saw him walking through walls, walking on the air, silhouetted among treetops. And wherever he went, he was accompanied by a large black cat which had the same ability to transcend the laws of time and space. Nor did my dreams have any progression or even, each within itself, any unity; they were a mixed-up sequence of scenes in which my great-grandfather, his cat, his house, and his property took part as in unrelated tableaux. They were distinctly related to my dreams of the previous night, and accompanied again by all the extra-dimensional trappings of those first nocturnal experiences, differing only in that they possessed greater clarity. These dreams insistently disturbed me throughout the night.

I was thus in no mood to learn from the architect that there would be some further delay in the resumption of work at the Peabody place. He seemed reticent or reluctant to explain, but I pressed him to do so, until at last he admitted that the workmen he had hired had all notified him early this morning that none of them wished to work on this 'job'. Nevertheless, he assured me, he would have no difficulty hiring some inexpensive Polish or Italian labourers from Boston, if I would be a little patient with him. I had no alternative, but, in fact, I was not as much annoyed as I pretended to be, for I began to have certain doubts about the wisdom of making all the alterations I had intended. After all, a part of the old house must necessarily stand with no more than re-inforcement, for much of the charm of the old place lay in its age; I adjured him, therefore, to take his time, and went out to make such purchases as I had intended to make when I came into Wilbraham.

I had hardly begun to do so before I was aware of a most sullen attitude on the part of the natives. Whereas, heretofore, they had either paid me no attention at all, since many of them did not know me, or they had greeted me perfunctorily, if they had made my acquaintance, I found them on that morning of one mind – no one wished to speak to me or to be seen speaking to me. Even the storekeepers were unnecessarily short, if not downright unpleasant, their manner suggesting plainly that they would appreciate my taking my trade elsewhere. It was possible, I reflected, that they had learned of my plans to renovate the old Peabody house, and might be opposed to it on twin grounds – either that the renovation would contribute to the destruction of its charm, or that it would, on the other hand, give another and longer lease of life to a piece of property that surrounding farmers would much have preferred to cultivate, once the house and the woods were gone.

My first thoughts, however, soon gave way to indignation. I was not a pariah, and I did not deserve to be shunned like one, and when, finally, I stopped in at the office of Ahab Hopkins, I unburdened myself to him rather more volubly than was my custom, even though, as I could see, I made him uneasy.

'Ah, well, Mr Peabody,' he said, seeking to soothe my ruffled composure, 'I would not take that too seriously. After all, these people have had a grievous shock, and they are in an ugly, suspicious mood. Besides, they are basically a superstitious lot. I am an old man, and I have never known them to be otherwise.'

Hopkins's gravity gave me pause. 'A shock, you say. You must forgive me – I've heard nothing.'

He favoured me with a most curious look, at which I was quite taken aback. 'Mr Peabody, two miles up the road from your place lives a family by the name of Taylor. I know George well. They have ten children. Or perhaps I had better say "had". Last night, their second youngest, a child of slightly over two years of age, was taken from his bed and carried off without a trace.'

'I am sorry to hear it. But what has that got to do with me?'

'Nothing, I'm sure, Mr Peabody. But you're a comparative stranger here, and, well – you must know it sooner or later – the name of Peabody is not looked on with pleasure – in fact, I may say it is hated – by many people of the community.'

I was astounded and did not attempt to hide it. 'But why?'

'Because there are many people who believe every kind of gossip and muttered talk, no matter how ridiculous it is,' Hopkins answered. 'You are an old enough man to realise that it is so, even if you're unfamiliar with our rural countryside, Mr Peabody. There were all manner of stories common about your great-grandfather, when I was a child, and, since during the years of his incumbency of the homestead, there were certain ugly disappearances of little children, of whom no trace was ever found, there is possibly a natural inclination to connect these two events – a new Peabody on the homestead, and a recurrence of a kind of event associated with another Peabody's residence there.'

'Monstrous!' I cried.

'Undoubtedly,' Hopkins agreed with an almost perverse amiability, 'but so it is. Besides, it is now April. Walpurgis Night is scarce a month away.'

I fear my face must have been so blank as to disconcert him.

'Oh, come, Mr Peabody,' said Hopkins with false joviality, 'you are surely aware that your great-grandfather was consider-ed to be a warlock!'

I took my leave of him, gravely disturbed. Despite my shock and outrage, despite my indignation at the manner in which the natives showed their scorn and – yes, fear – of me, I was even more upset by the nagging suspicion that there was a disquieting logic to the events of the previous night and this day. I had dreamed of my great-grandfather in strange terms indeed, and now I heard him spoken of in far more significant terms. I knew only enough to know that the natives had looked upon my great-grandfather superstitiously as the male counterpart of a witch – a warlock or wizard; by whatever name they called him, so they had seen him. I made no further attempt to be even decently courteous to the natives who turned their heads when I came walking toward them, but got into my car and drove out to the homestead. There my patience was still further tried, for I found nailed to my front door a crude warning – a sheet of tablet paper upon which some illiterate, ill-intentioned neigh-bour had scrawled in pencil: '*Git out – or els.*'

Possibly because of these distressing events, my sleep that night was far more troubled by dreams than it had been on pre-vious nights. Save for one major difference – there was more continuity in the scenes I saw while I tossed in restless slumber. Again it was my great-grandfather, Asaph Peabody, who occupied them, but he seemed now to have grown so sinister in appearance as to be threatening, and his cat moved with him with the hair of its neck ruffled, its pointed ears forward, and tail erect – a monstrous creature, which glided or floated along beside or behind him. He carried something – something white, or flesh-coloured, but in the murkiness of my dream would not permit me to recognise it. He went through woods, over countryside, among trees; he travelled in narrow passageways, and once, I was certain, he was in a tomb or vault. I recognised, too, certain parts of the house. But he was not alone in his dreams – lingering always in the background was a shadowy, but monstrous Black Man – not a Negro, but a man of such vivid blackness as to be literally darker than night, but with flaming eyes which seemed to be of living fire. There were all manner of lesser creatures about the old man – bats, rats, hideous little beings which were half human, half rat. Moreover, I was given to auditory hallucinations simultaneously, for from time to time, I seemed to hear muffled crying, as if a child were in pain, and, at the same time, a hideous, cackling laughter, and a chanting voice saying: 'Asaph will *be* again. Asaph will *grow* again.'

Indeed, when at last I woke from this continuing nightmare, just as the dawn light was making itself manifest in the room, I could have sworn that the crying of a child still sounded in my ears, as if it came from within the very walls itself. I did not sleep again, but lay wide-eyed, wondering what the coming night would bring, and the next, and the next after that.

The coming of the Polish workmen from Boston put my dreams temporarily from my mind. They were a stolid, quiet lot. Their foreman, a thick-set man named Jon Cieciorka, was matter-of-fact and dictatorial with the men under him; he was a well-muscled fellow of fifty or thereabouts, and the three men whom he directed moved in haste at his command, as if they feared his wrath. They had told the architect that they could not come for a week, the foreman explained, but another job had been postponed, and here they were; they had driven up from Boston after sending the architect a telegram. But they had his plans, and they knew what must be done.

Their very first act was to remove the plaster from the north wall of the room immediately beneath the hidden room. They had to work carefully, for the studding which supported the second storey could not be disturbed, nor need it be. Plaster and lathing, which, I saw as they began, was of that old-fashioned kind made by hand, had to be taken off and replaced; the plaster had begun to discolour and to break loose years before, so that the room was scarcely habitable. It had been so, too, with that corner of the house which I now occupied, but, since I had made greater changes there, the alterations had taken longer.

I watched the men work for a little while, and had just become accustomed to the sounds of their pounding, when suddenly, they ceased. I waited a moment, and then started up and went out into the hall. I was just in time to see all four of them, clustered near the wall, cross themselves superstitiously, back away a little, and then break and run from the house. Passing me, Cieciorka flung an epithet at me in horror and anger. Then they were out of the house, and while I stood as if rooted to the spot, I heard their car start and leap away from my property.

Utterly bewildered, I turned towards where they had been working. They had removed a considerable section of the plaster and lathing; indeed, several of their tools were still scattered about. In their work, they had exposed that section of the wall which lay behind the baseboard, and all the accumulated detritus of the years which had come to rest in that place. It was not until I drew close to the wall that I saw what they must have seen and understood what had sent these superstitious louts running in fear and loathing from the house.

For at the base of the wall, behind the baseboard, there lay, among long yellowed papers half gnawed away by mice, yet still bearing on their surfaces the unmistakably cabalistic designs of some bygone day, among wicked implements of death and destruction -- short, dagger-like knives rusted by what must surely have been blood -- *the small skulls and bones of at least three children!*

I stared unbelievingly, for the superstitious nonsense I had heard only a day before from Ahab Hopkins now took on a more sinister cast. So much I realised on the instant. Children had disappeared during my great-grandfather's aegis; he had been suspected of wizardry, of witchcraft, of playing roles in which the sacrifice of little children was an integral part; now here, within the walls of his house, were such remains as lent weight to the native suspicions of his nefarious activities!

Once my initial shock had passed, I knew I must act with despatch. If this discovery were made known, then indeed my tenure here would be bitterly unhappy, made so by the god-fearing natives of the neighbourhood. Without hesitating further, I ran for a cardboard box and, returning to the wall with it, gathered up every vestige of bone I could find, and carried this gruesome burden to the family vault, where I emptied the bones into the cubicle which had once held the remains of Jedediah Peabody, now long since gone to dust. Fortunately, the small skulls disintegrated, so that anyone searching there would find only the remains of someone long dead, and only an expert would have been able to determine the origin of the bones which remained sufficiently unimpaired to offer any key. By the time any report from the Polish workmen came back to the architect, I would be able to deny the truth of them, though for this report I was destined to wait in vain, for the fear-ridden Poles never revealed to the architect a word of their real reason for deserting their job.

I did not wait to learn this from the architect, who was bound eventually to find someone who would undertake such alteration as I wished made, but guided by an instinct I did not know I possessed, I made my way to the hidden room, carrying a powerful flashlight, determined to subject it to the most painstaking examination. Almost at once upon entering it, however, I made a spine-chilling discovery; though the marks the architect and I had made in our brief foray into the room were still identifiably evident, there were other, more recent marks which suggested that someone – or something – had been in this room since I had last entered it. The marks were plain to be seen – of a man, bare of foot, and, equally unmistakably, the prints of a cat. But these were not the most terrifying evidences of some sinister occupation – they began out of the north-east corner of the curiously angled room, at a point where it was impossible for a man to stand, and scarcely high enough for a cat; yet it was here that they materialised in the room, and from this point that they came forward, proceeding in the direction of the black desk – where there was something far worse, though I did not notice it until I was almost upon the desk in following the footsteps.

The desk had been freshly stained. A small pool of some viscous fluid lay there, as if it had boiled up out of the wood – scarcely more than three inches in diameter, next to a mark in the dust as if the cat or a doll or a bundle of some kind had lain there. I stared at it, trying to determine what it might be in the glow of my flashlight, sending my light ceiling-ward to detect, if possible, any opening through which rain might have come, until I remembered that there had been no rainfall since my first and only visit to this strange secret room. Then I touched my index finger to the pool and held it in the light. The colour was red – the colour of blood – and simultaneously I knew without being told that this was what it was. Of how it came there I dared not think.

By this time the most terrifying conclusions were crowding to mind, but without any logic. I backed away from the desk, pausing only long enough to snatch up some of the leather-

bound books, and the manuscript which reposed there; and
with these in my possession, I retreated from the room into the
more prosaic surroundings outside – where the rooms were not
constructed of seemingly impossible angles, suggesting dimensions beyond the knowledge of mankind. I hastened almost
guiltily to my quarters below, hugging the books carefully to my
bosom.

Curiously, as soon as I opened the books, I had an uncanny
conviction that I knew their contents. Yet I had never seen them
before, nor, to the best of my knowledge, had I ever encountered
such titles as *Malleus Maleficarum* and the *Daemonialitas* of Sin-
istrari. They dealt with witch-lore and wizardry, with all manner of spells and legends, with the destruction of witches and
warlocks by fire, with their methods of travel – 'Among their chief
operations are being bodily transported from place to place . . .
seduced by the illusions and phantasms of devils, do actually,
as they believe and profess, ride in the night-time on certain
beasts . . . or simply walk upon the air out of the openings built
for them and for none other. Satan himself deludes in dreams
the mind which he holds captive, leading it through devious
ways. . . . They take the unguent, which they made at the devil's
instruction from the limbs of children, particularly of those
whom they have killed, and anoint with it a chair or a broomstick; whereupon they are immediately carried up into the air,
either by day or by night, and either visibly or, if they wish,
invisibly . . .' But I read no more of this, and turned to Sinist-
rari.

Almost at once my eye fell upon this disturbing passage –
'*Promittunt Diabolo statis temporibus sacrificia, et oblationes;
singulis quindecim diebus, vel singulo mense saltem, necem alicujus
infantis, aut mortale veneficium, et singulis hebdomadis alia mala
in damnum humani generis, ut grandines, tempestates, incendia,
mortem animalium . . .*' setting forth how warlocks and witches
must bring about, at stated intervals, the murder of a child, or

some other homicidal act of sorcery, the mere reading of which filled me with an indescribable sense of alarm, as a result of which I did no more than glance at the other books I had brought down, the *Vitae sophistrarum* of Eunapius, Anania's *De Natura Daemonum*, Stampa's *Fuga Satanae*, Bouget's *Discours des Sorciers*, and that untitled work by Olaus Magnus, bound in a smooth black leather, which only later I realised was human skin.

The mere possession of these books betokened a more than ordinary interest in the lore of witchcraft and wizardry; indeed, it was such manifest explanation for the superstitious beliefs about my great-grandfather which abounded in and about Wilbraham, that I understood at once why they should have persisted for so long. Yet there must have been something more, for few people could have known about these books. What more? The bones in the wall beneath the hidden chamber spoke damningly for some hideous connection between the Peabody house and the unsolved crimes of other years. Even so, this was surely not a public one. There must have been some overt feature of my great-grandfather's life which established the connection in their minds, other than his reclusiveness and his reputation for parsimony, of which I knew. There was not likely to be any key to the riddle among these things from the hidden room, but there might well be some clue in the files of the Wilbraham *Gazette*, which were available in the public library.

Accordingly, half an hour later found me in the stacks of that institution, searching through the back issues of the *Gazette*. This was a time-consuming effort, since it involved a blind search of issue after issue during the later years of my great-grandfather's life, and not at all certain to be rewarding, though the newspapers of his day were less hampered and bound by legal restrictions than those of my own time. I searched for over an hour without coming upon a single reference to Asaph Peabody, though I did pause to read accounts of the 'outrages' perpetrated upon people – primarily children – of the countryside in the vicinity of the Peabody place, invariably accompanied by editorial queries about the 'animal' which was 'said to be a large black creature of some kind, and it has been reported to be of different sizes – sometimes as large as a cat, and sometimes as big as a lion' – which was a circumstance no doubt due solely to the imagination of the reporting witnesses, who were principally children under ten, victims of mauling or biting, from which they had made their escape, happily more fortunate in this than younger children who had vanished without trace at intervals during the year in which I read: 1905. But throughout all this, there was no mention of my great-grandfather; and, indeed, there was nothing until the year of his death.

Then, and only then, did the editor of the *Gazette* put into print what must have represented the current belief about Asaph Peabody. 'Asaph Peabody is gone. He will long be remembered. There are those among us who have attributed to him powers which belonged rather more to an era in the past than to our own time. There was a Peabody among those charged at Salem; indeed, it was from Salem that Jedediah Peabody removed when he came to build his home near Wilbraham. The pattern of superstition knows no reason. It is perhaps mere coincidence that Asaph Peabody's old black cat has not been seen since his death, and it is undoubtedly mere ugly rumour that the Peabody coffin was not opened before interment because there was some alteration in the body tissues or in the conventions of burial to make such opening unwise. This is again lending credence to old wives' tales – that a warlock must be buried face downward and never thereafter disturbed, save by fire. . . .'

This was a strange, oblique method of writing. Yet it told me much, perhaps uncomfortably more than I had anticipated. My great-grandfather's cat had been looked upon as his familiar – for every witch or warlock has his personal devil in any shape it might care to assume. What more natural than my great-grandfather's cat should be mistaken for his familiar, for it had evidently in life been as constant a companion to him as it was in my dreams of the old man? The one disturbing note struck by the editorial comment lay in the reference to his interment, for I knew what the editor could have not have known – that Asaph Peabody had indeed been buried face downward. I knew more – that he had been disturbed, and should not have been. And I suspected yet more – that something other than myself walked at the old Peabody homestead, walking in my dreams and over the countryside and in the air!

That night, once more, the dreams came, accompanied by that same exaggerated sense of hearing, which made it seem as if I were attuned to cacophonous sound from other dimensions. Once again my great-grandfather went about his hideous business, but this time it seemed that his familiar, the cat, stopped several times and turned to face squarely at me, with a wickedly triumphant grin on its evil face. I saw the old man in a conical black hat and a long black robe walking from woodland seemingly through the wall of a house, coming forth into a darkened room, spare of furnishings, appearing then before a black altar, where the Black Man stood waiting for the sacrifice which was too horrible to watch, yet I had no alternative, for the power of my dreams was such that I must look upon this hellish deed. And I saw him and his cat and the Black Man again, this time in the midst of a deep forest, far from Wilbraham, together with many others, before a large outdoors altar, to celebrate the Black Mass and the orgies that followed upon it. But they were not always so clear; sometimes the dreams were only arrow-swift descents through unlimited chasms of strangely coloured twilight and bafflingly cacophonous sound, where gravity had no meaning, chasms utterly alien to nature, but in which I was always singularly perceptive on an extra-sensory plane, able to hear and see things I would never have been aware of while waking. Thus I heard the eldritch chants of the Black Mass, the screams of a dying child, the discordant music of pipes, the inverted prayers of homage, the orgiastic cries of celebrants, though I could not always see them. And on occasion, too, my dreams conveyed portions of conversations, snatches of words, meaningless of themselves, but capable of dark and disquieting explication.

'Shall he be chosen?'

'By Belial, by Beelzebub, by Sathanus . . .

'Of the blood of Jedediah, of the blood of Asaph, companioned by Balor.'

'Bring him to the Book!'

Then there were those curious figments of dreams in which I myself appeared to be taking part, particularly one in which I was being led, alternately by my great-grandfather and by the cat, to a great black-bound book in which were written names in glowing fire, countersigned in blood, and which I was instructed to sign, my great-grandfather guiding my hand, while the cat, whom I heard Asaph Peabody call Balor, having clawed at my wrist to produce blood into which to dip the pen, capered and danced about. There was about this dream one aspect which had a more disturbing bond to reality. In the course of the way through the woods to the meeting place of the coven, the path led beside a marsh where we walked in the black mud of the sedge, near to foetid slough in a place where there was a charnel odour of decay; I sank into the mud repeatedly in that place, though neither the cat nor great-grandfather seemed to more than float upon its surface.

And in the morning, when at last I awoke after sleeping over long, I found upon my shoes, which had been clean when I went to bed, a drying black mud which was the substance of my dream. I started from bed at the sight of them, and followed the tracks they had made easily enough, tracing them backwards, out of the room, up the stairs, into the hidden room on the second storey – and, once there, inexorably, to that same bewitched corner of peculiar angle from which the footprints in the dust had led into the room! I stared in disbelief, yet my eyes did not deceive me. This was madness, but it could not be denied. Nor could the scratch on my wrist be wished out of existence.

I literally reeled from the hidden room, beginning at last vaguely to understand why my parents had been loath to sell the Peabody homestead; something had come down to them of its lore from my grandfather, for it must have been he who had had great-grandfather buried with his face downward in the family crypt. And, however much they may have scorned the superstitious lore they had inherited, they were unwilling to chance its defiance. I understood, too, why periods of rental had failed, for the house itself was a sort of focal point for forces beyond the comprehension or control of any one person, if indeed any human being; and I knew that I was already infected with the aura of the habitation, that, indeed, in a sense I was a prisoner of the house and its evil history.

I now sought the only avenue of further information open to me. The manuscript of the journal kept by my great-grandfather. I hastened to it directly, without pausing for breakfast, and found it to be a sequence of notes, set down in his flowing script, together with clippings from letters, newspapers, magazines, and even books, which had seemed to him pertinent, though these were peculiarly unconnected, yet all dealing with inexplicable events – doubtless, in great-grandfather's eyes, sharing a common origin in witchcraft. His own notes were spare, yet revealing.

'Did what had to be done today. J taking on flesh, incredibly. But this is part of the lore. Once turned over, all begins again. The familiar returns, and the clay takes shape again a little more with each sacrifice. To turn him back would be futile now. There is only the fire.'

And again:

'Something in the house. A cat? I see him, but cannot catch him.'

'Definitely a black cat. Where he came from, I do not know. Disturbing dreams. Twice at a Black Mass.'

'In dream the cat led me to the Black Book. Signed.'

'In dream an imp called Balor. A handsome fellow. Explained the bondage.'

And soon after:

'Balor came to me today. I would not have guessed him the same. He is as handsome a cat as he was a young imp. I asked him whether this was the same form in which he had served J. He indicated that it was. Led the way to the corner with a strange and extra-dimensional angle which is the door to outside. J had so constructed it. Showed me how to walk through it . . .

I could bear to read no further. Already I had read far too much.

I knew now what had happened to the remains of Jedediah Peabody. And I knew what I must do. However fearful I was of what I must find, I went without delay to the Peabody crypt, entered it, and forced myself to go to the coffin of my great-grandfather. There, for the first time, I noticed the bronze plate attached beneath the name of Asaph Peabody, and the engraving upon it: 'Woe betide him who disturbs his rest!'

Then I raised the lid.

Though I had every reason to expect what I saw, I was horrified no less. For the bones I had last seen were terribly altered. What had been but bone and fragments, dust and tatters of clothing, had begun a shocking alteration. Flesh was beginning to grow once again on the remains of my great-grandfather, Asaph Peabody — flesh that took its origin from the evil upon which he had begun to live anew when I had so witlessly turned over his mortal remains — and from that other thing within his coffin – the poor, shrivelling body of that child which, though it had vanished from the home of George Taylor less than ten days ago, already had a leathern, parchment appearance, as if it were drained of all substance, and partially mummified!

I fled the vault, numb with horror, but only to build the pyre I knew I must gather together. I worked feverishly, in haste lest someone surprise me at my labours, though I knew that the people had shunned the Peabody homestead for decades. And then, this done, I laboured alone to drag Åsaph Peabody's coffin and its hellish contents to the pyre, just as, decades before, Asaph himself had done to Jedediah's coffin and what it had contained! Then I stood by, while the holocaust consumed coffin and contents, so that I alone heard the high shrill wail of rage which rose from the flames like the ghost of a scream.

All that night the diminishing ashes of that pyre still glowed. I saw it from the windows of the house.

And inside, I saw something else.

A black cat which came to the door of my quarters and leered wickedly in at me.

And I remembered the path through the marsh I had taken, the muddied footprints, the mud on my shoes. I remembered the scratch on my wrist, and the Black Book I had signed. Even as Asaph Peabody had signed it.

I turned to where the cat lurked in the shadows and called it gently. 'Balor!'

It came and sat on its haunches just inside the door.

I took my revolver from the drawer of my desk and deliberately shot it.

It kept right on regarding me. Not so much as a whisker twitched.

Balor. One of the lesser devils.

This, then, was the Peabody heritage. The house, the grounds, the woods – these were only the superficial, material aspects of the extra-dimensional angles in the hidden room, the path through the marsh to the coven, the signatures in the Black Book. . . .

Who, I wonder, after I am dead, if I am buried as the others were, will turn me over?

3

The Witch's Vengeance

W B Seabrook

*There cannot be many writers who have had such a close
personal experience of the Black Arts as W B Seabrook, a
famous American explorer-author who lived during the first
half of the century. He wandered endlessly around the world
and saw Black Magic in Africa, Witchcraft in Europe and
was even initiated into a Voodoo cult in Haiti – the first
white man ever to be allowed to share the secrets of this
ritual. The book which he wrote about his experiences,*
Voodoo Island, *is still considered thirty years later to be one
of the most authentic ever written on the subject. In this
story, however, Mr Seabrook has taken Witchcraft as his
theme and written a sinister tale of the power of its devotees.*

THE QUARREL BETWEEN Mère Tirelou and my young friend
Philippe Ardet grew out of the fact that he had fallen in love
with Maguelonne, the old woman's granddaughter.

Although Maguelonne was past nineteen, by far the prettiest
girl in the village, she had no suitors among the local youths, for
the native peasants of Les Baux, this savage mountain hamlet in
the south of France which I had been visiting at intervals for
years, were steeped in superstition and believed that old Mère
Tirelou was a *sorcière*, a sort of witch.

Maguelonne, orphaned by the war, lived alone with the old
woman in an ancient tumbledown stone *mas*, somewhat isolated
from the village proper, among the ruins of the seigniorial castle
close above it, and gossip whispered that Mère Tirelou had involved the girl, willingly or unwillingly, in her dark practices.
They were not persecuted or hated – in fact the peasants and
shepherds of Les Baux and the surrounding mountainside sometimes consulted Mère Tirelou in certain emergencies – but save
for such special consultations, paid for usually with a rabbit, a

jug of wine or oil, the old beldam and her granddaughter 'apprentice', if such she really was, were generally avoided if not actually disliked and feared.

Philippe, however, who considered himself to be now of the great world – he had been to technical school in Marseilles and was working in an aeroplane plant at Toulon – regarded all this local superstition as stuff and nonsense. He had come up vacationing from Toulon on his motor-cycle. We had known each other at Les Baux the previous summer. He and I were now staying at the same little hotel, the Hotel René, perched on the edge of the cliff, run by Philippe's aunt, Madame Plomb, and her husband Martin. And Philippe, as I have said, had fallen in love with Maguelonne.

This was the situation, briefly outlined, when the strange series of events began which first involved me only as a chance onlooker, but finally as an active participant.

They began one hot mid-afternoon when I lay reading in my room, which was in an angle of the wall with windows overlooking the valley and a side window immediately above the medieval rampart gate from which the road serpentined downward.

Close beneath this window, all at once, I heard and recognised Mère Tirelou's querulous croaking voice raised angrily, and Philippe's in reply, half amiable, half derisive.

It was hazard rather than eavesdropping, impossible not to hear them, and then after some muttering the old woman raised her voice again, but this time in such a curious, unnatural tone that I got up to see what was occurring.

They were standing in the sunshine just beneath the window, he tall, blondish, ruddy, tousle-haired, bareheaded, in knickers and sports shirt; she grey, bent and hawk-like – bat-like, rather, in her Arlésienne *coiffe* and cloak, with arms outstretched barring his path. And she was intoning a weird, singsong doggerel, at the same time weaving in the air with her claw-like hands:

Go down, go down, my pretty youth,
But you will not come up again.
Tangled foot will twist and turn,
And tangled brain will follow.
You will go down, my pretty one,
But you will not come up again.
So tangle, tangle, twist and turn,
Cobwebs and spider webs are woven.

She was now no longer barring Philippe's path but standing aside, inviting him to pass, so that her back was turned to me, while Philippe stood so that I could see his face and the expressions which flitted over it – first an interested, incredulous, surprised attention as if he couldn't believe his own ears, then a good-humoured but derisive and defiant grin as the old woman repeated her doggerel.

'No, no, Mère Tirelou,' he said laughing. 'You can't scare me off with stuff like that. Better get a broomstick if you want to drive me away. Save your cobwebs and incantations for Bléo and the shepherds.'

So with a defiant, gay salute and an *au revoir* he was off down the road whistling, while the old woman screamed after him, 'Down, down, down you go, but not up, my pretty boy; not up, not up, not up!'

I watched Philippe descending the winding road into the valley while Mère Tirelou, leaning over the parapet, watched him too, until he became tiny far below and disappeared behind the orchard wall which skirts the road by the pavilion of the Reine-Jeanne. Then she picked up her stick, called Bléo her dog, and hobbled in through the gate.

'So,' thought I, 'that old woman really believes herself a witch, and probably thinks she has put an effective curse on Philippe!'

But it didn't occur to me to be in the least disturbed. I knew, or thought I knew, a good deal about witchcraft technically. I believed it all reduced finally to suggestion and autosuggestion. I had known it to produce tangible results, but only in cases when the victim himself (usually among primitives or savages) was deeply superstitious and consequently amenable to fear. I felt absolutely sure that complete, hard-headed, sceptical disbelief, derision, laughter, constituted a stronger 'counter-magic' than any amount of exorcism and holy water, and therefore it did not occur to me for an instant that Philippe could be in the slightest danger.

Holding these convictions, and therefore regarding the safe return of Philippe as a foregone conclusion, I thought little more of the matter that afternoon; finished my reading, dined early, strolled to the top of the cliff to watch the sunset and went early to bed.

Usually after ten o'clock at night the whole village of Les Baux, including the interior of the Hotel René, is sound asleep and silent as the grave. It was the noise of hurrying footsteps clattering along the stone floor of the hotel corridor which awoke me late in the night, but at the same time I heard lowered voices in the road beneath my window, saw lights flashing; heard sabots clacking along the cobbled street.

I struck a light, saw that it was shortly past midnight, dressed and went downstairs. Martin Plomb was talking to a group of neighbours. His wife was standing in the doorway, wrapped in a quilted dressing-gown.

'What has happened?' I asked her.

'We are worried about Philippe,' she replied. 'He went for a walk this afternoon down in the valley, and he hasn't returned. They are going to search for him. We thought nothing of it that he didn't come back for dinner, but it is now past midnight and we are afraid he may have had an accident.'

Already the men, in groups of twos and threes, some with old-fashioned farm lanterns, a few with electric flash lamps, were starting down the mountain side. I joined Martin Plomb, who was at the gate instructing them to go this way or that and to keep in touch with one another by shouting. He himself was going to search upward on the other slope, towards the Grotte des Fées where Philippe sometimes climbed, fearing that he might have fallen down a ravine. I went along with him. . . .

It was just before dawn, after hours of fruitless search, that we heard a different shouting from the head of the valley. I could not distinguish the words, but Martin immediately said, 'They've found him.' We worked our way across and climbed toward the road along which we now could see lights flashing, returning toward Les Baux.

They were carrying Philippe on an improvised litter made with two saplings and pine branches interwoven. He was conscious; his eyes were open; but he seemed to be in a stupor and had been unable, they said, to explain what had happened to him. No bones were broken nor had he suffered any other serious physical injury, but his clothes were badly torn, particularly the knees of his knickerbockers, which were ripped and abraded as if he had been dragging himself along on his hands and knees.

They all agreed as to what had probably happened: he had been climbing bareheaded among the rocks in the heat of the late afternoon and had suffered an *insolation*, a prostrating but not fatal sunstroke, had partially recovered and in seeking help, still delirious, had lost his way. He should be all right in a day or two, Martin said. They would have a doctor up from Arles in the morning.

Of course I had thought more than once that night about Mère Tirelou and had considered mentioning the matter to Martin Plomb, but his explanation was so reasonable, adequate, natural, that it seemed to me absurd now to view the episode as anything more than a pure coincidence, so I said nothing.

It was dawn when we reached Les Baux and got Philippe to

bed, and when I awoke towards noon the doctor had already come and gone.

'He had a bad stroke,' Martin told me. 'His head is clear — but there's still something the matter that the doctor couldn't understand. When Philippe tried to get up from the bed, he couldn't walk. Yet his legs aren't injured. It's queer. We are afraid it may be something like paralysis. He seemed to twist and stumble over his own feet.'

Sharply, as he spoke, the belated certainty came to me that here was an end to all coincidence; that I had been wrong; that something as sinister and darkly evil as I had ever known in the jungle had been happening here in Les Baux under my very eyes.

'Martin,' I said, 'something occurred yesterday afternoon which you do not know about. I am not prepared to say yet what it was. But I must see Philippe at once and talk with him. You say his mind is perfectly clear?'

'But assuredly,' said Martin, puzzled; 'though I can't understand what you're driving at. He will want to see you.'

Philippe was in bed. He looked depressed rather than ill, and was certainly in complete possession of his senses.

I said, 'Philippe, Martin tells me there is something wrong with your legs. I think perhaps I can tell you what——'

'Why, were you ever a doctor?' he interrupted eagerly. 'If we'd known that! The fellow who came up from Arles didn't seem to be much good.'

'No, I'm not a doctor. But I'm not sure this is a doctor's job. I want to tell you something. You know where my room is. I happened to be at the window yesterday and I heard and saw everything that occurred between you and Mère Tirelou. Haven't you thought that there may be some connection?'

He stared at me in surprise, and also with a sort of angry disappointment.

'*Tiens!*' he said. 'You, an educated modern American, you

believe in that fantastic foolishness! Why, I come from these mountains, I was born here, and yet I know that stuff is silly nonsense. I thought about it, of course, but it doesn't make any sense. How could it?'

'Maybe it doesn't,' I said, 'but just the same will you please tell me as well as you can remember what happened to you yesterday afternoon and last night?'

'Confound it, you know what happened. I had a stroke. And it has left me like this. Lord, I'd rather be dead than crippled or helpless.'

He lapsed into sombre silence. But I had heard enough. There are people who have lain paralysed in bed for life through no organic ailment but only because they *believed* they couldn't arise and walk. If I helped him now, it could be only by overwhelming proof. My business was with Mère Tirelou. . . .

Neither the old woman nor her granddaughter had been near the hotel that morning. I climbed the winding cobbled street and tapped at their door. Presently Maguelonne reluctantly opened. I made no effort to enter, but said:

'I've come to see Mère Tirelou – about a serious matter.'

She looked at me with worried, guarded eyes, as if uncertain how to answer, and finally said, 'She is not here. She went over the mountain last night, beyond Saint-Remy. She will be gone several days.' Sensing my doubt, she added defensively, almost pleadingly, 'You can come in and see if you wish. She is not here.'

The girl was obviously in great distress and I realised that she knew or suspected why I had come.

'In that case,' I said, 'we must talk. Shall it be like this, or would you prefer to have me come in?'

She motioned me inside.

I said: 'Ma'm'selle Maguelonne, I beg you to be honest with me. You know what people say about your grandmother – and there are some who say it also about you. I hope that part isn't true. But your grandmother has done something which I am determined to have undone. I am so certain of what I know that if necessary I am going to take Martin Plomb into my confidence and go with him to the police at Arles. Ma'm'selle, I feel that you know exactly what I am talking about. It's Philippe – and I want to ask if you——'

'No, no, no!' the girl cried pitifully, interrupting. 'I had nothing to do with it! I tried to stop it! I warned him! I begged him not to see me any more. I told him that something dreadful would happen, but he only laughed at me. He doesn't believe in such things. I have helped my grandmother in other things – she has forced me to help her – but never in anything so wicked as this – and against Philippe! No, no, Monsieur, never would I help in such a thing, not even if she——' Suddenly the girl began to sob, 'Oh, what ought I to do?'

I said, 'Do you mean there is something you could do?'

'I am afraid,' she said – 'afraid of my grandmother. Oh, if you knew! I don't dare go in there – and besides, the door is locked – and it may not be in there.'

'Maguelonne,' I said gently, 'I think you care for Philippe, and I think he cares for you. Do you know that he has lost the use of his legs?'

'Oh, oh, oh!' she sobbed; then she gathered courage and said, 'Yes, I will do it, if my grandmother kills me. But you must find something to force the lock, for she always carries the key with her.'

She led me to the kitchen which was at the rear, built into the side of the cliff almost beneath the walls of the old castle ruins. While she was lighting a lamp I found a small hatchet.

'It is through there,' she said, pointing to a closet whose entrance was covered by a drawn curtain.

At the back of the closet hidden by some old clothes hung on nails was a small door, locked. It was made of heavy wood, but I had little difficulty forcing the lock, opening the door to disclose a narrow flight of steps, winding downward into the darkness.

(There was nothing mysterious in the fact that such a stairway should exist there. The whole side of the cliff beneath the castle was honeycombed with similar passages.)

The girl went first and I followed close, lighting our way with the lamp held at her shoulder. The short stairway curved sharply downward, then emerged directly into an old forgotten rectangular chamber which at one time must have been a wine cellar or store room of the castle. But it now housed various strange and unpleasant objects on which the shadows flickered as I set the lamp in a niche and began to look about me. I had known that actual witches, practising almost in the direct medieval tradition, still existed in certain parts of Europe, yet I was surprised to see the definite material paraphernalia of the craft so literally surviving.

No need to describe all of it minutely – the place was evil and many of the objects were grotesquely evil; against the opposite wall an altar surmounted by a pair of horns, beneath them 'I N R I' reversed with the letters distorted into obscene symbols; dangling nearby a black, shrivelled Hand of Glory – and there on the floor, cunningly contrived with infinite pains, covering a considerable space, was the thing which we had come to find and which, for all my efforts to rationalise, sent a shiver through me as I examined it.

Four upright wooden pegs had been set in the floor, like miniature posts, making a square field about five feet in diameter, surrounded by cords which ran from peg to peg. Within this area and attached to the surrounding cords was stretched a criss-cross, labyrinthine, spiderweb-like maze of cotton thread.

Tangled in its centre like an insect caught in a web was a figure some eight inches high – a common doll, it had been, with china head sewed on its stuffed sawdust body; a doll such as might be bought for three francs in any toy-shop – but whatever baby dress it may have worn when it was purchased had been removed and a costume crudely suggesting a man's plus-four sports garb had been substituted in its place. The eyes of this manikin were bandaged with a narrow strip of black cloth; its feet and legs tangled, fastened, enmeshed in the criss-cross maze of thread.

It slumped, sagging there at an ugly angle, neither upright nor fallen, grotesquely sinister, like the body of a wounded man caught in barbed wire. All this may seem perhaps silly, childish in the telling. But it was not childish. It was vicious, wicked.

I disentangled that manikin gently and examined it carefully to see whether the body had been pierced with pins or needles. But there were none. The old woman had at least stopped short of attempted murder.

And then Maguelonne held it to her breast, sobbing, 'Ah, Philippe! Philippe!'

I picked up the lamp and we prepared to come away. The place, however, contained one other object which I have not thus far mentioned and which I now examined more closely. Suspended by a heavy chain from the ceiling was a life-sized, open, cage-like contrivance of wood and blackened leather straps and iron – as perversely devilish a device as twisted human ingenuity ever invented, for I knew its name and use from old engravings in books dealing with the obscure sadistic element in medieval sorcery. It was a Witch's Cradle. And there was something about the straps that made me wonder. . . .

Maguelonne saw me studying it and shuddered.

'Ma'm'selle,' I said, 'is it possible——?'

'Yes,' she answered, hanging her head; 'since you have been here there is nothing more to conceal. But it has always been on my part unwillingly.'

'But why on earth haven't you denounced her; why haven't you left her?'

'Monsieur,' she said, 'I have been afraid of what I knew. And where would I go? And besides, she is my grandmother.'

I was alone with Philippe in his bedroom. I had brought the manikin with me, wrapped in a bit of newspaper. If this were fiction, I should have found him magically cured from the moment the threads were disentangled. But magic in reality operates by more devious processes. He was exactly as I had left him, even more depressed. I told him what I had discovered.

He was at the same time sceptical, incredulous and interested, and when I showed him the manikin crudely dressed to represent himself and it became clear to him that Mère Tirelou had deliberately sought to do him a wicked injury, he grew angry, raised up from his pillows and exclaimed:

'Ah, the old hag! She really meant to harm me!'

I judged that the moment had come.

I stood up. I said, 'Philippe, forget all this now! Forget all of it and get up! There is only one thing necessary. Believe that you can walk, and you will walk.'

He stared at me helplessly, sank back and said, 'I do not believe it.'

I had failed. His mind lacked, I think, the necessary conscious imagination. But there was one more thing to try.

I said gently: 'Philippe, you care for Ma'm'selle Maguelonne, do you not?'

'I love Maguelonne,' he replied.

And then I told him brutally, briefly, almost viciously, of the thing that hung there in that cellar – and of its use.

The effect was as violent, as physical, as if I had suddenly struck him in the face. 'Ah! Ah! *Tonnerre de Dieu! La coquine! La vilaine coquine!*' he shouted, leaping from his bed like a crazy man.

The rest was simple. Philippe was too angry and concerned

about Maguelonne to have much time for surprise or even gratitude at his sudden complete recovery, but he was sensible enough to realise that for the girl's sake it was better not to make a public row. So when he went to fetch Maguelonne away he took his aunt with him, and within the hour she was transferred with her belongings to Madame Plomb's room.

Martin Plomb would deal effectively with old Mère Tirelou. He was to make no accusation concerning the part she had played in Philippe's misadventure – an issue difficult of legal proof – but to warn her that if ever she tried to interfere with Maguelonne or the impending marriage he would swear out a criminal warrant against her for ill treatment of a minor ward.

There remain two unsolved elements in this case which require an attempted explanation. The belief which I have always held concerning malevolent magic is that it operates by imposed auto-suggestion, and that therefore no incantation can work evil unless the intended victim believes it can. In this case, which seemed to contradict that thesis, I can only suppose that while Philippe's conscious mind reacted with complete scepticism, his unconscious mind (his family came from these same mountains) retained certain atavistic, superstitious fears which rendered him vulnerable.

The second element is, of course, the elaborate mummery of the enmeshed manikin, the doll, own cousin to the waxen images which in the Middle Ages were pierced with needles or slowly melted before a fire. The witch herself, if not a charlatan, implicitly believes that there is a literal, supernatural transference of identities.

My own belief is that the image serves simply as a focus for the concentrated, malevolent willpower of the witch. I hold, in short, that sorcery is a real and dangerous force, but that its ultimate explanation lies not in any supernatural realm, but rather in the field of pathological psychology.

4

The Snake

Dennis Wheatley

———

4

'Black Magic is a very real danger in the world today – it should neither be ignored nor underestimated.' These are the considered words of the man whose name has become inextricably linked with Satanism,—Dennis Wheatley. Although he has never participated in a Black Mass – or any other Witchcraft ceremony – Mr Wheatley probably knows as much about the power of Evil as anyone alive. During the half century in which he has been writing novels about Black Magic his daily post has never failed to bring him new details about the cult – both from those who belong to it and are proud of the fact and from those unfortunates who tangled with it lightheartedly and are now trying desperately to escape. Mr Wheatley rarely writes short stories, so this little masterpiece of horror is undoubtedly one of the gems of the collection.

I DIDN'T KNOW Carstairs at all well, mind you, but he was our nearest neighbour and a stranger to the place. He'd asked me several times to drop in for a chat, and that weekend I'd been saddled with a fellow called Jackson.

He was an engineer who had come over from South America to report on a mine my firm were interested in. We hadn't got much in common and the talk was getting a bit thin, so on the Sunday evening I thought I'd vary the entertainment by looking up Carstairs and take Jackson with me.

Carstairs was pleased enough to see us; he lived all on his own but for the servants. What he wanted with a big place like that I couldn't imagine, but that was his affair. He made us welcome and we settled down in comfortable armchairs to chat.

It was one of those still summer evenings with the scent of the flowers drifting in through the open windows, and the peace of it all makes you think for the moment that the city, on Monday morning, is nothing but a rotten bad dream.

I think I did know in a vague way that Carstairs had made his money mining, but when, or where, I hadn't an idea. Anyhow, he and young Jackson were soon in it up to the neck, talking technicalities. That never has been my end of the business; I was content to lend them an ear while I drank in the hush of the scented twilight; a little feller was piping away to his mate for all he was worth in the trees at the bottom of the garden.

It was the bat that started it; you know how they flit in on a summer's night through the open windows, absolutely silently, before you are aware of them. How they're here one moment — and there the next, in and out of the shadows while you flap about with a newspaper like a helpless fool. They're unclean things, of course, but harmless enough, yet never in my life have I seen a big man so scared as Carstairs.

'Get it out!' he yelled. 'Get it out,' and he buried his bald head in the sofa cushions.

I think I laughed; anyhow, I told him it was nothing to make a fuss about, and switched out the light.

The bat zig-zagged from side to side once or twice, and then flitted out into the open as silently as it had come.

Carstairs' big red face had gone quite white when he peeped out from beneath his cushions. 'Has it gone?' he asked in a frightened whisper.

'Of course it has,' I assured him. 'Don't be silly — it might have been the Devil himself from the fuss you made!'

'Perhaps it was,' Carstairs said seriously. As he sat up I could see the whites of his rather prominent eyes surrounding the blue pupils — I should have laughed if the man hadn't been in such an obvious funk.

'Shut the windows,' he said sharply, as he moved over to the whisky and mixed himself a pretty stiff drink. It seemed a sin on a night like that, but it was his house, so Jackson drew them.

Carstairs apologised in a half-hearted sort of way for making such a scene, then we settled down again.

In the circumstances it wasn't unnatural that the talk should turn to witchcraft and things like that.

Young Jackson said he'd heard some pretty queer stories in the forests of Brazil, but that didn't impress me, because he looked a good half-dago himself, for all his English name, and dagos always believe in that sort of thing.

Carstairs was a different matter; he was as British as could be, and when he asked me seriously if I believed in Black Magic – I didn't laugh, but told him just as seriously that I did not.

'You're wrong, then,' he declared firmly, 'and I'll tell you this, I shouldn't be sitting here if it wasn't for Black Magic.'

'You can't be serious,' I protested.

'I am,' he said. 'For thirteen years I roamed the Union of South Africa on my uppers, a "poor white", if you know what that means. If you don't – well, it's hell on earth. One rotten job after another with barely enough pay to keep body and soul together and, between jobs, not even that, so that at times you'd even lower yourself to chum up to a black for the sake of a drink or a bit of a meal. Never a chance to get up in the world, and despised by natives and whites alike – well, I suppose I'd be at it still but that I came up against the Black Art, and that brought me big money. Once I had money I went into business. That's twenty-two years ago – I'm a rich man now, and I've come home to take my rest.'

Carstairs evidently meant every word he said, and I must confess I was impressed. There was nothing neurotic about him, he was sixteen stone of solid, prosaic Anglo-Saxon; in fact, he looked just the sort of chap you'd like to have with you in a tight corner. That's why I'd been so surprised when he got in such a blue funk about the bat.

'I'm afraid I'm rather an unbeliever,' I admitted, 'but per-

haps that's because I've never come up against the real thing –
won't you tell us some more about it?'

He looked at me steadily for a moment with his round, blue
eyes. 'All right,' he said, 'if you like; help yourself to another
peg, and your friend, too.'

We refilled our glasses and he went on: 'When I as good as
said just now, "that bat may be the Devil in person", I didn't
mean quite that. Maybe there are people who can raise the
Devil – I don't know, anyhow, I've never seen it done; but
there is a power for evil drifting about the world – suffused in
the atmosphere, as you might say, and certain types of animals
seem to be sensitive to it – they pick it up out of the ether just
like a wireless receiving set.

'Take cats – they're uncanny beasts; look at the way they can
see in the dark; and they can do more than that; they can see
things that we can't in broad daylight. You must have seen them,
before now, walk carefully round an object in a room that simply
wasn't there.

'These animals are harmless enough in themselves, of course,
but where the trouble starts is when they become used as a focus
by a malignant human will. However, that's all by the way. As I
was telling you, I'd hiked it up and down the Union for
thirteen years, though it wasn't the Union in those days.
From Durban to Damaraland, and from the Orange River
to Matabele, fruit farmer, miner, salesman, wagoner, clerk –
I took every job that offered, but for all the good I'd done
myself I might as well have spent my time on the Breakwater
instead.

'I haven't even made up my mind today which is the tougher
master – the Bible-punching Dutchman, with his little piping
voice, or the whisky-sodden South African Scot.

'At last I drifted into Swaziland; that's on the borders of
Portuguese East, near Lourenço Marques and Delagoa Bay. As
lovely a country as you could wish to see; it's all been turned

into native reserve now, but in those days there were a handful of white settlers scattered here and there.

'Anyhow, it was there in a saloon at Mbabane that I met old Benny Isaacsohn, and he offered me a job. I was down and out, so I took it, though he was one of the toughest-looking nuts that I'd ever come across. He was a bigger man than I am, with greasy black curls and a great big hook of a nose. His face was as red as a turkey-cock, and his wicked black eyes were as shifty as sin. He said his storekeeper had died on him sudden, and the way he said it made me wonder just what had happened to that man.

'But it was Benny or picking up scraps from a native kraal – so I went along with him there and then.

'He took me miles up country to his famous store – two tins of sardines and a dead rat were about all he had in it, and of course I soon tumbled to it that trading honest wasn't Benny's real business. I don't doubt he'd sized me up and reckoned I wouldn't be particular. I was careful not to be too curious, because I had a sort of idea that that was what my predecessor had died of.

'After a bit he seemed to get settled in his mind about me, and didn't take much trouble to conceal his little games. He was doing a bit of gun-running for the natives from over the Portuguese border and a handsome traffic in illicit booze. Of course all our customers were blacks; there wasn't another white in a day's march except for Rebecca – Benny's old woman.

'I kept his books for him; they were all fake, of course. Brown sugar meant two dummy bullets out of five, and white, three. I remember; the dummies were cardboard painted to look like lead – cartridges come cheaper that way! Anyhow, Benny knew his ledger code all right.

'He didn't treat me badly on the whole; we had a shindy one hot night soon after I got there, and he knocked me flat with one blow from his big red fist. After that I used to go and walk it off if I felt my temper getting the best of me – and I did at times when I saw the way he used to treat those niggers. I'm not exactly squeamish myself, but the things he used to do would make you sick.

'When I got into the game, I found that gun-running and liquor weren't the end of it. Benny was a money-lender as well – that's where he over-reached himself and came up against the Black Art.

'Of the beginnings of Benny's dealings with Umtonga, the witch doctor, I know nothing. The old heathen would come to us now and again all decked out in his cowrie shells and strings of leopards' teeth, and Benny always received him in state. They'd sit drinking glass for glass of neat spirit for hours on end until Umtonga was carried away dead drunk by his men. The old villain used to sell off all the surplus virgins of his tribe to Benny, and Benny used to market them in Portuguese East, together with the wives of the poor devils who were in his clutches and couldn't pay the interest on their debts.

'The trouble started about nine months after I'd settled there; old Umtonga was a spender in his way, and there began to be a shortage of virgins in the tribe, so he started to borrow on his own account and then he couldn't pay. The interviews weren't so funny then – he began to go away sober and shaking his big black stick.

'That didn't worry Benny. He'd been threatened by people before, and he told Umtonga that if he couldn't raise enough virgins to meet his bill he'd better sell off a few of his wives himself.

'I was never present at the meetings, but I gathered a bit from what old Benny said in his more expansive moments, and I'd picked up enough Swazi to gather the gist of Umtonga's views when he aired them at parting on the stoep.

'Then one day Umtonga came with three women – it seemed that they were the equivalent of the original debt, but Benny had a special system with regard to his loans. Repayment of capital was nothing like enough – and the longer the debt was out-standing the greater the rate of interest became. By that time he wanted about thirty women, and good ones at that, to clear Umtonga off his books.

'The old witch doctor was calm and quiet; contrary to cus-tom, he came in the evening and did not stay more than twenty minutes. The walls were thin, I heard most of what went on – he offered Benny the three women – or death before the morning.

'If Benny had been wise he would have taken the women, but he wasn't. He told Umtonga to go to the Devil – and Umtonga went.

'His people were waiting for him outside, about a dozen of them, and he proceeded to make a magic. They handed him a live black cock and a live white cock, and Umtonga sat down before the stoep and he killed them in a curious way.

'He examined their livers carefully, and then he began to rock backwards and forwards on his haunches, and in his cracked old voice he sang a weird, monotonous chant. The others lay down flat on the ground and wriggled round him one after the other on their bellies. They kept that up for about half an hour, and then the old wizard began to dance. I can see his belt of monkey tails swirling about him now, as he leapt and spun. You wouldn't have thought that lean old savage had the strength in him to dance like that.

'Then all of a sudden he seemed to have a fit – he went abso-lutely rigid and fell down flat. He dropped on his face, and when his people turned him over we could see he was frothing at the mouth. They picked him up and carried him away.

'You know how the night comes down almost at once in the tropics. Umtonga started his incantation in broad daylight, and it didn't take so very long, but by the time he'd finished it was as dark as pitch, with nothing but the Southern Cross and the Milky Way to light the hidden world.

'In those places most people still act by Nature's clock. We had the evening meal, old Rebecca, Benny, and I; he seemed a bit preoccupied, but that was no more than I would have been in the circumstances. Afterwards he went into his office room to see what he'd made on the day, as he always did, and I went off to bed.

'It was the old woman roused me about two o'clock – it seems she'd dropped off to sleep, and woke to find that Benny had not come up to bed.

'We went along through the shanty, and there he was with his eyes wide and staring, gripping the arms of his office chair and all hunched up as though cowering away from something.

'He had never been a pretty sight to look at, but now there was something fiendish in the horror on his blackened face, and of course he'd been dead some hours.

'Rebecca flung her skirts over her head, and began to wail fit to bring the house down. After I'd got her out of the room, I went back to investigate – what could have killed Benny Isaacsohn? I was like you in those days – I didn't believe for a second that that toothless old fool Umtonga had the power to kill from a distance.

'I made a thorough examination of the room, but there was no trace of anybody having broken in, or even having been there. I had a good look at Benny – it seemed to me he'd died of apoplexy or some sort of fit, but what had brought it on? He'd seen something, and it must have been something pretty ghastly.

'I didn't know then that a week or two later I was to see the same thing myself.

'Well, we buried Benny the next day – there was the usual kind of primitive wake, with the women howling and the men getting free drinks – half Africa seemed to have turned up; you know how mysteriously news travels in the black man's country.

'Umtonga put in an appearance; he expressed neither regret nor pleasure but stood looking on. I didn't know what to make of it. The only evidence against him was the mumbo-jumbo of the night before, and no sane European could count that as proof of murder. I was inclined to think that the whole thing was an amazing coincidence.

'When the burying was over he came up to me. "Why you no kill house-boys attend Big Boss before throne of Great Spirit?" he wanted to know.

'I explained that one killing in the house was quite enough at a time. Then he demanded his stick, said he had left it behind in Benny's office the night before.

'I was pretty short with him, as you can imagine, but I knew the old ruffian's stick as well as I knew my own hairbrush; so I went in to get it.

'There it was lying on the floor – a four-foot snake stick. I dare say you've seen the sort of thing I mean; they make them shorter for Europeans. They are carved out of heavy wood, the snake's head is the handle, the tail the ferrule. Between, there are from five to a dozen bands; little markings are carved all down it to represent the scales. Umtonga's was a fine one – quite thin, but as heavy as lead. It was black, and carved out of ebony, I imagine. Not an ounce of give in it, but it would have made a splendid weapon. I picked it up and gave it to him without a word.

'For about ten days I saw no more of him. Old Rebecca stopped her wailing, and got down to business. Benny must have told her about most of his deals that mattered, for I found that she knew pretty much how things stood. It was agreed that I should carry on as a sort of manager for her, and after a bit we came to the question of Umtonga. I suggested that the interest was pretty hot, and that the man might be really dangerous. But she wouldn't have it; you would have thought I was trying to draw her eye-teeth when I suggested forgoing the interest! She fairly glared at me.

' "What is it to do with you?" she screamed. "I need money, I have the future of my—er—myself to think of. Send a boy with a message that you want to see him, and when he comes – make him pay."

'Well, there was nothing to do but to agree; the old shrew was worse than Benny in some ways. I sent a boy the following morning, and the day after Umtonga turned up.

'I saw him in Benny's office while his retinue waited outside; I was sitting in Benny's chair – the chair he'd died in – and I came to the point at once.

'He sat there for a few minutes just looking at me; his wizened old face was like a dried-up fruit that had gone bad. His black boot-button eyes shone with a strange, malignant fire, then he said very slowly, "You – very brave young Baas."

' "No," I said, "just business-like, that's all."

' "You know what happen to old Baas – he die – you want to go Great Spirit yet?"

'There was something evil and powerful in his steady stare; it was horribly disconcerting, but I wouldn't give in to it, and I told him I didn't want anything except his cash that was due, or its equivalent.

' "You forget business with Umtonga?" he suggested. "You do much good business, other mens. You no forget, Umtonga make bad magic – you die."

'Well, it wasn't my business – it was the old woman's. I couldn't have let him out if I'd wanted to – so there was only one reply, the same as he'd got from Benny.

'I showed him Benny's gun, and told him that if there were any monkey tricks I'd shoot on sight. His only answer was one of the most disdainful smiles I've ever seen on a human face. With that he left me and joined his bodyguard outside.

'They then went through the same abracadabra with another black cock and another white cock – wriggled about on their bellies, and the old man danced till he had another fit and was carried away.

'Night had fallen in the meantime, and I was none too easy in my mind. I thought of Benny's purple face and staring eyes.

'I had supper with the old hag, and then I went to Benny's room. I like my tot, but I'd been careful not to take it; I meant to remain stone cold sober and wide-awake that night.

'I had the idea that one of Umtonga's people had done something to Benny, poisoned his drink perhaps.

'I went over his room minutely, and after I'd done, there wasn't a place you could have hidden a marmoset. Then I shut the windows carefully, and tipped up a chair against each so that no one could get in without knocking it down. If I did drop off, I was bound to wake at that. I turned out the light so that they should have no target for a spear or an arrow, and then I sat down to wait.

'I never want another night like that as long as I live; you know how you can imagine things in the darkness – well, what I didn't imagine in those hours isn't worth the telling.

'The little noises of the veldt came to me as the creeping of the enemy – half a dozen times I nearly lost my nerve and put a bullet into the blacker masses of the shadows that seemed to take on curious forms, but I was pretty tough in those days and I stuck it out.

'About eleven o'clock the moon came up; you would have thought that made it better, but it didn't. It added a new sort of terror – that was all. You know how eerie moonlight can be; it is unnatural somehow, and I believe there's a lot in what they say about there being evil in the moon. Bright bars of it stood out in rows on the floor, where it streamed in silent and baleful through the slats in the jalousies. I found myself counting them over and over again. It seemed as if I were becoming mesmerised by that cold, uncanny light. I pulled myself up with a jerk.

'Then I noticed that something was different about the desk in front of me. I couldn't think what it could be – but there was something missing that had been there a moment before.

87

'All at once I realised what it was, and the palms of my hands became clammy with sweat. Umtonga had left his stick behind again – I had picked it up off the floor when I searched the office and leant it against the front of the desk; the top of it had been there before my eyes for the last three hours in the semi-darkness – standing up stiff and straight – and now it had disappeared.

'It couldn't have fallen, I should have heard it – my eyes must have been starting out of my head. A ghastly thought had come to me – just supposing that stick was not a stick?

'And then I saw it – the thing was lying straight and still in the moonlight, with its eight to ten wavy bands, just as I'd seen it a dozen times before; I must have dreamed I propped it against the desk – it must have been on the floor all the time, and yet I knew deep down in me that I was fooling myself and that it had moved of its own accord.

'My eyes never left it – and I watched, holding my breath to see if it moved – but I was straining so that I couldn't trust my eyesight. The bright bars of moonlight on the floor began to waver ever so slightly, and I knew that my sight was playing me tricks; when I opened them again the snake had raised its head.

'My vest was sticking to me, and my face was dripping wet. I knew now what had killed old Benny – I knew, too, why his face had gone black. Umtonga's stick was no stick at all, but the deadliest snake in all Africa – a thing that can move like lightning, can overtake a galloping horse, and kill its rider, so deadly that you're stiff within four minutes of its bite – I was up against a black mamba.

'I had my revolver in my hand, but it seemed a stupid, useless thing – there wasn't a chance in a hundred that I could hit it. A shot-gun's the only thing that's any good; with that I might have blown its head off, but the guns weren't kept in Benny's room and, like a fool, I'd locked myself in.

'The brute moved again as I watched it; it drew up its tail

with a long slithering movement. There could be no doubt now; Umtonga was a super snake-charmer, and he'd left this foul thing behind to do his evil work.

'I sat there petrified, just as poor Benny must have done, wondering what in heaven's name I could do to save myself, but my brain simply wouldn't work.

'It was an accident that saved me. As it rose to strike, I slipped in my attempt to get to my feet and kicked over Benny's wicker wastepaper basket; the brute went for that instead of me. The force with which they strike is tremendous – it's like the blow from a hammer or the kick of a mule. Its head went clean through the side of the basket and there it got stuck; it couldn't get its head out again.

'As luck would have it, I had been clearing out some of Benny's drawers that day, and I'd thrown away a whole lot of samples of quartz; the basket was about a third full of them and they weigh pretty heavy; a few had fallen out when it fell over, but the rest were enough to keep the mamba down.

'It thrashed about like a gigantic whiplash, but it couldn't free its head, and I didn't waste a second; I started heaving ledgers on its tail. That was the end of the business as far as the mamba was concerned – I'd got it pinned down in half the time it took you to drive out that bat. Then I took up my gun again. "Now my beauty," I thought, "I've got you where I want you, and I'll just quietly blow your head off – I'm going to have a dam fine pair of shoes out of your skin."

'I knelt down to the job and levelled my revolver; the snake struck twice, viciously, in my direction, but it couldn't get within a foot of me and it no more than jerked the basket either time.

'I looked down the barrel of the pistol within eighteen inches of its head, and then a very strange thing happened – and this is where the Black Magic comes in.

'The moonlit room seemed to grow dark about me, so that

the baleful light faded before my eyes – the snake's head disappeared from view – the walls seemed to be expanding and the queer, acrid odour of the native filled my nostrils.

'I knew that I was standing in Umtonga's hut, and where the snake had been a moment before I saw Umtonga sleeping – or in a trance, if you prefer it. He was lying with his head on the belly of one of his women, as is the custom of the country, and I stretched out a hand toward him in greeting. It seemed that, although there was nothing there, I had touched something – and then I realised with an appalling fear that my left hand was holding the wastepaper basket in which was the head of the snake.

'There was a prickling sensation on my scalp, and I felt my hair lifting – stiff with the electricity that was streaming from my body. With a tremendous effort of willpower I jerked back my hand. Umtonga shuddered in his trance – there was a thud, and I knew that the snake had struck in the place where my hand had been a moment before.

'I was half-crazy with fear, my teeth began to chatter, and it came to me suddenly that there was an icy wind blowing steadily upon me. I shivered with the deadly cold – although in reality it was a still, hot night. The wind was coming from the nostrils of the sleeping Umtonga full upon me; the bitter coldness of it was numbing me where I stood. I knew that in another moment I should fall forward on the snake.

'I concentrated every ounce of willpower in my hand that held the gun – I could not see the snake, but my eyes seemed to be focused upon Umtonga's forehead. If only my frozen finger could pull the trigger – I made a supreme effort, and then there happened a very curious thing.

'Umtonga began to talk to me in his sleep – not in words, you understand, but as spirit talks to spirit. He turned and groaned and twisted where he lay. A terrible sweat broke out on his forehead and round his skinny neck. I could see him as clearly as I can see you – he was pleading with me not to kill him, and in that deep, silent night, where space and time had ceased to exist, I knew that Umtonga and the snake were one.

'If I killed the snake, I killed Umtonga. In some strange fashion he had suborned the powers of evil, so that when at the end of the incantation he fell into a fit, his malignant spirit passed into the body of his dread familiar.

'I suppose I ought to have killed that snake and Umtonga, too, but I didn't. Just as it is said that a drowning man sees his whole life pass before him at the moment of death – so, I saw my own. Scene after scene out of my thirteen years of disappointment and failure flashed before me – but I saw more than that.

'I saw a clean, tidy office in Jo'burg, and I was sitting there in decent clothes. I saw this very house as you see it from the drive – although I'd never seen it in my life before – and I saw other things as well.

'At that moment I had Umtonga in my power, and he was saying as clearly as could be "All these things will I give unto you – if only you will spare my life."

'Then the features of Umtonga faded. The darkness lightened and I saw again the moonlight streaming through the slats of old Benny's office – and the mamba's head!

'I put my revolver in my pocket, unlocked the door, and locking it again behind me, went up to bed.

'I slept as though I'd been on a ten-day march, I was so exhausted; I woke late, but everything that had happened in the night was clear in my memory – I knew I hadn't dreamed it. I loaded a shot-gun and went straight to Benny's office.

'There was the serpent still beside the desk – its head thrust through the wicker basket and the heavy ledgers pinning down its body. It seemed to have straightened out, though, into its usual form, and when I knocked it lightly with the barrel of the gun it remained absolutely rigid. I could hardly believe it to be anything more than a harmless piece of highly polished wood and yet I knew that it had a hideous, hidden life, and after that I left it very carefully alone.

'Umtonga turned up a little later, as I felt sure he would; he seemed very bent and old. He didn't say very much, but he spoke again about his debt, and asked if I would not forgo some part of it – he would pay the whole if he must, but it would ruin him if he did. To sell his wives would be to lose authority with his tribe.

'I explained that it wasn't my affair, but Rebecca's; she owned everything now that Benny was dead.

'He seemed surprised at that; natives don't hold with women owning property. He said he'd thought that the business was mine and that all I had to do was to feed Rebecca till she died.

'Then he wanted to know if I would have helped him had that been the case. I told him that extortion wasn't my idea of business, and with that he seemed satisfied; he picked up his terrible familiar and stumped away without another word.

'The following week I had to go into Mbabane for stores. I was away a couple of nights and when I got back Rebecca was dead and buried; I heard the story from the houseboys. Umtonga had been to see her on the evening that I left. He'd made his magic again before the stoep, and they'd found her dead and black in the morning. I asked if by any chance he'd left his stick behind him, although I knew the answer before I got it – "Yes, he'd come back for it the following day."

'I started in to clear up Benny's affairs, and board by board to pull the shanty down. Benny didn't believe in banks and I knew there was a hoard hidden somewhere. It took me three weeks, but I found it. With that, and a reasonable realisation of what was outstanding, I cleared up a cool ten thousand. I've turned that into a hundred thousand since, and so you see that it was through the Black Art that I come to be sitting here.'

As Carstairs came to the end of the story, something made me turn and look at Jackson; he was glaring at the older man, and his dark eyes shone with a fierce light in his sallow face.

'Your name's not Carstairs,' he cried suddenly in a harsh voice. 'It's Thompson – and mine is Isaacsohn. I am the child that you robbed and abandoned.'

Before I could grasp the full significance of the thing he was on his feet – I saw the knife flash as it went home in Carstairs's chest, and the young Jew shrieked, 'You fiend – you paid that devil to kill my mother.'

5

Prince Borgia's Mass

August Derleth

———

5

No enthusiast of horror stories needs an introduction to the work of August Derleth. His stories have established him as one of the finest modern writers in the genre while his numerous anthologies reveal him as a discerning editor with access to the very best material. Derleth is also an expert on the Occult and lives in Sauk City, Wisconsin, one of the dark, witch-infested corners of America where legends of evil die hard. History also fascinates him and in this rare early story – which Derleth himself suggested for this collection – he weaves a tale of Black Magic around one of the great monsters of all time, Cesare Borgia.

CESARE, THE PRINCE Borgia, Duke of Valentinois and Romagna, Lord of Imola and Forli, of Rimini and Pesaro, of Faenza and Urbino, stretched forth his imperial hand and took from the lackey the paper he extended. At the same moment two figures moved out of the shadows behind the Borgia and peered over his shoulder at the paper. The younger of the two, he with the incipient moustache, nervously stroked the down on his sharp chin; the other, an older, grey-haired man in military costume, betrayed by nought save the narrowing of his eyes the intensity of his interest.

Cesare, the Prince Borgia, grunted suddenly. 'Three more!' he exclaimed with sullen vehemence.

'Devil's work,' muttered the military man.

'Three more,' repeated the young man under his breath.

'Some action must be taken, Highness,' said the military man in a jerky voice. 'This thing cannot . . . must not continue.'

'It is not fitting that you rebuke me thus, Captain,' returned the Prince Borgia shortly. 'Be assured; action has already been taken. This very night shall see the end of this satanic business.'

He turned abruptly to the lackey, who at once began to bow with the rapidity and regularity of an automaton. 'Summon before me the mage, René!'

The lackey, still bowing, backed himself out of the spacious tent. The young man sank into a chair at the side of the Prince Borgia.

'What would you with René, Highness? Is it that you need magic now to combat this vandalism?'

Cesare, the Prince Borgia, turned his gaze on his companion. 'Your mind is yet too young, Midi, to know this thing. Think you common vandals come to steal the bodies of my dead . . . such bodies already denuded of all things costly and of value? Pah!'

'It is good to think not, Highness. But if it is not vandals who do this thing, who then?'

The captain leaned forward. 'You suspect, then, Highness? Shall we take them this night?'

'They shall die before the dawn!'

'That is well,' said the captain. 'Yes, that is well.'

Cesare nodded.

The flap of the tent was drawn aside, and into the large, dimly-lit space shuffled the bent, wizened figure of René, the mage, and his grotesque, bird-like shadow followed behind, trailing the wall of the tent. He approached the Prince Borgia.

'Highness!' he murmured, and inclined his head.

'René, this night have three more bodies gone.' Cesare paused for the full import of his words to reach the mage. In a moment he continued: 'These, my men, have died an honourable death in battle, and it is fitting that an honourable burial be given them. But their bodies have been taken, and burial is not to be for them. Yet, you were set to watch them with a purpose. Have you accomplished that purpose, René?'

The mage bowed low. 'My commission is fulfilled; it is as you had foreseen, Highness. If a body of retainers is summoned together, I shall guide Highness to the spot where the bodies have been taken. There Highness shall see and know the guilty and shall devise for them fit punishment. Fourteen bodies now in all have gone; these three we can yet save from indignity.'

'Well done, my worthy René; go now and array yourself for the journey.' The Prince Borgia turned. 'And you, Captain, give orders for picked men to be in readiness to accompany us within the hour.'

The captain murmured, inclined his head, and left the tent, the crabbed figure of René trailing slowly in his wake.

A half-hour's hard riding brought the group of men to the base of a small knoll some distance from the camp, where René indicated that the Prince Borgia should give the signal to dismount. The Borgia relayed a curt order to his captain, and in a moment the body of men was creeping silently up the slope, René, with the Prince Borgia, Midi, and the captain in the lead. Topping the rise, René turned and raised a hand to enjoin silence. Then he bent to the three around him.

'Recollect, Highness,' he muttered in a low voice, 'tonight is Walpurgis night; this night do all the demons of the earth, the air, the fire, and the water come together to serve through earthly men at the Black Mass. See there!' He crouched low, and pointed.

Before them, in a slight depression at the base of the knoll, there stood a grove of trees; in the midst of this grove could be discerned vague, black shadows, moving to and fro in the flickering light of huge candles. Midi gasped. The Prince Borgia gave the order for the men to surround the grove in silence; at his call they were to take those in the grove. Then the four, again led by the mage, crept forward, and came at last to a vantage-point, where they stood to watch the horrible ritual taking place before them. Midi, the young companion of Cesare, started forward, the better to see, but Cesare drew him softly back.

There were nine men in the grove, and each was robed in black from head to toe, and upon each face there was a grotesque mask. Their robes, the watchers could see, were decorated with furs. Midi turned a startled, puzzled face to René.

'Mockery, Messer,' said the mage softly. 'The furs of panther, lynx, and cat are worn always in these rituals. And those candles, Highness,' he went on, turning now to the Prince Borgia, 'those candles are made from the fat of corpses. See, too, how they are made, each in the form of an inverted cross. Their bowls are skulls, and their fires are fed with cypress branches, and with the wood of gibbets. Soon they will consecrate a black host before that huge inverted cross they have stolen somewhere.'

The air was heavy with the stench of sulphur and evil-smelling asafoetida. The watchers saw the nine in the grove walk upon an earth covered with triangles, columns, stars, penta-grams and all manner of cabalistic signs. Now one of the nine separated himself and strode forward alone, where, with incred-ible obscenities, he held aloft a black host, and at once there arose from the eight before him a low chant, a calling upon Beelzebub and Ahriman, a paean to Satan on high.

But the Prince Borgia was not inclined to grant the nine sufficient time to complete their rituals; for suddenly he gave a sharp command, and at once there came rushing from all sides the retainers, who threw themselves upon the black priests in fury. 'Alive!' called Cesare. 'I want them brought to me alive!' He turned and began to walk rapidly to where his horse was tethered. 'Come,' he said to the three with him, 'I shall punish them to fit the crime; they shall celebrate with me a Mass of my own devising . . . and that their last!'

They rode swiftly back to the camp, where Cesare gave a quick order, rousing his troops from their sleep. At his order, too, men started to fashion nine inverted crosses, to set them in the ground when they were completed. Then he, with Midi and the mage, sat to await the coming of his retainers with the nine black priests.

They came at last, with the nine, a sorry group, stripped of their robes, securely bound. Cesare, the Prince Borgia, scrutinised them closely. Then he motioned for them to be brought forward and flung to their knees; again he studied the faces before him. He leaned forward to speak to them.

'Did you not know this the camp of the Borgia Prince, eh? . . . And yet you took from it the bodies of its dead! . . . Swine! Know that you are about to die; prepare to go before your black master.' He motioned to the men. 'Strip these of all clothing, and nail them upon the crosses . . . see to it that their heads do not touch upon the earth.' He turned now to René. 'Take with you their black hosts, and by your magic make them white.'

The mage bowed and shambled away.

'Look you to it that upon each cross there is placed a portion of the tallow candles these swine have used,' the Prince addressed his men. 'These must be placed and lit so that each drop of hot wax strikes the faces of the men below; let it remind them of their eternity.'

René appeared suddenly, in his hands nine of the white wafers which had been black only a moment before. These he gave to Cesare, and stood aside to await the further orders of the Prince Borgia.

'To fight these carrion,' murmured Cesare, 'I can use either white or black magic . . . and it is my pleasure to use black. Think you not the black more fitting, René?'

'Highness knows best.' The mage inclined his head. 'Black, too, is the more dangerous.'

'And the better then,' said Cesare, and strode forward. 'Come!'

Obediently René followed him. The Prince Borgia paused before the first of the nine, and with his own fingers forced into the man's mouth one of the unconsecrated white wafers. At the same moment René mumbled a short ritual in Latin. Cesare waited until the mage had finished; then he moved to the second, repeated his process, and the mage again said the ritual. Thus the nine were served. Now Cesare turned once more to the retainers.

'Bring to me the skull-bowls these carrion have used.'

Two retainers moved forward with the bowls, which the mage took carefully in his hands. The Prince Borgia moved forward in his turn and dipped his hands into the fluid in the bowl; then he turned and began to sprinkle the bodies on the crosses with the fluid. This completed, he stepped away and gave the ritual into the charge of the mage.

René cast from him the skulls, so that they fell before the crosses, and more of the fluid splattered upward into the straining faces of the nine. Then he took from one of the retainers a black robe, which had been worn in the grove that night, and put it over his clothes. Now he fell to gesticulating and shouting and at last, with incredible rapidity, began to repeat the entire ritual of the Black Mass backward, and at its conclusion pronounced in a loud voice the name of Beelzebub seven times.

Hardly had the sound of his voice died away when there came from the depths of the sky a dense black cloud resembling nothing so much as a mass of dull black velvet suspended in the air. This hovered for a moment above the crosses; then descended suddenly, and immediately the air became intolerable for the smell of sulphur saturating it. Instinctively the soldiers crowded back; but René held his ground. For a moment the black cloud clung to the crosses, writhing and weaving about them; then suddenly there came a bluish pallor, and at once a brilliant flash of flame . . . and it was gone.

Then the startled soldiers saw that though the crosses remained as fresh as they had been made, the bodies of the nine were gone, and with them the skull-bowls, and the tallow candles — but below each cross there lay a tiny heap of ashes!

'My Mass is over,' said Cesare, the Prince Borgia. 'And I am very tired . . . and you, Midi? Come.'

Together the two moved away, and behind them in silence came the crabbed, weary figure of the mage, René.

Secret Worship

Algernon Blackwood

Few people's names are more closely linked with the Super-natural than that of Algernon Blackwood – in fact, because of his great interest in the lore of the Occult, he has become widely known as 'The Ghost Man'. Born in 1869, he spent much of his young life travelling and had a variety of jobs (most of them involving hard, manual work) before turning to writing and scoring an overnight success. His wide ex-perience of life is reflected in his work and his books are noted for their authenticity. His best-sellers include such dark tales as The Empty House *and* The Dance of Death. *Algernon Blackwood had more than a passing knowledge of Black Magic which he demonstrates to great effect in this story.*

HARRIS, THE SILK merchant, was in South Germany on his way home from a business trip when the idea came to him suddenly that he would take the mountain railway from Strasbourg and run down to revisit his old school after an interval of something more than thirty years. And it was to this chance impulse of the junior partner in Harris Brothers of St Paul's Churchyard that John Silence owed one of the most curious cases of his whole experience, for at that very moment he happened to be tramping these same mountains with a holiday knapsack, and from different points of the compass the two men were actually converging towards the same inn.

Deep down in the heart that for thirty years had been con-cerned chiefly with the profitable buying and selling of silk, Harris's school had left the imprint of its peculiar influence, and, though perhaps unknown to Harris, had strongly coloured the whole of his subsequent existence. It belonged to the deeply religious life of a small Protestant community (which it is unnecessary to specify), and his father had sent him there at the age of fifteen, partly because he would learn the German requisite for the conduct of the silk business, and partly because the discipline was strict, and discipline was what his soul and body needed just then more than anything else.

The life, indeed, had proved exceedingly severe, and young Harris benefited accordingly; for though corporal punishment was unknown, there was a system of mental and spiritual correction which somehow made the soul stand proudly erect to receive it, while it struck at the very root of the fault and taught the boy that his character was being cleaned and strengthened, and that he was not merely being tortured in a kind of personal revenge.

That was over thirty years ago, when he was a dreamy and impressionable youth of fifteen; and now, as the train climbed slowly up the winding mountain gorges, his mind travelled back somewhat lovingly over the intervening period, and forgotten details rose vividly again before him out of the shadows. The life there had been very wonderful, it seemed to him, in that remote mountain village, protected from the tumults of the world by the love and worship of the devout Brotherhood that ministered to the needs of some hundred boys from every country in Europe. Sharply the scenes came back to him. He smelt again the long stone corridors, the hot pinewood rooms, where the sultry hours of summer study were passed with bees droning through open windows in the sunshine, and German characters struggling in the mind with dreams of English lawns – and then the sudden awful cry of the master in German –

'Harris, stand up! You sleep!'

And he recalled the dreadful standing motionless for an hour, book in hand, while the knees felt like wax and the head grew heavier than a cannonball.

The very smell of the cooking came back to him – the daily *Sauerkraut*, the watery chocolate on Sundays, the flavour of the

stringy meat served twice a week at *Mittagessen*; and he smiled
to think again of the half-rations that was the punishment for
speaking English. The very odour of the milk-bowls – the hot
sweet aroma that rose from the soaking peasant-bread at the six
o'clock breakfast – came back to him pungently, and he saw the
huge *Speisesaal* with the hundred boys in their school uniform,
all eating sleepily in silence, gulping down the coarse bread and
scalding milk in terror of the bell that would presently cut them
short – and, at the far end where the masters sat, he saw the
narrow slit windows with the vistas of enticing field and forest
beyond.

And this, in turn, made him think of the great barn-like room
on the top floor where all slept together in wooden cots, and he
heard in memory the clamour of the cruel bell that woke them
on winter mornings at five o'clock and summoned them to the
stone-flagged *Waschkammer*, where boys and masters alike, after
scanty and icy washing, dressed in complete silence.

From this his mind passed swiftly, with vivid picture-
thoughts, to other things, and with a passing shiver he remembered how the loneliness of never being alone had eaten into him,
and how everything – work, meals, sleep, walks, leisure – was
done with his 'division' of twenty other boys and under the eyes
of at least two masters. The only solitude possible was by asking
for half an hour's practice in the cell-like music rooms, and
Harris smiled to himself as he recalled the zeal of his violin
studies.

Then, as the train puffed laboriously through the great pine
forests that cover these mountains with a giant carpet of velvet,
he found the pleasanter layers of memory giving up their dead,
and he recalled with admiration the kindness of the masters,
whom all addressed as Brother, and marvelled afresh at their
devotion in burying themselves for years in such a place, only to
leave it, in most cases, for the still rougher life of missionaries in
the wild places of the world.

He thought once more of the still, religious atmosphere that hung over the little forest community like a veil, barring the distressful world; of the picturesque ceremonies at Easter, Christmas, and New Year; of the numerous feast-days and charming little festivals. The *Beschehr-Fest*, in particular, came back to him – the feast of gifts at Christmas – when the entire community paired off and gave presents, many of which had taken weeks to make or the savings of many days to purchase. And then he saw the midnight ceremony in the church at New Year, with the shining face of the *Prediger* in the pulpit – the village preacher who, on the last night of the old year, saw in the empty gallery beyond the organ loft the faces of all who were to die in the ensuing twelve months, and who at last recognised himself among them, and, in the very middle of his sermon, passed into a state of rapt ecstasy and burst into a torrent of praise.

Thickly the memories crowded upon him. The picture of the small village dreaming its unselfish life on the mountain tops, clean, wholesome, simple, searching vigorously for its God, and training hundreds of boys in the grand way, rose up in his mind with all the power of an obsession. He felt once more the old mystical enthusiasm, deeper than the sea and more wonderful than the stars; he heard again the winds sighing from leagues of forest over the red roofs in the moonlight; he heard the Brothers' voices talking of the things beyond this life as though they had actually experienced them in the body; and, as he sat in the jolting train, a spirit of unutterable longing passed over his seared and tired soul, stirring in the depths of him a sea of emotions that he thought had long since frozen into immobility.

And the contrast pained him – the idealistic dreamer then, the man of business now – so that a spirit of unworldly peace and beauty known only to the soul in meditation laid its feathered finger upon his heart, moving strangely the surface of the waters.

Harris shivered a little and looked out of the window of his empty carriage. The train had long passed Hornberg, and far below the streams tumbled in white foam down the limestone rocks. In front of him, dome upon dome of wooded mountain stood against the sky. It was October, and the air was cool and sharp, wood-smoke and damp moss exquisitely mingled in it with the subtle odours of the pines. Overhead, between the tips of the highest firs, he saw the first stars peeping, and the sky was a clean, pale amethyst that seemed exactly the colour all these memories clothed themselves with in his mind.

He leaned back in his corner and sighed. He was a heavy man, and he had not known sentiment for years; he was a big man, and it took much to move him, literally and figuratively; he was a man in whom the dreams of God that haunt the soul in youth, though overlaid by the scum that gathers in the fight for money, had not, as with the majority, utterly died the death.

He came back into this little neglected pocket of the years where so much fine gold had collected and lain undisturbed, with all his semi-spiritual emotions aquiver; and, as he watched the mountain tops come nearer, and smelt the forgotten odours of his boyhood, something melted on the surface of his soul and left him sensitive to a degree he had not known since, thirty years before, he had lived here with his dreams, his conflicts, and his youthful suffering.

A thrill ran through him as the train stopped with a jolt at a tiny station and he saw the name in large black lettering on the grey stone building, and below it, the number of metres it stood above the level of the sea.

'The highest point on the line!' he exclaimed. 'How well I remember it – Sommerau – Summer Meadow. The very next station is mine!'

And, as the train ran downhill with brakes on and steam shut off, he put his head out of the window and one by one saw the old familiar landmarks in the dusk. They stared at him like dead faces in a dream. Queer, sharp feelings, half poignant, half sweet, stirred in his heart.

'There's the hot, white road we walked along so often with the two Brüders always at our heels,' he thought; 'and there, by jove, is the turn through the forest to "*Die Galgen*", the stone gallows where they hanged the witches in olden days!'

He smiled a little as the train slid past.

'And there's the copse where the Lilies of the Valley powdered the ground in spring; and, I swear' – he put his head out with a sudden impulse – 'if that's not the very clearing where Calame, the French boy, chased the swallow-tail with me, and Brüder Pagel gave us half-rations for leaving the road without permission, and for shouting in our mother tongues!' And he laughed again as the memories came back with a rush, flooding his mind with vivid detail.

The train stopped, and he stood on the grey gravel platform like a man in a dream. It seemed half a century since he last waited there with corded wooden boxes, and got into the train for Strasbourg and home after the two years' exile. Time dropped from him like an old garment and he felt a boy again. Only, things looked so much smaller than his memory of them; shrunk and dwindled they looked, and the distances seemed on a curiously smaller scale.

He made his way across the road to the little Gasthaus, and, as he went, faces and figures of former schoolfellows – German, Swiss, Italian, French, Russian – slipped out of the shadowy woods and silently accompanied him. They flitted by his side, raising their eyes questioningly, sadly, to his. But their names he had forgotten. Some of the Brothers, too, came with them, and most of these he remembered by name – Brüder Röst, Brüder Pagel, Brüder Schliemann, and the bearded face of the old preacher who had seen himself in the haunted gallery of those about to die – Brüder Gysin. The dark forest lay all about him like a sea that any moment might rush with velvet waves upon the scene and sweep all the faces away. The air was cool and wonderfully fragrant, but with every perfumed breath came also a pallid memory. . . .

Yet, in spite of the underlying sadness inseparable from such an experience, it was all very interesting, and held a pleasure peculiarly its own, so that Harris engaged his room and ordered supper feeling well pleased with himself, and intending to walk up to the old school that very evening. It stood in the centre of the community's village, some four miles distant through the forest, and he now recollected for the first time that this little Protestant settlement dwelt isolated in a section of the country that was otherwise Catholic. Crucifixes and shrines surrounded the clearing like the sentries of a beleaguering army. Once beyond the square of the village, with its few acres of field and orchard, the forest crowded up in solid phalanxes, and beyond the rim of trees began the country that was ruled by the priests of another faith. He vaguely remembered, too, that the Catholics had showed sometimes a certain hostility toward the little Protestant oasis that flourished so quietly and benignly in their midst. He had quite forgotten this. How trumpery it all seemed now with his wide experience of life and his knowledge of other countries and the great outside world! It was like stepping back, not thirty years, but three hundred.

There were only two others besides himself at supper. One of them, a bearded, middle-aged man in tweeds, sat by himself at the far end, and Harris kept out of his way because he was English. He feared he might be in business, possibly even in the silk business, and that he would perhaps talk on the subject. The other traveller, however, was a Catholic priest. He was a little man who ate his salad with a knife, yet so gently that it was almost inoffensive, and it was the sight of 'the cloth' that recalled his memory of the old antagonism. Harris mentioned by way of conversation the object of his sentimental journey, and the priest looked up sharply at him with raised eyebrows and an expression of surprise and suspicion that somehow piqued him. He ascribed it to his difference of belief.

'Yes,' went on the silk merchant, pleased to talk of what his mind was so full, 'and it was a curious experience for an English boy to be dropped down into a school of a hundred foreigners. I well remember the loneliness and intolerable *Heimweh* of it at first.' His German was very fluent.

The priest opposite looked up from his cold veal and potato salad and smiled. It was a nice face. He explained quietly that he did not belong here, but was making a tour of the parishes of Württemberg and Baden.

'It was a strict life,' added Harris. 'We English, I remember, used to call it *Gefängnisleben* – prison life!'

The face of the other, for some unaccountable reason, darkened. After a slight pause, and more by way of politeness than because he wished to continue the subject, he said quietly:

'It was a flourishing school in those days, of course. Afterwards, I have heard——' He shrugged his shoulders slightly, and the odd look – it almost seemed a look of alarm – came back into his eyes. The sentence remained unfinished.

Something in the tone of the man seemed to his listener uncalled for – in a sense reproachful, singular. Harris bridled in spite of himself.

'It has changed?' he asked. 'I can hardly believe——'

'You have not heard, then?' observed the priest gently, making a gesture as though to cross himself, yet not actually completing it. 'You have not heard what happened there before it was abandoned——?'

It was very childish, of course, and perhaps he was overtired and overwrought in some way, but the words and manner of the little priest seemed to him so offensive – so disproportionately offensive – that he hardly noticed the concluding sentence. He recalled the old bitterness and the old antagonism, and for a moment he almost lost his temper.

'Nonsense,' he interrupted with a forced laugh, '*Unsinn!* You must forgive me, sir, for contradicting you. But I was a pupil there myself. I was at school there. There was no place like it. I cannot believe that anything serious could have happened to — to take away its character. The devotion of the Brothers would be difficult to equal anywhere——'

He broke off suddenly, realising that his voice had been raised unduly and that the man at the far end of the table might understand German; and at the same moment he looked up and saw that this individual's eyes were fixed upon his face intently. They were peculiarly bright. Also they were rather wonderful eyes, and the way they met his own served in some way he could not understand to convey both a reproach and a warning. The whole face of the stranger, indeed, made a vivid impression upon him for it was a face, he now noticed for the first time, in whose presence one would not willingly have said or done anything unworthy. Harris could not explain to himself how it was he had not become conscious sooner of its presence.

But he could have bitten off his tongue for having so far forgotten himself. The little priest lapsed into silence. Only once he said, looking up and speaking in a low voice that was not intended to be overheard, but that evidently *was* overheard, 'You will find it different.' Presently he rose and left the table with a polite bow that included both the others, and, after him, from the far end rose also the figure in the tweed suit, leaving Harris by himself.

He sat on for a bit in the darkening room, sipping his coffee and smoking his fifteen-pfennig cigar, till the girl came in to light the oil lamps. He felt vexed with himself for his lapse from good manners, yet hardly able to account for it. Most likely, he reflected, he had been annoyed because the priest had unintentionally changed the pleasant character of his dream by introducing a jarring note. Later he must seek an opportunity to make amends. At present, however, he was too impatient for his walk to the school, and he took his stick and hat and passed out into the open air.

And, as he crossed before the Gasthaus, he noticed that the priest and the man in the tweed suit were engaged already in such deep conversation that they hardly noticed him as he passed and raised his hat.

He started off briskly, well remembering the way, and hoping to reach the village in time to have a word with one of the Brüders. They might even ask him in for a cup of coffee. He felt sure of his welcome, and the old memories were in full possession once more. The hour of return was a matter of no consequence whatever.

It was then just after seven o'clock, and the October evening was drawing in with chill airs from the recesses of the forest. The road plunged straight from the railway clearing into its depths, and in a very few minutes the trees engulfed him and the clack of his boots fell dead and echoless against the serried stems of a million firs. It was very black; one trunk was hardly distinguishable from another. He walked smartly, swinging his holly stick. Once or twice he passed a peasant on his way to bed, and the guttural '*Gruss Gott*', unheard for so long, emphasised the passage of time, while yet making it seem as nothing. A fresh group of pictures crowded his mind. Again the figures of former schoolfellows flitted out of the forest and kept pace by his side, whispering of the doings of long ago. One reverie stepped hard upon the heels of another. Every turn in the road, every clearing of the forest, he knew, and each in turn brought forgotten associations to life. He enjoyed himself thoroughly.

He marched on and on. There was powdered gold in the sky till the moon rose, and then a wind of faint silver spread silently between the earth and stars. He saw the tips of the fir trees shimmer, and heard them whisper as the breeze turned their needles towards the light. The mountain air was indescribably sweet. The road shone like the foam of a river through the gloom.

White moths flitted here and there like silent thoughts across his path, and a hundred smells greeted him from the forest caverns across the years.

Then, when he least expected it, the trees fell away abruptly on both sides, and he stood on the edge of the village clearing.

He walked faster. There lay the familiar outlines of the houses, sheeted with silver; there stood the trees in the little central square with the fountain and small green lawns; there loomed the shape of the church next to the Gasthof der Brüdergemeinde; and just beyond, dimly rising into the sky, he saw with a sudden thrill the mass of the huge school building, blocked castle-like with deep shadows in the moonlight, standing square and formidable to face him after the silences of more than a quarter of a century.

He passed quickly down the deserted village street and stopped close beneath its shadow, staring up at the walls that had once held him prisoner for two years – two unbroken years of discipline and homesickness. Memories and emotions surged through his mind; for the most vivid sensations of his youth had focused about this spot, and it was here he had first begun to live and learn values. Not a single footstep broke the silence, though lights glimmered here and there through cottage windows; but when he looked up at the high walls of the school, draped now in shadow, he easily imagined that well-known faces crowded to the windows to greet him – closed windows that really reflected only moonlight and the gleam of stars.

This, then, was the old school building, standing foursquare to the world, with its shuttered windows, its lofty, tiled roof, and the spiked lightning conductors pointing like black and taloned fingers from the corners. For a long time he stood and stared. Then, presently, he came to himself again, and realised to his joy that a light still shone in the windows of the *Brüderstube*.

He turned from the road and passed through the iron railings; then climbed the twelve stone steps and stood facing the black wooden door with the heavy bars of iron, a door he had once loathed and dreaded with the hatred and passion of an imprisoned soul, but now looked upon tenderly with a sort of boyish delight.

Almost timorously he pulled the rope and listened with a tremor of excitement to the clanging of the bell deep within the building. And the long-forgotten sound brought the past before him with such a vivid sense of reality that he positively shivered. It was like the magic bell in the fairy-tale that rolls back the curtain of Time and summons the figures from the shadows of the dead. He had never felt so sentimental in his life. It was like being young again. And, at the same time, he began to bulk rather large in his own eyes with a certain spurious importance. He was a big man from·the world of strife and action. In this little place of peaceful dreams would he, perhaps, not cut something of a figure?

'I'll try once more,' he thought after a long pause, seizing the iron bell-rope, and was just about to pull it when a step sounded on the stone passage within, and the huge door slowly swung open.

A tall man with a rather severe cast of countenance stood facing him in silence.

'I must apologise – it is somewhat late,' he began a trifle pompously, 'but the fact is I am an old pupil. I have only just arrived and really could not restrain myself.' His German seemed not quite so fluent as usual. 'My interest is so great. I was here in 'seventy.'

The other opened the door wider and at once bowed him in with a smile of genuine welcome.

'I am Brüder Kalkmann,' he said quietly in a deep voice. 'I myself was a master here about that time. It is a great pleasure always to welcome a former pupil.' He looked at him very keenly for a few seconds, and then added, 'I think, too, it is splendid of you to come – very splendid.'

'It is a very great pleasure,' Harris replied, delighted with his reception.

The dimly-lighted corridor with its flooring of grey stone, and the familiar sound of a German voice echoing through it – with the peculiar intonation the Brothers always used in speaking – all combined to lift him bodily, as it were, into the dream-atmosphere of long-forgotten days. He stepped gladly into the building and the door shut with the familiar thunder that completed the reconstruction of the past. He almost felt the old sense of imprisonment, of aching nostalgia, of having lost his liberty.

Harris sighed involuntarily and turned towards his host, who returned his smile faintly and then led the way down the corridor.

'The boys have retired,' he explained, 'and, as you remember, we keep early hours here. But, at least, you will join us for a little while in the *Brüderstube* and enjoy a cup of coffee.' This was precisely what the silk merchant had hoped, and he accepted with an alacrity that he intended to be tempered by graciousness. 'And tomorrow,' continued the Brüder, 'you must come and spend a whole day with us. You may even find acquaintances, for several pupils of your day have come back here as masters.'

For one brief second there passed into the man's eyes a look that made the visitor start. But it vanished as quickly as it came. It was impossible to define. Harris convinced himself it was the effect of a shadow cast by the lamp they had just passed on the wall. He dismissed it from his mind.

'You are very kind, I'm sure,' he said politely. 'It is perhaps a greater pleasure to me than you can imagine to see the place again. Ah' – he stopped short opposite a door with the upper half of glass and peered in – 'surely there is one of the music rooms where I used to practise the violin. How it comes back to me after all these years!'

Brüder Kalkmann stopped indulgently, smiling, to allow his guest a moment's inspection.

'You still have the boys' orchestra? I remember I used to play "*zweite Geige*" in it. Brüder Schliemann conducted at the piano. Dear me, I can see him now with his long black hair and – and ——' He stopped abruptly. Again the odd, dark look passed over the stern face of his companion. For an instant it seemed curiously familiar.

'We still keep up the pupils' orchestra,' he said, 'but Brüder Schliemann, I am sorry to say——' he hesitated an instant, and then added, 'Brüder Schliemann is dead.'

'Indeed, indeed,' said Harris quickly. 'I am sorry to hear it.' He was conscious of a faint feeling of distress, but whether it arose from the news of his old music teacher's death – or from something else – he could not quite determine. He gazed down the corridor that lost itself among shadows. In the street and village everything had seemed so much smaller than he remembered, but here, inside the school building, everything seemed so much bigger. The corridor was loftier and longer, more spacious and vast, than the mental picture he had preserved. His thoughts wandered dreamily for an instant.

He glanced up and saw the face of the Brüder watching him with a smile of patient indulgence.

'Your memories possess you,' he observed gently, and the stern look passed into something almost pitying.

'You are right,' returned the man of silk, 'they do. This was the most wonderful period of my whole life in a sense. At the time I hated it——' He hesitated, not wishing to hurt the Brother's feelings.

'According to English ideas it seemed strict, of course,' the other said persuasively, so that he went on.

'——Yes, partly that; and partly the ceaseless nostalgia, and the solitude which came from never being really alone. In English schools the boys enjoy peculiar freedom, you know.'

Brüder Kalkmann, he saw, was listening intently.

'But it produced one result that I have never wholly lost,' he continued self-consciously, 'and am grateful for.'

'*Ach! Wie so, denn!*'

'The constant inner pain threw me headlong into your religious life, so that the whole force of my being seemed to project itself towards the search for a deeper satisfaction – a real resting-place for the soul. During my two years here I yearned for God in my boyish way as perhaps I have never yearned for anything since. Moreover, I have never quite lost that sense of peace and inward joy which accompanied the search. I can never quite forget this school and the deep things it taught me.'

He paused at the end of his long speech, and a brief silence fell between them. He feared he had said too much, or expressed himself clumsily in the foreign language, and when Brüder Kalkmann laid a hand upon his shoulder, he gave a little involuntary start.

'So that my memories perhaps do possess me rather strongly,' he added apologetically; 'and this long corridor, these rooms, that barred and gloomy front door, all touch chords that – that——' His German failed him and he glanced at his companion with an explanatory smile and gesture. But the Brother had removed his hand from his shoulder and was standing with his back to him, looking down the passage.

'Naturally, naturally so,' he said hastily without turning round. '*Es ist doch selbstverständlich.* We shall all understand.'

Then he turned suddenly, and Harris saw that his face had turned most oddly and disagreeably sinister. It may only have been the shadows again playing their tricks with the wretched oil lamps on the wall, for the dark expression passed instantly as they retraced their steps down the corridor, but the Englishman somehow got the impression that he had said something to give offence, something that was not quite to the other's taste. Opposite the door of the *Brüderstube* they stopped. Harris realised that it was late and he had possibly stayed talking too long. He made a tentative effort to leave, but his companion would not hear of it.

'You must have a cup of coffee with us,' he said firmly as though he meant it, 'and my colleagues will be delighted to see you. Some of them will remember you, perhaps.'

The sound of voices came pleasantly through the door, men's voices talking together. Brüder Kalkmann turned the handle and they entered a room ablaze with light and full of people.

'Ah – but your name?' he whispered, bending down to catch the reply; 'you have not told me your name yet.'

'Harris,' said the Englishman quickly as they went in. He felt nervous as he crossed the threshold, but ascribed the momentary trepidation to the fact that he was breaking the strictest rule of the whole establishment, which forbade a boy under severest penalties to come near this holy of holies where the masters took their brief leisure.

'Ah, yes, of course – Harris,' repeated the other as though he remembered it. 'Come in, Herr Harris, come in, please. Your visit will be immensely appreciated. It is really very fine, very wonderful of you to have come in this way.'

The door closed behind them and, in the sudden light which made his sight swim for a moment, the exaggeration of the language escaped his attention. He heard the voice of Brüder Kalkmann introducing him. He spoke very loud, indeed, unnecessarily – absurdly loud, Harris thought.

'Brothers,' he announced, 'it is my pleasure and privilege to introduce to you Herr Harris from England. He has just arrived to make us a little visit, and I have already expressed to him on behalf of us all the satisfaction we feel that he is here. He was, as you remember, a pupil in the year 'seventy.'

It was very formal, a very German introduction, but Harris rather liked it. It made him feel important and he appreciated the tact that made it almost seem as though he had been expected.

The black forms rose and bowed; Harris bowed; Kalkmann bowed. Everyone was very polite and very courtly. The room swam with moving figures; the light dazzled him after the gloom of the corridor; there was thick cigar smoke in the atmosphere. He took the chair that was offered to him between two of the Brothers, and sat down, feeling vaguely that his perceptions were not quite as keen and accurate as usual. He felt a trifle dazed perhaps, and the spell of the past came strongly over him, confusing the immediate present and making everything dwindle oddly to the dimensions of long ago. He seemed to pass under the mastery of a great mood that was a composite reproduction of all the moods of his forgotten boyhood.

Then he pulled himself together with a sharp effort and entered into the conversation that had begun again to buzz round him. Moreover, he entered into it with keen pleasure, for the Brothers – there were perhaps a dozen of them in the little room – treated him with a charm of manner that speedily made him feel one of themselves. This, again, was a very subtle delight to him. He felt that he had stepped out of the greedy, vulgar, self-seeking world, the world of silk and markets and profit-making – stepped into the cleaner atmosphere where spiritual ideals were paramount and life was simple and devoted. It all charmed him inexpressibly, so that he realised – yes, in a sense – the degradation of his twenty years' absorption in business. This keen atmosphere under the stars where men thought only of their souls, and of the souls of others, was too rarefied for the world he was now associated with. He found himself making comparisons to his own disadvantage – comparisons with the mystical little dreamer that had stepped thirty years before from the stern peace of this devout community, and the man of the world that he had since become – and the contrast made him shiver with a keen regret and something like self-contempt.

He glanced round at the other faces floating towards him

through tobacco smoke – this acrid cigar smoke he remembered so well: how keen they were, how strong, placid, touched with the nobility of great aims and unselfish purposes. At one or two he looked particularly. He hardly knew why. They rather fascinated him. There was something so very stern and uncompromising about them, and something, too, oddly, subtly, familiar, that yet just eluded him. But whenever their eyes met his own they held undeniable welcome in them; and some held more – a kind of perplexed admiration, he thought, something that was between esteem and deference. This note of respect in all the faces was very flattering to his vanity.

Coffee was served presently, made by a black-haired Brother who sat in the corner by the piano and bore a marked resemblance to Brüder Schliemann, the musical director of thirty years ago. Harris exchanged bows with him when he took the cup from his white hands, which he noticed were like the hands of a woman. He lit a cigar, offered to him by his neighbour, with whom he was chatting delightfully, and who, in the glare of the lighted match, reminded him sharply for a moment of Brüder Pagel, his former room-master.

'*Es ist wirklich merkwürdig,*' he said, 'how many resemblances I see, or imagine. It is really *very* curious!'

'Yes,' replied the other, peering at him over his coffee cup, 'the spell of the place is wonderfully strong. I can well understand that the old faces rise before your mind's eye – almost to the exclusion of ourselves perhaps.'

They both laughed pleasantly. It was soothing to find his mood understood and appreciated. And they passed on to talk of the mountain village, its isolation, its remoteness from the worldly life, its peculiar fitness for meditation and worship, and for spiritual development – of a certain kind.

'And your coming back in this way, Herr Harris, has pleased us all so much,' joined in the Brother on his left. 'We esteem you for it most highly. We honour you for it.'

Harris made a deprecating gesture. 'I fear, for my part, it is only a very selfish pleasure,' he said a trifle unctuously.

'Not all would have had the courage,' added the one who resembled Brüder Pagel.

'You mean,' said Harris, a little puzzled, 'the disturbing memories——?'

Brüder Pagel looked at him steadily, with unmistakable admiration and respect. 'I mean that most men hold so strongly to life, and can give up so little for their beliefs,' he said gravely.

The Englishman felt slightly uncomfortable. These worthy men really made too much of his sentimental journey. Besides, the talk was getting a little out of his depth. He hardly followed it.

'The worldly life still has *some* charms for me,' he replied smilingly, as though to indicate that sainthood was not yet quite within his grasp.

'All the more, then, must we honour you for so freely coming,' said the Brother on his left; 'so unconditionally!'

A pause followed, and the silk merchant felt relieved when the conversation took a more general turn, although he noted that it never travelled very far from the subject of his visit and the wonderful situation of the lonely village for the men who wished to develop their spiritual powers and practise the rites of a high worship. Others joined in, complimenting him on his knowledge of the language, making him feel utterly at his ease, yet at the same time a little uncomfortable by the excess of their admiration. After all, it was such a very small thing to do, this sentimental journey.

The time passed along quickly; the coffee was excellent, the cigars soft and of the nutty flavour he loved. At length, fearing to outstay his welcome, he rose reluctantly to take his leave. But the others would not hear of it. It was not often a former pupil returned to visit them in this simple, unaffected way. The night was young. If necessary they could even find him a corner in the great *Schlafzimmer* upstairs. He was easily persuaded to stay a little longer. Somehow he had become the centre of the little party. He felt pleased, flattered, honoured.

'And perhaps Brüder Schliemann will play something for us – now.'

It was Kalkmann speaking, and Harris started visibly as he heard the name, and saw the black-haired man by the piano turn with a smile. For Schliemann was the name of his old music director, who was dead. Could this be his son? They were so exactly alike.

'If Brüder Meyer has not put his Amati to bed, I will accompany him,' said the musician suggestively, looking across at a man whom Harris had not yet noticed, and who, he now saw, was the very image of a former master of that name.

Meyer rose and excused himself with a little bow, and the Englishman quickly observed that he had a peculiar gesture as though his neck had a false join on to the body just below the collar and feared it might break. Meyer of old had this trick of movement. He remembered how the boys used to copy it.

He glanced sharply from face to face, feeling as though some silent, unseen process were changing everything about him. All the faces seemed oddly familiar. Pagel, the Brother he had been talking with, was of course the image of Pagel, his former room-master; and Kalkmann, he now realised for the first time, was the very twin of another master whose name he had quite forgotten, but whom he used to dislike intensely in the old days. And, through the smoke, peering at him from the corners of the room, he saw that all the Brothers about him had the faces he had known and lived with long ago – Rost, Fluheim, Meinert, Rigel, Gysin.

He stared hard, suddenly grown more alert, and everywhere saw, or fancied he saw, strange likenesses, ghostly resemblances – more, the identical faces of years ago. There was something queer about it all, something not quite right, something that made him feel uneasy. He shook himself, mentally and actually, blowing the smoke from before his eyes with a long breath, and as he did so he noticed to his dismay that everyone was fixedly staring. They were watching him.

This brought him to his senses. As an Englishman, and a foreigner, he did not wish to be rude, or to do anything to make himself foolishly conspicuous and spoil the harmony of the evening. He was a guest, and a privileged guest at that. Besides, the music had already begun. Brüder Schliemann's long white fingers were caressing the keys to some purpose.

He subsided into his chair and smoked with half-closed eyes that yet saw everything.

But the shudder had established itself in his being, and, whether he would or not, it kept repeating itself. As a town, far up some inland river, feels the pressure of the distant sea, so he became aware that the mighty forces from somewhere beyond his ken were urging themselves up against his soul in this smoky little room. He began to feel exceedingly ill at ease.

And as the music filled the air his mind began to clear. Like a lifted veil there rose up something that had hitherto obscured his vision. The words of the priest at the railway inn flashed across his brain unbidden: 'You will find it different.' And also, though why he could not tell, he saw mentally the strong, rather wonderful eyes of that other guest at the supper table, the man who had overheard his conversation, and had later got into earnest talk with the priest. He took out his watch and stole a glance at it. Two hours had slipped by. It was already eleven o'clock.

Schliemann, meanwhile, utterly absorbed in his music, was playing a solemn measure. The piano sang marvellously. The power of a great conviction, the simplicity of great art, the vital spiritual message of a soul that had found itself – all this, and more, were in the chords, and yet somehow the music was what can only be described as impure – atrociously and diabolically

impure. And the piece itself, although Harris did not recognise it as anything familiar, was surely the music of a
Mass – huge, majestic, sombre? It stalked through the smoky
room with slow power, like the passage of something that was
mighty, yet profoundly intimate, and as it went there stirred
into each and every face about him the signature of the enor-
mous forces of which it was the audible symbol. The countenances round him turned sinister, but not idly, negatively sinister:
they grew dark with purpose. He suddenly recalled the face of
Brüder Kalkmann in the corridor earlier in the evening. The
motives of their secret souls rose to the eyes, and mouths, and
foreheads, and hung there for all to see like the black banners of
an assembly of ill-starred and fallen creatures. Demons – was
the horrible word that flashed through his brain like a sheet of
fire.

When this sudden discovery leaped out upon him, for a
moment he lost his self-control. Without waiting to think and
weigh his extraordinary impression, he did a very foolish but a
very natural thing. Feeling himself irresistibly driven by the
sudden stress to some kind of action, he sprang to his feet – and
screamed! To his own utter amazement he stood up and
shrieked aloud!

But no one stirred. No one, apparently, took the slightest
notice of his absurdly wild behaviour. It was almost as if no one
but himself had heard the scream at all – as though the music
had drowned it and swallowed it up – as though after all perhaps
he had not really screamed as loudly as he imagined, or had not
screamed at all.

Then, as he glanced at the motionless, dark faces before him,
something of utter cold passed into his being, touching his very
soul. . . . All emotion cooled suddenly, leaving him like a
receding tide. He sat down again, ashamed, mortified, angry
with himself for behaving like a fool and a boy. And the music,
meanwhile, continued to issue from the white and snake-like

fingers of Brüder Schliemann, as poisoned wine might issue from the weirdly-fashioned necks of antique phials.

And, with the rest of them, Harris drank it in.

Forcing himself to believe that he had been the victim of some kind of illusory perception, he vigorously restrained his feelings. Then the music presently ceased, and every one applauded and began to talk at once, laughing, changing seats, complimenting the player and behaving naturally and easily as though nothing out of the way had happened. The faces appeared normal once more. The Brothers crowded round their visitor, and he joined in their talk and even heard himself thanking the gifted musician.

But, at the same time, he found himself edging towards the door, nearer and nearer, changing his chair when possible, and joining the groups that stood closest to the way of escape.

'I must thank you all *tausendmal* for my little reception and the great pleasure – the very great honour you have done me,' he began in decided tones at length, 'but I fear I have trespassed far too long already on your hospitality. Moreover, I have some distance to walk to my inn.'

A chorus of voices greeted his words. They would not hear of his going – at least not without first partaking of refreshment. They produced pumpernickel from one cupboard, and rye-bread and sausage from another, and all began to talk again and eat. More coffee was made, fresh cigars lighted, and Brüder Meyer took out his violin and began to tune it softly.

'There is always a bed upstairs if Herr Harris will accept it,' said one.

'And it is difficult to find the way out now, for all the doors are locked,' laughed another loudly.

'Let us take our simple pleasures as they come,' cried a third. 'Brüder Harris will understand how we appreciate the honour of this last visit of his.'

They made a dozen excuses. They all laughed, as though the

politeness of their words was but formal, and veiled thinly —
more and more thinly — a very different meaning.

'And the hour of midnight draws near,' added Brüder
Kalkmann with a charming smile, but in a voice that sounded to
the Englishman like the grating of iron hinges.

Their German seemed to him more and more difficult to
understand. He noted that they called him 'Brüder' too, classing
him as one of themselves.

And then suddenly he had a flash of keener perception, and
realised with a creeping of his flesh that he had all along misinterpreted — grossly misinterpreted — all they had been saying.
They had talked about the beauty of the place, its isolation and
remoteness from the world, its peculiar fitness for certain kinds
of spiritual development and worship — yet hardly, he now
grasped, in the sense in which he had taken the words. They had
meant something different. Their spiritual powers, their desire
for loneliness, their passion for worship, were not the powers,
the solitude, or the worship that *he* meant and understood. He
was playing the part in some horrible masquerade; he was among
men who cloaked their lives with religion in order to follow
their real purposes unseen of men.

What did it all mean? How had he blundered into so equivocal
a situation? Had he blundered into it at all? Had he not rather
been led into it, deliberately led? His thoughts grew dreadfully
confused, and his confidence in himself began to fade. And why,
he suddenly thought again, were they so impressed by the mere
fact of his coming to revisit his old school? What was it they so
admired and wondered at in his simple act? Why did they set
such store upon his having the courage to come, to 'give himself
so freely', 'unconditionally' as one of them had expressed it with
such a mockery of exaggeration?

Fear stirred in his heart most horribly, and he found no answer
to any of his questionings. Only one thing he now understood
quite clearly: it was their purpose to keep him here. They did not

intend that he should go. And from this moment he realised that they were sinister, formidable and, in some way he had yet to discover, inimical to himself, inimical to his life. And the phrase one of them had used a moment ago — 'this *last* visit of his' — rose before his eyes in letters of flame.

Harris was not a man of action, and had never known in all the course of his career what it meant to be in a situation of real danger. He was not necessarily a coward, though, perhaps, a man of untried nerve. He realised at last plainly that he was in a very awkward predicament indeed, and that he had to deal with men who were utterly in earnest. What their intentions were he only vaguely guessed. His mind, indeed, was too confused for definite ratiocination, and he was only able to follow blindly the strongest instincts that moved in him. It never occurred to him that the Brothers might all be mad, or that he himself might have temporarily lost his senses and be suffering under some terrible delusion. In fact, nothing occurred to him — he realised nothing except that he meant to escape — and the quicker the better. A tremendous revulsion of feeling set in and overpowered him.

Accordingly, without further protest for the moment, he ate his pumpernickel and drank his coffee, talking meanwhile as naturally and pleasantly as he could, and when a suitable interval had passed, he rose to his feet and announced once more that he must now take his leave. He spoke very quietly, but very decidedly. No one hearing him could doubt that he meant what he said. He had got very close to the door by this time.

'I regret,' he said, using his best German, and speaking to a hushed room, 'that our pleasant evening must come to an end, but it is now time for me to wish you all good-night.' And then, as no one said anything, he added, though with a trifle less assurance, 'And I thank you all most sincerely for your hospitality.'

'On the contrary,' replied Kalkmann instantly, rising from his chair and ignoring the hand the Englishman had stretched out to him, 'it is we who have to thank you; and we do so most gratefully and sincerely.'

And at the same moment at least half a dozen of the Brothers took up their position between himself and the door.

'You are very good to say so,' Harris replied as firmly as he could manage, noticing this movement out of the corner of his eye, 'but really I had no conception that – my little chance visit could have afforded you so much pleasure.' He moved another step nearer the door, but Brüder Schliemann came across the room quickly and stood in front of him. His attitude was uncompromising. A dark and terrible expression had come into his face.

'But it was *not* by chance that you came, Brüder Harris,' he said so that all the room could hear; 'surely we have not misunderstood your presence here?' He raised his black eyebrows.

'No, no,' the Englishman hastened to reply. 'I was – I am delighted to be here. I told you what pleasure it gave me to find myself among you. Do not misunderstand me, I beg.' His voice faltered a little, and he had difficulty in finding the words. More and more, too, he had difficulty in understanding *their* words.

'Of course,' interposed Brüder Kalkmann in his iron bass, '*we* have not misunderstood. You have come back in the spirit of true and unselfish devotion. You offer yourself freely, and we all appreciate it. It is your willingness and nobility that have so completely won our veneration and respect.' A faint murmur of applause ran round the room. 'What we all delight in – what our great Master will especially delight in – is the value of your spontaneous and voluntary——'

He used a word Harris did not understand. He said '*Opfer*'. The bewildered Englishman searched his brain for the translation, and searched in vain, for the life of him he could not remember what it meant. But the word, for all his inability to translate it, touched his soul with ice. It was worse, far worse, than anything he had imagined. He felt like a lost, helpless creature, and all power to fight sank out of him from that momment.

'It is magnificent to be such a willing——' added Schliemann, sidling up to him with a dreadful leer on his face. He made use of the same word – '*Opfer*'

God! What could it all mean? 'Offer himself'! 'True spirit of devotion'! 'Willing', 'unselfish', 'magnificent'! *Opfer, Opfer, Opfer!* What in the name of heaven did it mean, that strange, mysterious word that struck such terror into his heart?

He made a valiant effort to keep his presence of mind and hold his nerves steady. Turning, he saw that Kalkmann's face was a dead white. Kalkmann! He understood that well enough. *Kalkmann* meant 'Man of Chalk'; he knew that. But what did '*Opfer*' mean? That was the real key to the situation. Words poured through his disordered mind in an endless stream – unusual, rare words he had perhaps heard but once in his life – while '*Opfer*', a word in common use, entirely escaped him. What an extraordinary mockery it all was!

Then Kalkmann, pale as death, but his face hard as iron, spoke a few low words that he did not catch, and the Brothers standing by the walls at once turned the lamps down so that the room became dim. In the half light he could only just discern their faces and movements.

'It is time,' he heard Kalkmann's remorseless voice continue just behind him. 'The hour of midnight is at hand. Let us prepare. He comes! He comes; Brüder Asmodelius comes!' His voice rose to a chant.

And the sound of that name, for some extraordinary reason, was terrible – utterly terrible; so that Harris shook from head to foot as he heard it. Its utterance filled the air like soft thunder, and a hush came over the whole room. Forces rose all about him, transforming the normal into the horrible, and the spirit of craven fear ran through all his being, bringing him to the verge of collapse.

Asmodelius! Asmodelius! The name was appalling. For he understood at last to whom it referred and the meaning that lay between its great syllables. At the same instant, too, he suddenly understood the meaning of that unremembered word. The import of the word *'Opfer'* flashed upon his soul like a message of death.

He thought of making a wild effort to reach the door, but the weakness of his trembling knees, and the row of black figures that stood between, dissuaded him at once. He would have screamed for help, but remembering the emptiness of the vast building, and the loneliness of the situation, he understood that no help could come that way, and he kept his lips closed. He stood still and did nothing. But he knew now what was coming.

Two of the brothers approached and took him gently by the arm.

'Brüder Asmodelius accepts you,' they whispered; 'are you ready?'

Then he found his tongue and tried to speak. 'But what have I to do with this Brüder Asm – Asmo——?' he stammered, a desperate rush of words crowding vainly behind the halting tongue.

The name refused to pass his lips. He could not pronounce it as they did. He could not pronounce it at all. His sense of helplessness then entered the acute stage, for this inability to speak the name produced a fresh sense of quite horrible confusion in his mind, and he became extraordinarily agitated.

'I came here for a friendly visit,' he tried to say with a great effort, but, to his intense dismay, he heard his voice saying something quite different, and actually making use of that very word they had all used: 'I came here as a willing *Opfer*,' he heard his own voice say, *'and I am quite ready.'*

He was lost beyond all recall now! Not alone his mind, but the very muscles of his body had passed out of control. He felt that he was hovering on the confines of a phantom or demon-world –

a world in which the name they had spoken constituted the Master-name, the word of ultimate power.

What followed he heard and saw as in a nightmare!

'In the half light that veils all truth, let us prepare to worship and adore,' chanted Schliemann, who had preceded him to the end of the room.

'In the mists that protect our faces before the Black Throne, let us make ready the willing victim,' echoed Kalkmann in his great bass.

They raised their faces, listening expectantly, as a roaring sound, like the passing of mighty projectiles, filled the air, far, far away, very wonderful, very forbidding. The walls of the room trembled.

'He comes! He comes! He comes!' chanted the Brothers in chorus.

The sound of roaring died away, and an atmosphere of still and utter cold established itself over all. Then Kalkmann, dark and unutterably stern, turned in the dim light and faced the rest.

'Asmodelius, our *Haupbrüder*, is about us,' he cried in a voice that even while it shook was yet a voice of iron; 'Asmodelius is about us. Make ready.'

There followed a pause in which no one stirred or spoke. A tall Brother approached the Englishman; but Kalkmann held up his hand.

'Let the eyes remain uncovered,' he said, 'in honour of so freely giving himself.' And to his horror Harris then realised for the first time that his hands were already fastened to his sides.

The Brother retreated again silently, and in the pause that followed all the figures about him dropped to their knees, leaving him standing alone, and as they dropped, in voices hushed with mingled reverence and awe, they cried softly, odiously, appallingly the name of the Being whom they momentarily expected to appear.

Then, at the end of the room, where the windows seemed to

have disappeared so that he saw the stars, there rose into view far up against the night sky, grand and terrible, the outline of a man. A kind of grey glory enveloped it so that it resembled a steel-cased statue, immense, imposing, horrific in its distant splendour; while, at the same time, the face was so spiritually mighty, yet so proudly, so austerely sad, that Harris felt as he stared, that the sight was more than his eyes could meet, and that in another moment the power of vision would fail him altogether, and he must sink into utter nothingness.

So remote and inaccessible hung this figure that it was impossible to gauge anything as to its size, yet at the same time so strangely close, that when the grey radiance from its mightily broken visage, august and mournful, beat down upon his soul, pulsing like some dark star with the powers of spiritual evil, he felt almost as though he were looking into a face no farther removed from him in space than the face of any one of the Brothers who stood by his side.

And then the room filled and trembled with sounds that Harris understood full well were the failing voices of others who had preceded him in a long series down the years. There came first a plain, sharp cry, as of a man in the last anguish, choking for his breath, and yet, with the very final expiration of it, breathing the name of the Worship – of the dark Being who rejoiced to hear it. The cries of the strangled; the short, running gasp of the suffocated; and the smothered gurgling of the tightened throat, all these, and more, echoed back and forth between the walls, the very walls in which he now stood a prisoner, a sacrificial victim. The cries, too, not alone of the broken bodies, but – far worse – of beaten, broken souls. And as the ghastly chorus rose and fell, there came also the faces of the lost and unhappy creatures to whom they belonged, and, against that curtain of pale grey light, he saw float past him in the air, an array of white and piteous human countenances that seemed to beckon and gibber at him as though he were already one of themselves.

Slowly, too, as the voices rose, and the pallid crew sailed past, that giant form of grey descended from the sky and approached the room that contained the worshippers and their prisoner. Hands rose and sank about them in the darkness, and he felt that he was being draped in other garments than his own; a circlet of ice seemed to run about his head, while round the waist, enclosing the fastened arms, he felt a girdle tightly drawn. At last, about his very throat, there ran a soft and silken touch which, better than if there had been full light, and a mirror held to his face, he understood to be the cord of sacrifice — and of death.

At this moment the Brothers, still prostrate upon the floor, began again their mournful, yet impassioned chanting, and as they did so a strange thing happened. For, apparently without moving or altering its position, the huge Figure seemed, at once and suddenly, to be inside the room, almost beside him, and to fill the space around him to the exclusion of all else.

He was now beyond all ordinary sensations of fear, only a drab feeling as of death — the death of the soul — stirred in his heart. His thoughts no longer even beat vainly for space. The end was near, and he knew it.

The dreadfully chanting voices rose about him in a wave: 'We worship! We adore! We offer!' The sounds filled his ears and hammered, almost meaningless, upon his brain.

Then the majestic grey face turned slowly downwards upon him, and his very soul passed outwards and seemed to become absorbed in the sea of those anguished eyes. At the same moment a dozen hands forced him to his knees, and in the air before him he saw the arm of Kalkmann upraised, and felt the pressure about his throat grow strong.

It was in this awful moment, when he had given up all hope, and the help of gods or men seemed beyond question, that a strange thing happened. For before his fading and terrified vision, there slid, as in a dream of light — yet without apparent rhyme or reason — wholly unbidden and unexplained — the face of that other man at the supper table of the railway inn. And the sight, even mentally, of that strong, wholesome, vigorous English face, inspired him suddenly with a new courage.

It was but a flash of fading vision before he sank into a dark and terrible death, yet, in some inexplicable way, the sight of that face stirred in him unconquerable hope and the certainty of deliverance. It was a face of power, a face, he now realised, of simple goodness such as might have been seen by men of old on the shores of Galilee; a face, by heaven, that could conquer even the devils of outer space.

And, in his despair and abandonment, he called upon it, and called with no uncertain accents. He found his voice in this over-whelming moment to some purpose; though the words he actually used, and whether they were in German or English, he could never remember. Their effect, nevertheless, was instant-aneous. The Brothers understood, and that grey Figure of evil understood.

For a second the confusion was terrific. There came a great shattering sound. It seemed that the very earth trembled. But all Harris remembered afterwards was that voices rose about him in the clamour of terrified alarm —

'A man of power is among us! A man of God!'

The vast sound was repeated — the rushing through space as of huge projectiles — and he sank to the floor of the room, un-conscious. The entire scene had vanished, vanished like smoke over the roof of a cottage when the wind blows.

And, by his side, sat down a slight un-German figure — the figure of the stranger at the inn — the man who had the 'rather wonderful eyes'.

When Harris came to himself he felt cold. He was lying under the open sky, and the cool air of field and forest was blowing upon his face. He sat up and looked about him. The memory of the late scene was still horribly in his mind, but no vestige of it remained. No walls or ceiling enclosed him; he was no longer in a room at all. There were no lamps turned low, no cigar smoke, no black forms of sinister worshippers, no tremendous grey Figure hovering beyond the windows.

Open space was about him, and he was lying on a pile of bricks and mortar, his clothes soaked with dew, and the kind stars shining brightly overhead. He was lying, bruised and shaken, among the heaped-up debris of a ruined building.

He stood up and stared about him. There, in the shadowy distance, lay the surrounding forest, and here, close at hand, stood the outline of the village buildings. But, underfoot, beyond question, lay nothing but the broken heaps of stones that betokened a building long since crumbled to dust. Then he saw that the stones were blackened, and that great wooden beams, half burnt, half rotten, made lines through the general debris. He stood, then, among the ruins of a burnt and shattered building, the weeds and nettles proving conclusively that it had lain thus for many years.

The moon had already set behind the encircling forest, but the stars that spangled the heavens threw enough light to enable him to make quite sure of what he saw. Harris, the silk merchant, stood among these broken and burnt stones and shivered.

Then he suddenly became aware that out of the gloom a figure had risen and stood beside him. Peering at him, he thought he recognised the face of the stranger at the railway inn.

'Are *you* real?' he asked in a voice he hardly recognised as his own.

'More than real – I'm friendly,' replied the stranger; 'I followed you up here from the inn.'

Harris stood and stared for several minutes without adding anything. His teeth chattered. The least sound made him start: but the simple words in his own language, and the tone in which they were uttered, comforted him inconceivably.

'You're English too, thank God,' he said inconsequently. 'These German devils——' He broke off and put a hand to his eyes. 'But what's become of them all – and the room – and – and——' The hand travelled down to his throat and moved nervously round his neck. He drew a long, long breath of relief. 'Did I dream everything – everything?' he said distractedly.

He stared wildly about him, and the stranger moved forward and took his arm. 'Come,' he said soothingly, yet with a trace of command in the voice, 'we will move away from here. The high road or even the woods will be more to your taste, for we are standing now on one of the most haunted – and most terribly haunted – spots of the whole world.'

He guided his companion's stumbling footsteps over the broken masonry until they reached the path, the nettles stinging their hands, and Harris feeling his way like a man in a dream. Passing through the twisted iron railing they reached the path, and thence made their way to the road, shining white in the night. Once safely out of the ruins, Harris collected himself and turned to look back.

'But, how is it possible?' he exclaimed, his voice still shaking. 'How can it be possible? When I came in here I saw the building in the moonlight. They opened the door. I saw the figures and heard the voices and touched, yes touched, their very hands, and saw their damned black faces, saw them far more plainly than I see you now.' He was deeply bewildered. The glamour was still upon his eyes with a degree of reality stronger than the reality even of normal life. 'Was I so utterly deluded?'

Then suddenly the words of the stranger, which he had only half heard or understood, returned to him.

'Haunted?' he asked, looking hard at him; 'haunted, did you say?' He paused in the roadway and stared into the darkness where the building of the old school had first appeared to him. But the stranger hurried him forward.

'We shall talk more safely farther on,' he said. 'I followed you from the inn the moment I realised where you had gone. When I found you it was eleven o'clock——'

'Eleven o'clock,' said Harris, remembering with a shudder.

'——I saw you drop. I watched over you till you recovered consciousness of your own accord, and now – now I am here to guide you safely back to the inn. I have broken the spell – the glamour——'

'I owe you a great deal, sir,' interrupted Harris again, beginning to understand something of the stranger's kindness, 'but I don't understand it at all. I feel dazed and shaken.' His teeth still chattered, and spells of violent shivering passed over him from head to foot. He found that he was clinging to the other's arm. In this way they passed beyond the deserted and crumbling village and gained the high road that led homewards through the forest.

'That school building has long been in ruins,' said the man at his side presently; 'it was burnt down by order of the Elders of the community at least ten years ago. The village has been uninhabited ever since. But the simulacra of certain ghastly events that took place under that roof in past days still continue. And the "shells" of the chief participants still enact there the dreadful deeds that led to its final destruction, and to the desertion of the whole settlement. They were devil-worshippers!'

Harris listened with beads of perspiration on his forehead that did not come alone from their leisurely pace through the cool night. Although he had seen this man but once before in his life, and had never before exchanged so much as a word with him, he felt a degree of confidence and a subtle sense of safety and well-being in his presence that were the most healing influences he could possibly have wished after the experience he had been through. For all that, he still felt as if he were walking in a dream; and though he heard every word that fell from his companion's lips, it was only the next day that the full import of all he said became fully clear to him. The presence of this quiet stranger, the man with the wonderful eyes which he felt now, rather than saw, applied a soothing anodyne to his shattered spirit that healed him through and through. And this healing influence, distilled from the dark figure at his side, satisfied his first imperative need, so that he almost forgot to realise how strange and opportune it was that the man should be there at all.

It somehow never occurred to him to ask his name, or to feel any undue wonder that one passing tourist should take so much trouble on behalf of another. He just walked by his side, listening to his quiet words, and allowing himself to enjoy the very wonderful experience after his recent ordeal, of being helped, strengthened, blessed. Only once, remembering vaguely something of his reading of years ago, he turned to the man beside him, after some more than usually remarkable words, and heard himself, almost involuntarily it seemed, putting the question: 'Then are you a Rosicrucian, sir, perhaps?' But the stranger had ignored the words, or possibly not heard them, for he continued with his talk as though unconscious of any interruption, and Harris became aware that another somewhat unusual picture had taken possession of his mind, as they walked there side by side through the cool reaches of the forest, and that he had found his imagination suddenly charged with the childhood memory of Jacob wrestling with an angel -- wrestling all night with a being of superior quality whose strength eventually became his own.

'It was your abrupt conversation with the priest at supper that first put me upon the track of this remarkable occurrence,' he heard the man's quiet voice beside him in the darkness, 'and it was from him I learned after you left the story of the devil-worship that became secretly established in the heart of this simple and devout little community.'

'Devil-worship! Here——!' Harris stammered, aghast.

'Yes – here – conducted secretly for years by a group of Brothers before unexplained disappearances in the neighbourhood led to its discovery. For where could they have found a safer place in the whole wide world for their ghastly traffic and perverted powers than here, in the very precincts – under cover of the very shadow of saintliness and holy living?'

'Awful, awful!' whispered the silk merchant, 'and when I tell you the words they used to me——'

'I know it all,' the stranger said quietly. 'I saw and heard everything. My plan first was to wait till the end and then to take steps for their destruction, but in the interest of your personal safety' – he spoke with the utmost gravity and conviction – 'in the interest of the safety of your soul, I made my presence known when I did, and before the conclusion had been reached——'

'My safety! The danger, then, was real. They were alive and——' Words failed him. He stopped in the road and turned towards his companion, the shining of whose eyes he could just make out in the gloom.

'It was a concourse of the shells of violent men, spiritually-developed but evil men, seeking after death – the death of the body – to prolong their vile and unnatural existence. And had they accomplished their object you, in turn, at the death of your body, would have passed into their power and helped to swell their dreadful purposes.'

Harris made no reply. He was trying hard to concentrate his mind upon the sweet and common things of life. He even thought of silk and St Paul's Churchyard and the faces of his partners in business.

'For you came all prepared to be caught,' he heard the other's voice like someone talking to him from a distance; 'your deeply introspective mood had already reconstructed the past so vividly, so intensely, that you were *en rapport* at once with any forces of those days that chanced still to be lingering. And they swept you up all unresistingly.'

Harris tightened his hold upon the stranger's arm as he heard. At the moment he had room for one emotion only. It did not seem to him odd that this stranger should have such intimate knowledge of his mind.

'It is, alas, chiefly the evil emotions that are able to leave their photographs upon surrounding scenes and objects,' the other added, 'and who ever heard of a place haunted by a noble deed, or of beautiful and lovely ghosts revisiting the glimpses of the moon? It is unfortunate. But the wicked passions of men's hearts alone seem strong enough to leave pictures that persist; the good are ever too lukewarm.'

The stranger sighed as he spoke. But Harris, exhausted and shaken as he was to the very core, paced by his side, only half listening. He moved as in a dream still. It was very wonderful to him, this walk home under the stars in the early hours of the October morning, the peaceful forest all about them, mist rising here and there over the small clearings, and the sound of water from a hundred little invisible streams filling in the pauses of the talk. In after-life he always looked back to it as something magical and impossible, something that had seemed too beautiful, too curiously beautiful, to have been quite true. And, though at the time he heard and understood but a quarter of what the stranger said, it came back to him afterwards, staying with him till the end of his days, and always with a curious, haunting sense of unreality, as though he had enjoyed a wonderful dream of which he could recall only faint and exquisite portions.

But the horror of the earlier experience was effectually dispelled; and when they reached the railway inn, somewhere about three o'clock in the morning, Harris shook the stranger's hand gratefully, effusively, meeting the look of those rather wonderful eyes with a full heart, and went up to his room, thinking in a hazy, dream-like way of the words with which the stranger had brought their conversation to an end as they left the confines of the forest.

'And if thought and emotion can persist in this way so long after the brain that sent them forth has crumbled into dust, how vitally important it must be to control their very birth in the heart, and guard them with the keenest possible restraint.'

But Harris, the silk merchant, slept better than might have been expected, and with a soundness that carried him halfway through the day. And when he came downstairs and learned that the stranger had already taken his departure, he realised with keen regret that he had never once thought of asking his name.

'Yes, he signed in the visitors' book,' said the girl in reply to his question.

And he turned over the blotted pages and found there, the last entry, in a very delicate and individual handwriting –

'John Silence, London.'

7

The Devil-Worshipper

Francis Prevot

———————

Accounts of Black Magic frequently mention ancient books which describe the theory and practise of the evil rites. Their very names, like Discours Des Sorciers *and* Le Satanisme, *are almost enough to cause a shudder of horror, and it is perhaps as well that very few copies of the books exist outside the sealed cases of national libraries. However, when one does come into the hands of a member of the public – be he a student of the Occult or not – the results can be unpredictable to say the least. In this short story, Francis Prevot, who was a noted writer of ghost stories at the turn of the century, has worked a grisly tale around the malignant powers of a Black Book.*

SETTLING HIMSELF COMFORTABLY in his deep armchair, Turner adjusted the reading lamp, and began to examine with pleasurable anticipation the volume his bookseller had sent him. With it was a short note to the effect that here was an exceedingly rare manuscript that every student of witchcraft and black magic knew by name and reputation, but that few had ever seen or handled.

It proved to be a dumpy little volume bound in vellum that was yellow and stained with age and, Turner observed that it was of a quality and texture unlike that of any vellum he was acquainted with. On the back the title was written in bold black lettering, *De Mysteriis Dom Sathanas* – 'Of The Secret Rites of the Lord Satan'. Turner, who had a morbid hankering after forbidden things, whose bleak, acute intellect spent itself upon the study of the grim rites performed by those that worship evil, chuckled greedily.

Here, indeed, was a find and material for his studies that he had never hoped to see. Putting the book down, he rose and, going to his desk, wrote to the dealer, enclosing a cheque and asking, as it were by an afterthought, in what manner and from whom the book had been acquired. It was seldom that such a carefully guarded treasure as this fell into a dealer's hands, and Turner was curious to know who its late owner had been, and in what circumstances he had come to part with it.

Then he returned to his chair and prepared to make a careful study of his new acquisition. Taking the squat little book into his hands, Turner experienced an odd, vague fear and a strange reluctance to open it and see its pages. Suddenly, and without any real reason, he thought of Rahling, of that strange individual who had known more of evil than it is good for any man to know, who had been found dead one morning by his servant, every bone in his body crushed to powder, yet with his skin white and fresh, uncut, unbruised, and unbroken. Rahling, he knew, had possessed a copy of this very book. Perhaps it was Rahling's own copy. The servant, he remembered, had gone mad, and from the moment he had seen the awful thing which had been his master, never again uttered an intelligible word.

Surprised and indignant at the current of his thoughts, Turner pulled himself together. It was unlike him to be hysterical like a woman, he thought, and with an irritable gesture he opened the book and began to read.

For an hour he read undisturbed, completely absorbed in the crabbed sentences of the medieval devil-worshipper who had composed the work, entirely unmoved by the loathsome abominations proclaimed on every page. Then something happened, he knew not precisely what, and he leaped to his feet with a muffled shriek of sheer terror.

He was instantly furious with himself for this fresh display of what he called schoolgirl nerves. But in spite of himself waves of horror and dread swept over him. He looked at his hands, which felt wet and sticky, and was appalled to find them stained with blood!

Glancing at the book which lay on the floor, he realised with a shudder that it was bound in human skin. Little beads of blood were starting from every pore on its surface, and it seemed to twitch and shrink as though it were suffering intolerable agony.

Stunned and scarcely capable of coherent thought, horrible ideas flitted through his mind. He thought again of Rahling and wondered if the powers of evil of this book were greater than he thought, and whether there were hidden forces that were beyond man's control, that brought destruction upon all that sought to master them. Or might that force be the servant of some long dead, avenging victim?

In an instant what remained of Turner's self-control snapped and with a shriek of pain from his parched lips he threw himself on the floor, writhing in agony. The feeling had come over him that his hands and feet were bound with thongs. And that his body was laid on a hard stone altar. Unseen hands moved him to and fro, unseen lips murmered abominable blasphemies over him that filled him with horror. Then came the ultimate agony as he felt the sharp blade of the sacrificial knife thrust into his flesh. . . .

A cheerful party returning from the theatre to the flat above heard a strange sound as they passed Turner's door. One of the men ventured to open it and peeped in. He slammed the door suddenly as though to prevent Something from escaping.

'I don't think we'll go in just yet,' he muttered faintly. 'Let's get a clergyman, quickly.'

8

Archives of the Dead

Basil Copper

———

8

Basil Copper, the author of this claustrophobic piece of modern Satanism, is one of the most promising horror-story writers to emerge in Britain in recent years. A life-long enthusiast and student of the Occult, he is a journalist by training and brings a newspaperman's objective eye and care for detail to his writing. He does much of his writing in a lovely old French château and many of his stories are notable for their haunting, Gothic quality. Archives of the Dead was written specially for this collection – don't turn the lights down too low before starting to read it.

ROBERT TRUMBLE ARRIVED at Linnet Ridge as a thin, persistent rain was beginning to fall. The house was in a remote part of Surrey and the sombre drive up through avenues of pines and fir had not prepared him for the sight of the building itself; painted white, standing four-square to the bracing winds of the uplands, it did not seem to Trumble to typify the reputation of Dr Ramon Fabri as one of the foremost authorities on the occult.

And yet why should it? Trumble smiled wryly to himself. Surprising how one's mind still moved on conventional lines in some respects. He still found it difficult to conceal his bitterness at some facets of the world as he found it; a minor poet of some brilliance, he had somehow failed to live up to his early promise. As is the way with poets, the public had omitted to buy his works in any great numbers, the editions had passed out of print and Trumble had been reduced to tutoring and hack work over the past years in order to make a living.

This was why Dr Fabri's Personal advertisement in *The Times* had seemed so attractive; a secretaryship, though not really the sort of thing to which a minor poet aspired, would at least see him financially stable until he should set forth again on some other literary adventure. From what he had gathered at a London interview with Dr Fabri his duties would not be too onerous; furthermore, the salary was generous in proportion to Trumble's slender secretarial experience; he would live in and live well, judging by Dr Fabri's reputation as a gourmet; and the post would leave him time for his literary endeavours. He had closed at once and, three days later, had driven down in his old, second-hand two-seater.

As always, the hood had leaked all the way, though the rain had held off its main attack until he was past Reigate; from then on its steady encroachment had made driving a misery and Trumble saw with relief the lodge gates of his destination compose themselves before the thin beams of his headlights in the filmy April dusk.

His tyres crunched over gravel as he drove up a well-kept drive between smooth lawns and on to the impressive Georgian façade of Dr Fabri's residence. He carried up his two shabby suitcases between the gleaming white splendour of the pillared entrance porch and saw light shining through the circular windows that flanked the pale yellow front door. Before he could set down his cases to ring the bell, a tall, lean figure blocked out the light that spilled from the open entry.

The man was some sort of general handyman, Trumble judged by his striped waistcoat and the green baize apron he wore round his waist like a domestic servant in a faded pre-war comedy. The man had razor-sharp features with yellow skin stretched over a sharply-etched skull; his bald head echoed his face in the lamplight as he stooped to pick up Trumble's bags.

'Dr Fabri's waiting in the study, sir,' he said in correct, clipped tones. 'He says he would like you to go straight through.'

Trumble murmured some commonplace and then turned towards his car; he found the bald man at his elbow. A hand closed over his arm and he was held softly but immovably. The pressure lasted only a moment but the fellow must have had immense strength.

'Dr Fabri said at once, sir,' he said with slight emphasis on the last words. 'I'll attend to your car if you'll give me the keys.'

Trumble looked at the man's impassive features and handed them over. The grip on his arm was instantly relaxed. The man in the striped waistcoat slid swiftly behind the wheel of Trumble's old machine.

'Straight down the hall, sir, first door on the right,' he called, his flat, clipped voice without echoes in the dusk and the thin, whispering rain. 'I'll bring your baggage after.'

Trumble went through the porch and into the hall, leaving his bags where they were, as the car trundled away round the drive towards some unseen destination in the rear. Rather an odd character for chauffeur-butler, he felt, though no doubt Dr Fabri might have use of such a person living in the lonely spot he had chosen to make his home.

It was none of his business; and in any case the fellow had been polite enough. It was just his attitude; withdrawn strength and confidence, just this side of insolence, which rankled somewhere inside Trumble's mind. He felt he must be getting hypersensitive; rejection by the larger literary world of which he had once had such inordinate hopes might be the reason behind it. He closed the door softly behind him and blinked in the bright light of the inner hall.

He walked in over a tiled floor of extraordinary beauty. Light reflected back the smooth greens, reds and blues of the convoluted designs; Trumble recognised the pentacle and something which looked like the seal of Cagliostro. Dr Fabri, as he knew, was deeply read in literature which dwelt on dark and hidden things and Trumble himself was intensely interested in the subject; indeed, one of his earlier volumes of poetry, *On Goety*, had been based on the Seven Seals, which may well have originally drawn his name to Dr Fabri's attention.

He was charmed, too, to see that his future employer carried his interests to the length of including them in the decor of his house; the post promised to be one of unexpected delights. He passed several oil paintings on his way to the door of which the servant had spoken; they were undoubtedly genuine works of art, of obvious value and chosen with unfailing taste to illustrate Dr Fabri's chosen pursuits. Trumble was astonished to notice a magnificent Bosch which he did not think had existed outside a museum in Amsterdam; though, like all of Bosch's work, it had a haunting and vivid quality that one with tender nerves would find disquieting, to say the least.

Even Trumble was not sure that he cared all that much for the subject; screaming forms which fled through what appeared to be looped sections of viscera. But he did not have time for more than an admiring glance at the canvas; in a moment more he was at the door and, knocking on it, heard Dr Fabri call out for him to enter.

Fabri was a man in his middle forties with a powerful frame and a tanned complexion; despite his comparative youth his hair was completely white but cut very short like a young man. His deep-set eyes were brilliant and penetrating and his square tortoiseshell spectacles gave his face a quizzical look and reinforced its strength. His jaw was square also and the glasses echoed the cubistic theme. He rose from a red-leather-topped desk to greet Trumble with obvious pleasure.

'I trust you had a good journey?'

His voice was dark-toned and deep and its timbre recalled to the new secretary that Dr Fabri had been famous for his lecture-tours on the Continent a dozen or so years before; a celebrated series that at one time threatened to launch him into the dubious career of a television celebrity. Fortunately, Dr Fabri had the good taste to draw back and his scholarship and erudition were henceforth confined to those comparatively small numbers of people who bought tickets of entry to the halls of learned institutions in London, Paris, Rome, Berlin and other leading capitals. Trumble had, of course, spent almost an hour in Dr Fabri's company at his previous interview but he was now seeing the doctor in his own surroundings for the first time and he studied his employer's milieu with more than casual interest.

As the two men exchanged a few remarks, Trumble's eyes wandered about the vast study in which they sat; it was one of the most curious places he had ever seen. There was a large globe covered with zodiac signs whose use was obscure to him; tapestries decorated with cabalistic insignia writhed over the far wall while the massed shelves contained thousands of volumes of works in Greek and Latin. So far as he could make out, many of the books were rare and valuable originals. Trumble felt his spirits reviving.

At the far end of the chamber was a large platform enclosed by iron railings; a spiral staircase ascended to it from the main floor of the library. Trumble could see chemical retorts and a Bunsen-burner on one of the benches gave off a bluish-green flame in the dusk. Blue velvet curtains partitioned off part of the other end of the room and the shadowy forms of images of ancient gods ranged round those parts of the walls not given over to books.

'I see that you approve of my surroundings,' said Dr Fabri, shooting him a shrewd glance. 'My collection is not so comprehensive as I should wish, but I have begun to make a start. Life is not long enough for the amassing of knowledge, my friend.' Fabri laughed and then rose abruptly from his seat.

'Forgive me, but I am forgetting my manners. You must be hungry. Joseph will have a meal prepared shortly.'

He led the way out of the study and into an adjoining apartment, conventionally furnished as a dining-room but with panelled walls of some charm and with great glazed doors looking on to the ruin of a once considerable garden. Fabri pulled the curtains over the sombre scene outside the window and led the way over to a cabinet; whisky splashed into long crystal glasses and there came the friendly tinkle of ice. A moment later Dr Fabri handed him the glass and they toasted one another silently by a fire of logs which spluttered contentedly to itself in a handsome stone fireplace. Trumble sank into a high-backed chair and gazed into the fire as his host excused himself; he felt that he would enjoy his stay at Linnet Ridge.

He was aroused from his thoughts by a sound at his elbow and saw the man Joseph, who had met him in the porch, busying himself at the long teak dining-table. He laid two places silently and went out through the far door. Dr Fabri returned almost at once.

'Excuse my bad manners, my dear Trumble,' he said, pressing a thin book into his new secretary's hands, 'but I could not resist the opportunity. I am something of a collector, as you know, and your name was not unknown to me before we met. It would give me great pleasure if you would inscribe the work for me.'

Trumble saw with surprise that the book was a rare edition of his own *On Goety*, produced on hand-woven paper in a limited edition from a private press in Paris. So far as he knew there had been only two hundred copies produced. He felt his hands tremble as he took a pen from his pocket and composed something appropriate on the fly-leaf for Dr Fabri.

'You were surprised, eh?' said the doctor, as he examined Trumble's inscription and thanked him for it.

'There are so few copies and my work is so obscure,' said Trumble, his voice quivering slightly. 'One works so hard and yet it is so difficult to become known.'

Dr Fabri gazed at him in sympathy. 'One is known to those who are of importance and that is what counts,' he said simply. 'It is a great honour to have you under my roof. But now let us eat. Tomorrow it will give me pleasure to show you round my house. You will not find your duties onerous and I am sure we shall find many mutual interests to share.'

He led the way to the table. The meal passed in silence, the courses served impeccably by the man Joseph. There did not appear to be any other staff. Dr Fabri made no mention of Trumble's duties and for his part the poet was content for the moment to enjoy the good food and wine with which his new employer plied him. Shortly after half-past nine Dr Fabri excused himself. 'Joseph will show you your quarters,' he said. 'Until tomorrow, then.'

The big man led the way up a large oak staircase that opened from the hall and along a luxuriously carpeted corridor lined with oak doors. He flung open the third and switched on the light.

'If you require anything, sir, you have only to ring,' he said, indicating a brass push-button set into the wall next to a battery of light switches.

Trumble thanked him and closed the door behind him. His two shabby suitcases were standing in the centre of the room where Joseph had left them; his car keys were on the dressing-table. He smiled to himself; evidently Joseph was as efficient as his master. He unpacked quickly, stowed away his few belongings in the drawers and put the empty suitcases in the wardrobe.

He went idly to the window and looked down into the garden, now silvered by a moon which shone from a clear, rainless sky. It was then that he saw the window was covered with bars which followed the pattern of the leaded panes. He frowned. He went back over towards the door. It was, as he had somehow expected, locked. It was curious but it proved nothing, except possibly that to Dr Fabri he was an unknown quantity; a new employee loose in a household which contained many valuable paintings and *objets d'art*. He smiled to himself; he did not feel at all insulted. He stood irresolute for a moment, gazing at the door-lock and from there to the brass bell-push which would bring the servant Joseph to him within seconds.

Then he shrugged and turned away. He might take up the

matter tomorrow. He got into bed, his mind already embracing sleep, and switched off the light. He slept well, awakening only once at the high, sharp, piercing cry of an owl. He got up then and looked into the grounds but could see nothing. He went to the door before returning to the warmth of his bed; he tried the handle gently in the gloom. This time it was unlocked.

Trumble breakfasted alone in a small, pleasant room that opened on to the lawn. He was astonished to find that the garden, which had appeared such a ruin was, at closer acquaintance, obviously well-tended, with smooth lawns and well-kept beds. He was annoyed with himself for having made such a stupid error, and was just going outside when Dr Fabri entered with smiling apologies for his non-appearance at breakfast.

'I have much to do, you know,' he said jovially. He enquired politely how Trumble had slept; the latter had decided to say nothing about the locked bedroom door and privately meant to see whether it was his employer's intention to keep him segregated from the main house during the nights. In the meantime there was much to engage his attention; while Joseph cleared the table Dr Fabri and his new employee took a turn round the vast garden, which confirmed Trumble's estimate through the window. He resolved to have a look at his bedroom casement that evening; there might be some distorting quality in the glass.

The two men returned to the house half an hour later, chatting in a desultory way of Trumble's duties; he gathered that he would be expected to keep Dr Fabri's appointments' diary, work out his day for him, answer the telephone and do the indexing on the doctor's vast collection of books and documents. Apparently there were a great many more papers apart from the main library and it would take him a month or two to find his way around.

Trumble learned, with some pleasure, that he would have

most afternoons free but, in return, was expected to put in an hour or two in the evenings, as Dr. Fabri might require from time to time; he would also have to take some dictation and he was glad that he had once learned shorthand in the days when he was contributing to magazines; the facility would obviously come in useful.

At this point in their conversation the two men had returned to the vast study, where the doctor was engaged in pointing out various aspects of his indexing system in the large green filing cabinets which lined one corner of the room.

'There is one other part of the house which will be your special domain,' he said with a spark of humour in his eye, as he drew the young man down the shelving. 'I think you will find it not the least interesting aspect of your new duties.'

He beckoned to where the platform sprang from the floor of the main study. The two men ascended the spiral staircase, their steps echoing hollowly on the treads.

The shadowy statues leered darkly from their niches but Trumble had little time to take in their detail or any other particulars of the interesting minutiae strewn about in such profusion in this esoteric corner. Dr Fabri took him over to the curtains which he drew aside with a silken cord. Facing the two men was a large bronze door, about six feet high, whose golden surface caught the light in dull, undulating reflections.

Trumble then saw that the bas-relief design on the door, magnificently executed, depicted a Sabbat. Nude figures writhed in a circle on some deserted heathland and the artist, with a cunning amounting to genius, had made his horrific vision stand out with startling reality, doubly emphasised, of course, by the medium he had chosen. The figures seemed to move within the frame of the door and Trumble felt a great stir of the heart as he gazed in fascination. There was a rough altar in the centre of the design, he saw, and a goat-form conducting the rites.

A naked girl formed the top of the altar; there was a bowl on her stomach and another girl lay across her knees. Assistants supported the second girl and the goat-figure appeared to be cutting her throat over the bowl. Trumble gazed on with fascinated distaste. Fabri glanced at him with obvious pleasure. 'After Callot,' he said with great satisfaction. 'One of my little fancies.'

He pulled back the bronze catch of the great door and led the way into a large chamber; concealed lighting clicked on as he opened the door. It was a curious room, Trumble thought; perhaps the most curious he had ever seen, though it was also strangely commonplace. Walls and floor appeared to be lined with zinc; there were grills high up in the walls and in the ceiling, evidently to do with the air-conditioning, and racks of books, many with tattered leather bindings and faded gold inscriptions; Trumble noticed many rare works bound in vellum; among them *Vermis de Mysteris* by Ludvig Prinn, and *De Masticatione Mortuorum* by Philip Rohr; the *Dissertatio de Vampyris Seruinsibus* by Zopfius, Harenberg's extremely rare *Von Vampyren*, together with a contemporary account of the Salem Witch Trials. This section was an incongruous sight, set as it was among modern filing cabinets and a great shelf of ledgers, each numbered and indexed.

On a green-leather-topped desk which stood some yards within the chamber was an open ledger which was inscribed in green ink; and a bundle of newspaper cuttings. A faint humming filled the air.

'This room fulfils two functions,' said Dr Fabri, 'and will be the scene of your main duties. My most important and rarest manuscripts are stored here. The air-conditioning keeps them at a constant temperature.'

He ran his eyes over the packed shelves with satisfaction. He moved farther down the room and drew Trumble's attention to the ledgers. He chuckled softly.

'These are my records of notabilities, kept through the medium of newspaper cuttings and other material, sent me from all over the world. Obituaries, you understand, of all the celebrities and public persons whose careers interest me.'

He waved his hand towards the shelf of ledgers. 'I call them the Archives of the Dead.'

He moved back again to the desk. 'You will see from this daily ledger the name of the person or persons who are to be added to the scrapbooks. Then, when the material arrives by post, it is cut out and transferred to the appropriate ledger. The information is then cross-indexed in these filing cabinets. The system is simplicity itself.'

Trumble moved to the desk, his mind turning over the odd nature of the task; he saw that Fabri's records were incredibly detailed and contained much out of the way information not only from famous newspapers and magazines but obscure journals in German, French and Russian. He looked down the green-inked entries in the smaller book which stood open on the desk – like the Book of Judgement, he could not help thinking wryly to himself – and noted that the two latest names, in Fabri's impeccable hand-writing, were those of a scenic designer and a ballet dancer.

'If you have any queries, Mr Trumble,' said Dr Fabri, waving his hand to indicate the contents of the room, 'now is the time. You will be left much to yourself, I am afraid, as I have my own affairs to pursue. We are all alone here, except for Joseph, and the cleaning woman comes in during the mornings, twice a week.'

While Trumble put a few questions to Dr Fabri, his mind continued to debate his astonishing good fortune; for he had soon grasped that his duties for the moment would be merely nominal. He could not really see why Dr Fabri needed a secretary at all but on the other hand if he were prepared to pay so handsomely in return for such agreeably lightweight tasks, Trumble, for one, was not prepared to argue. The two men parted on the best of terms; Fabri was driving over to see some friends and would not be back until late afternoon. Joseph would prepare Trumble's lunch and he could work on at the indexing undisturbed during the afternoon, in order to get the doctor's records up to date.

Trumble sat at the desk, quietly jubilant for some minutes after the rumble of the doctor's car had died away down the drive. He glanced round at the massed volumes on the shelves and then down again to the material awaiting his attention; the air-conditioning hummed quietly to itself and the scent of the spring flowers, arranged in big jars round the main library, came to him through the bronze door of the room, which had been propped open with a large stone ornament.

He gazed at the doctor's green-ink entry once again. He picked up his pen and turned to the top of a large, blank page of the current ledger, which had been left open on the desk with the cuttings. In neat block capitals, underlined with a ruler, he wrote; FAENZA, BORIS b 1884. Then he set to work.

Three days passed. Three days in which Trumble gradually came to know the ascetic but not unpleasant routine of the Fabri household. In the mornings he took dictation from Dr Fabri in answer to the incoming mail; the doctor had an astonishing correspondence from all over the world, much of it from such exotic places as Venezuela or the Gulf of Mexico. Many of these were in the languages of the country of origin and Dr Fabri would peruse them and then rattle out his replies in English with machine-gun precision. More than once Trumble was glad that he had taken the trouble to thoroughly master shorthand during the earlier days of his career.

Occasionally, there would be time in the mornings for him to work on the Archives of the Dead; he had taken up Dr Fabri's remark, which he ascribed to his employer's somewhat grim vein of humour, and applied it in a mocking manner to the indexing upon which he was engaged. Dr Fabri's tastes appeared to be completely catholic and it almost seemed to Trumble that he was obsessed with recording the deaths of everyone of importance who died in the world, without regard to their profession or occupation. Trumble had also taken time to study the earlier ledgers, which went back a good many years, and was astonished to see the meticulous way in which the deaths of bishops, film stars, footballers, philosophers, politicians and university professors had been kept.

Writers, musicians and those in the graphic arts were recorded in separate volumes, coded blue, and Trumble, though of course he had never questioned Dr Fabri on the subject, concluded that the doctor had a special interest in those arts; particularly as many of the writers were also savants who had been authorities on witchcraft and the occult. In this respect the rare volumes in Latin and medieval French, which were evidently of immense value, came in useful, and already Trumble had had occasion to check a reference from an original source, when the printed information on his subject's career had been scanty.

The work had its own fascination, though Trumble might once have felt it to be morbid; it was certainly no more so than similar departments kept up by the major newspapers and known to their respective staffs as 'The Morgue'. In fact, Trumble felt Dr Fabri's own system was preferable as he understood the newspapers wrote their obituaries in advance, which did rather smack of the macabre, to his way of thinking. He put down the pen, looked at the completed page and replaced the ledger on the shelf with the others. He would do the indexing on these last items tomorrow.

Trumble ate dinner on his own that evening and was sitting in the lounge engrossed in a novel at about nine o'clock when he heard Dr Fabri's car in the drive. A few moments later the hall door slammed with hollow resonance and the measured tread of his employer passed up the staircase; shortly afterwards Dr

Fabri's bedroom door closed. Trumble picked up his half-finished drink and resumed his book.

The house was unnaturally quiet and occasionally he would put down the volume and listen briefly but the only sounds were the faint sputtering of wood from the fire, for the nights were still cold as yet, and the muted sounds of Joseph from his quarters at the back of the house. The mantel clock measured a few minutes after ten and Trumble was thinking about retiring to his own room when the sharp, peremptory strokes of the front door bell, jabbed by an impatient finger, startled him.

He gained the hall and was opening the door before Joseph had made his appearance. A tall, silvery-haired man of some distinction, wearing a dress suit and black tie under a dark raincoat, stood in the porch. In the background shimmered the gleaming bulk of a grey Mercedes. Trumble hesitated for a fraction and the man in the porch seemed slightly taken aback also. The older man was the first to recover himself.

'I would like to speak with Dr Fabri if it isn't too inconvenient,' he said. 'He is expecting me.'

Trumble introduced himself and the two men shook hands. 'I usually arrange his appointments but I am new here and the doctor may have forgotten to tell me,' said Trumble. He motioned the visitor forward into the hall and closed the door behind him. Joseph had now appeared and took the tall man's coat.

'However, if you made an appointment I have no doubt Dr Fabri is expecting you,' Trumble continued. 'He came in about an hour ago.'

The visitor seemed pleased at this, but just then the sound of Dr Fabri's footsteps sounded at the stairhead.

'Would you like me to announce you?' Trumble asked.

The visitor shook his head. 'That won't be necessary,' he said decisively. Joseph was hovering at the back of the hall but Dr Fabri was now halfway down the staircase, and he vanished in the direction of the kitchen.

'Delighted to see you, my dear fellow,' said Dr Fabri, shaking his visitor warmly by the hand. 'I was worried in case you might have been delayed.'

'Not this night. Certainly not this night of all nights,' said his visitor sharply.

Dr Fabri laughed shortly. 'No, no, of course not,' he said soothingly, laying his hand on the other's arm. 'You go ahead into the study and I will join you immediately.'

He turned to Trumble, his strong face impassive in the soft light of the hall lamps.

'I shan't require you any further tonight, Robert,' he said. 'We shall be quite late. I have told Joseph he may retire. I will show my guest out myself.'

Trumble nodded. He went back into the lounge and finished his drink. There was no sound from the direction of the study, into which both men had disappeared. He dragged the heavy brass guard over the remains of the fire, recovered his book from the armchair and switched off the lights. Joseph nodded to him darkly as he crossed the hall. The big, taciturn handyman was hovering near the study door, behind which could now be made out the low murmur of voices. Trumble walked up to the landing and sought his own room.

He quickly prepared for bed, drew the covers over him and again settled down to another chapter of his book; this time, for some indefinable reason, the texture of the writing did not seem to absorb him as it had done formerly and it was still a few minutes short of eleven when he put the book aside on the table and put out the lamp. Thin cracks of light came through under his bedroom door from farther down the landing; Trumble was just about to shift his position so that he would be facing the darker side of the room when he saw a shadow briefly cross the light coming in under the door. A moment later he heard the faint click of the key as someone locked the door from the outside.

Trumble smiled to himself in the semi-darkness; he supposed he ought to object to this rather peculiar procedure, but he could not say the practice inconvenienced him. He had a self-contained suite and if Dr Fabri liked to confine the occupants of his house to their own portions of the building during the dead hours of the night, he supposed that was his own business. Perhaps he would tackle the doctor about it when he had got to know him a little better.

His head occupied with these and similar thoughts Trumble soon slept. He found himself awake again in the still of the night. He lay trembling for some moments, trying to collect himself. What had awakened him, or rather what he fancied had awakened him, was a long, high scream which sounded like an animal in pain. Trumble had noted degrees of torment in animals, as in humans, and it seemed to him that the sound which had broken his sleep was of some creature in extremis. He looked at the luminous dial of his watch and saw that it was just after three o'clock. He had therefore slept for nearly four hours.

A glance towards the door showed him that the light on the landing had been extinguished. No sound broke the stillness but his own heavy breathing as he listened intently; the darkness of the night pressed heavily on the house and held it as though within a deep vault. Trumble felt perspiration in the roots of his hair and he was hot and sticky against his pyjamas.

Then an owl sounded, sharp and distinct, from the woods beyond the house and with this commonplace noise all the little sounds of the night crept back; Trumble felt his stiff hands relax their frenzied grip on the sheets and his body began to relax. Sleep was so subtle on this second occasion that he was not aware of it when unconsciousness finally overtook him.

The following day Dr Fabri did not appear in the morning though Trumble had heard his car earlier; he took his breakfast, as usual served by the unsmiling Joseph, and just before ten began his work in the small cabinet with the bronze door.

There was a large bronze handle, mate to the one on the face, on his own side of the door and, as if that were not enough, the massive bronze key, made specially to match, was on his own side to avoid him being locked in. It was this key which he handed to Joseph in the evenings when he had finished his scholarly work among the rare books.

But already this morning Dr Fabri must have been down, for as soon as Trumble was seated at his desk and had commenced to examine the material which awaited his attention, he saw that two new names had been added to the register ledger in the doctor's unmistakable green-inked hand. The first was that of Burnett Fairbarn, an internationally known architect. Trumble had heard his death announced on the news the night before; he had died in a mountaineering accident on a peak in the Andes the previous day. The latest name was that of Lyle Bassett, of whom Trumble had never heard.

The first information for documenting purposes would no doubt come from the evening papers that night. Trumble continued with his usual pursuits and the day slowly assumed the pattern of those preceding. Dr Fabri returned to the house for lunch; the two men walked in the garden; Trumble took some dictation and, a little later, drove over to Guildford for tea. He bought the two evening papers on his way back, intending to go through them after dinner.

But another session of note-taking followed and when Trumble returned to the archive room for more indexing at about half-past ten the newspapers were still on the desk unread. It was only when, his immediate task finished, Trumble turned to peruse the day's news that he saw a long story on an inside page of Fairbarn's climbing accident. There was over a column of space in both papers devoted to this, together with photographs of the architect, and some of his principal buildings.

When he had finished pasting these entries into the large book and had suitably indexed them, Trumble remembered the second entry on the ledger. He turned again to verify the name and then went through the inside pages. He found what he was looking for in a short item on the front page of the *Evening Standard*.

It merely said that the body of Lyle Bassett, a somewhat obscure ballet choreographer and composer, had been found dead in a blazing car near the Guildford By-pass in the early hours of the same day. Trumble entered the notice and found a smaller piece in the stop press column of the *Evening News*. It referred to another story on an inside page and this was an expanded version of the facts already known, but giving more details of Bassett's career. Trumble closed both books, tidied his desk and went to bed rather satisfied with his labours.

The midday post the following day contained a great deal of material for Dr Fabri's archives, together with a number of business letters which had to be answered and Trumble was not able to return to his indexing until nearly twenty-four hours later. He then saw that he had rather a lot of leeway to make up; Dr Fabri had added another four or five names in green ink in the ledger and the pile of clippings and magazine articles had reached alarming proportions.

Trumble went swiftly through the material, arranging it in piles and subject matter, preparatory to making the entries. His hand faltered when he picked up the last clipping which consisted of several inches of text and a large photograph; the room suddenly became hot and stuffy and Trumble put the cutting down on the desk with a hand which had begun to behave in an uncontrollable manner. He studied the face again; the picture was that of the man he had showed into the hall of Linnet Ridge a little over two days earlier. He checked back over the original entry; it was the man who had died in the wrecked car.

The name was Lyle Bassett.

Trumble did not mention this fact to Dr Fabri. His procedure was strange, even to himself, and no application of logic could account for it. Even more unusual was the fact that Dr Fabri himself did not bring up the subject; it was impossible that his guest's fatal accident could have escaped his attention, unless Joseph had placed the cuttings in position on the secretary's desk. In which case that would explain the matter; Trumble embraced this theory almost with relief. Joseph's taciturnity was notorious in the household and he might, in his extraordinary way, have kept his own counsel.

In the meantime Trumble avoided all conversation which might lead round to Bassett's visit to the house and hoped that the doctor himself might make the discovery while going through the record books. But in any case opportunities for conversation with the doctor were becoming more limited; as the weeks went by and the spring advanced he appeared more seldom at meals and apart from dictation and matters relating to business correspondence, Trumble had little contact with him.

He worked on in his cabinet and was left more and more to his own affairs, though he had no doubt that Joseph, who was undoubtedly in his employer's confidence, kept a discreet eye on the secretary's movements and reported back to the doctor how his time had been spent. Trumble did not resent this; after all, he reasoned to himself, the doctor was paying him well, he was living in some comfort and style and though the hours were sometimes irregular, he was not greatly inconvenienced and could not honestly say that he was overworked.

He slept more easily at nights also and he had noted during the last week that his room was no longer locked after he had gone up to bed; evidently he had proved his loyalty and the doctor had decided that he could be trusted with the run of the house. Trumble was wryly amused at the thought; Dr Fabri might have an international reputation as an authority on the black arts, but in private life he was perfectly proper and his household disappointingly normal, so far as Trumble could see.

Not that he expected any out-of-the-way happenings, but he had hoped that his employer would unlock some of the hidden treasures of his mind to him during the long summer evenings, especially as the doctor and the poet evidently shared many tastes and common viewpoints on matters normally considered forbidden among those in what, for want of a better phrase, was termed polite society.

And yet there was an incident a few days later which illustrated vividly to Trumble the darker side of Dr Fabri's nature. It had been unnaturally cold for an England poised on the threshold of May and fires had been lit in the principal rooms to supplement the central heating. For some reason or other the doctor and his secretary had forsaken the study and were seated at the dining-room table where Fabri had been dictating sections of one of a new series of lectures for the following autumn.

He had called this particular talk 'The Past Which is to Come', a title which had vividly impressed itself upon Trumble; in fact he wished he had thought of it himself. His pen scratched rapidly over the paper as Dr Fabri rattled on.

While dictating, Dr Fabri would turn his deep, piercing eyes ruminatively on Trumble as he searched for the apposite phrase; then he would proceed to deliver it unfalteringly, so that the secretary was hard put to it to keep up. Once he had found his thought, he would polish and assemble it in his mind before giving utterance, so that he never had to correct the typed word once it was on paper.

'The cancer of time eats inexorably at the fabric of human lives,' said Dr Fabri, the phrase seeming to hang on the hushed air of the dining-room.

'We drag our pasts behind us as a snail its slime.'

He paused for a moment, his cigar smoke rising steadily upwards towards the panelled ceiling with hardly a tremor, the air within the room was so still.

Trumble's pen raced on over the paper until, with relief, he heard Dr Fabri come to the end of his discourse. He flexed his hand to relieve the cramp, aware of the doctor's eyes fixed upon him with sardonic humour. Dr Fabri stretched himself in his chair.

'Is there anything there which you feel requires amplification, Robert?' he asked.

What he really meant, Trumble understood well enough, was whether the latter had managed to take down everything accurately and wanted him to check anything again. Trumble flipped through his pages of voluminous notes, hoping that he would have no difficult transcription problems.

'There was a point here, Doctor,' he said diffidently. 'I believe my note is accurate but I didn't quite understand the meaning.'

He searched for the passage while Dr Fabri waited politely, his dark eyes a startling contrast to his white hair and tufted eyebrows.

Trumble found the place and read, 'In this Key you may behold, as in a mirror, the distinct functions of the spirits, and how they are to be drawn into communication in all places, seasons and times.'

'Well?' said Dr Fabri, a little impatiently. 'It is a quotation, of course.'

'I understand that,' Trumble replied, 'and there are many such passages throughout your lecture. Am I to take it that this is intended to be taken literally?'

'Certainly,' said Dr Fabri calmly. 'I could give you a number of instances. It is, of course, a power given to very few and one certainly not to be abused. You are desirous of learning more of such things – from a personal aspect, that is?'

He pronounced the last words in a very soft and curious

manner and Trumble became suddenly aware that he was trespassing on very strange and dangerous ground.

'He who would learn the secrets of my Master must be prepared for long and arduous preparations. It is a hard and thorny way.'

The air seemed to have grown close and sultry and Trumble's head began to swim; he was aware of Dr Fabri's eyes which were now bright and sharp and boring into his.

'Your Master?' Trumble asked foolishly, trying to fight the nausea which threatened to overcome him.

'Of course,' said Dr Fabri.

'My Master,' he added softly. 'We are all the servants of One Master, Mr Trumble.'

Dr Fabri laughed quietly and with the laughter the tension and oppression lifted from the room and Trumble felt he could breathe again; he wiped his forehead, which was wet with perspiration.

'Are you well?' the doctor asked in some concern. He went to the sideboard and came back with a full glass which he thrust into his secretary's hand. Trumble drank the whisky as though it had been water and then felt normality returning to him. He gathered up his notes with a muttered apology to the doctor. They did not again return to the subject that evening.

Several more weeks passed and it was now mid-May. Despite the season the weather had continued cold; Trumble was by now thoroughly accustomed to his duties; he continued the odd task of indexing in the inner cabinet and felt he had thoroughly mastered the complexities of Dr Fabri's dictation style. Best of all, he had commenced to write again; the sheltered atmosphere of Linnet Ridge had released something long pent-up in him and in his spare time he began sketching out the movements of an epic poem in praise of the Old Gods.

Curiously enough, there abruptly came a day of great heat, among those of cold, wet January-like weather; Fabri and Trumble had been seated long after breakfast was cleared that morning, going over some proofs of a projected book by Dr Fabri on magic as practised by the older cultures of the world.

Quite casually, in the middle of their discussion on business matters, Dr Fabri turned to his secretary and said, 'By the way, I am expecting a number of people this evening. We shall be occupying the study so I would be grateful if you would arrange to vacate the ground floor of the house by nine-thirty tonight.'

Dr Fabri's tone was courteous and his words polite, but it was obvious to Trumble that his pronouncement was an order; so he did not question his employer, though he was naturally curious on the subject.

'Would you like me to wait up?' he asked. 'I could go into Guildford for the evening, if you wish, and return to the house late if you require any help in entertaining your guests.'

'That won't be necessary, Robert,' Dr Fabri said smoothly. 'I should appreciate it, though, if you would receive the visitors between eight and nine o'clock so I should cancel any arrangements you may have made regarding Guildford. Joseph will lock up later. He is used to our activities.'

When Trumble thought over the conversation later in the day he felt his curiosity roused by the phrasing of Dr Fabri's last sentence; he wondered idly what activities were meant. And if Joseph were used to them, how frequent they might be. Apart from the visit of the ill-fated Bassett there were few guests to Linnet Ridge, and those only during the afternoons. As the day wore on he found his thoughts turning more and more towards the evening and it was with something like impatience that he watched the clock during his long hours of indexing in the cabinet.

Just before dinner, which was earlier than usual that night, he cleared those of his personal papers which he felt he might require, and prepared his writing-table in the sitting-room of his own suite upstairs; he felt that if he were to be denied the use of the ground floor that night he would at least be able to put his time to good use in composition before retiring. He descended to the ground floor again just in time for dinner, to find Dr Fabri already at the table.

To his surprise Trumble noted that there was a third person already seated and in conversation with his employer. The two men rose as Trumble entered and Dr Fabri made haste to introduce his companion, though the secretary had already recognised the strong, clear-minted head of Zadek, the celebrated 'cellist, who was currently giving a series of concerts in the London area. Joseph, who had been standing in sullen silence, now bustled forward as Dr Fabri snapped his fingers, and served the soup.

When he had withdrawn once more, Dr Fabri put the two men at ease by talking smoothly and flowingly of general matters and gradually the meal was transformed into a pleasant arena of reminiscence and anecdote, of philosophical musings, all backed by a wide range of scholarship and cultured taste. Trumble had seldom heard his employer in this vein and indeed, it would have been hard to better his conversation; Trumble himself confined his own comments to brief generalities in answer to specific questions.

They had sat down to table early, a little after half-past six; and now it was nearly eight o'clock, Joseph had just come in to remind them. Trumble sipped his second liqueur with his black coffee and felt that he had more than upheld his own end of the conversation. Zadek had also heard of Trumble's efforts as a poet, to the secretary's barely-concealed astonishment and the two men had, in fact, treated him as their peer. Though flattered, Trumble did wonder, as the meal progressed, whether the 'cellist had not been briefed by Fabri before his arrival in the dining-room.

Even so, it was a pleasant thought of the doctor's and not for the first time the secretary felt his heart warming to him. He was a little strange, not to say eccentric in his ways, but no one could complain of their treatment under his roof. But now Joseph was standing at his elbow and communicating unmistakably by his manner that Trumble should prepare himself for the guests who were expected between eight and nine o'clock. So Trumble rose to his feet, excused himself and a few minutes later stationed himself within easy earshot of the front door.

He had not long to wait; it was just three minutes past eight before the first visitors announced themselves. These were a tall, thin woman in her mid-fifties, accompanied by a plump young man in his early thirties. Joseph, impassive as one of the wooden images in the doctor's collection, relieved them of their hats and coats while Trumble, murmuring polite conventionalities, showed them to the study. He did not enter himself but merely ushered them through and closed the door behind them.

In all, he must have passed through something like thirty people between eight and nine o'clock, when the flow finally began to slacken off. Though he recognised no one, Trumble felt there must have been more than one person of public eminence among the gathering; they were about evenly divided between men and women but the age range fell into two distinct patterns. The men were from about thirty to sixty at a rough guess, while the women's ages ranged between twenty to about fifty-five.

All were well-dressed and highly literate in their conversation and manner; without exception all seemed to have arrived by private car and none of them addressed Trumble in terms other than polite greetings normally exchanged among total strangers. To his fumbled attempts at small talk they maintained a discreet silence until they were beyond the study door. Joseph remained in the hall throughout the entire proceedings and stationed himself directly in front of the study whenever he was not engaged in dealing with hats and coats. His manner, too, did not encourage any approach from Trumble.

Finding himself ignored in this manner, the secretary retired to a side room with a novel and as nine-thirty chimed he found the silent-footed Joseph at his elbow.

'I think that is the last of the ladies and gentlemen, sir,' he said softly, in that politely insolent manner which the secretary found so offensive. He could not have made the situation more plain if he had said, 'I think it is time you followed your instructions and retired upstairs.' So Trumble elaborately stretched himself, smoothed out the cushion at his elbow and took his time in closing his book.

'Thank you, Joseph, that will be all,' he said by way of feeble revenge. The servant stared at him a moment longer with smouldering eyes, then abruptly turned and went silently out of the door. A moment later the main hall-light was extinguished. Trumble waited as long as he felt he dared – after all, he did not want to bring Dr Fabri out to see what was delaying him – and five minutes later ascended the oak staircase with as good grace as he could muster.

Joseph was still standing in front of the door; Trumble saw that he was wearing some sort of dark cloak like that of a coachman. The man's head was silhouetted against the deep pinks and greys of the convoluted intestines of the Bosch painting which had so disturbed him earlier; Trumble could not help but feel that it was an appropriate background for Joseph's saturnine features.

For more than two hours he wrestled in his room with the difficult metres of the verse-form he had chosen for his new work, but the felicitous phrase eluded him. He got up at length from the table; there was no noise at all in the house. He extinguished the lights in the sitting-room and passed through into the bedroom; a light shining from under the door which led on to the landing showed him that Dr Fabri's visitors had not yet gone.

It was nearly midnight and again Trumble felt tiredness sapping the strength of his limbs; once in his pyjamas he looked out at the garden but the night was dark and there was little to be seen. He got into bed, turned out the light and was soon asleep.

It seemed but a moment before he started awake; some unusual noise had aroused him from a deep sleep. Trumble was facing the wall, but as the room was in semi-darkness he reasoned that light was still shining in under his bedroom door. A glance over his shoulder confirmed this. His watch showed the time as being a quarter-past two and its steady tick reassured him. He sat up in bed then and pushed away the sheets, his mind quite alert. A moment later he again heard the sound which had penetrated the walls of sleep; the low murmur of voices, seemingly from far away.

He got out of bed and padded over towards the door. Again he found it unlocked. Trumble hesitated for a fraction and then once more heard the low, insidious noise that mumbled like a dark sea swirling on some lonely coast. His feet found the warmth of his carpet slippers instinctively; already he was shrugging on his thin silk dressing-gown. He opened the door cautiously but the corridor and landing were silent and deserted.

One solitary lamp burned in the dusk of the hall and keeping in the shadow, his form concealed by a thick corner post, his eyes searched the darkness below. To his relief Joseph was no longer standing sentinel. He felt no fear; curiosity had driven it out. He was impelled towards the mysterious noise which he was convinced was coming from the interior of Dr Fabri's study. The low, mumbling sound came again as he hesitated and then he went with a rush born of desperate courage down the staircase, as though the interruption had given him the confidence to move under its thick, muttered cover.

He reached the study door without incident and felt the smooth-fitting lock turn noiselessly at his pressure; he slipped inside into the comfort of almost complete darkness. He crouched behind a high-backed chair, his heart thudding uncomfortably in his throat. The darkness ahead of him was suddenly split by a soft red light which blossomed beyond the windows leading on to the garden; Trumble could see little in the fantastic flicker, but he noted once again the ruinous dereliction of the grounds in the faint glare. He moved over towards the windows, careful not to bump into the furniture, but when he reached them the pale fire had burnt to a dusky amber.

While he crouched irresolute, another low moaning murmur started up within the room; Trumble felt his legs turn to water and he crouched sweating in the shadow as the red glow grew within the garden. Then he saw the explanation; the light was coming not from the grounds but from within the house.

Somewhere below him, light was flickering and shimmering from a window within the house and staining the lawns with faint amber. With this he recovered something of his courage; his first thought was the large platform approached by the spiral staircase. The sounds appeared to be coming from within the cabinet where Trumble normally worked and yet he knew that it would have been impossible to contain thirty people within its narrow limits.

Instead, he compromised; somehow he dragged himself up the staircase and towards the blue curtains at the end of the room; lying in the comparative safety of a large settee which sheltered him, he cradled his head on his hands and listened intently. He felt he could go no farther without giving himself away, but at least he could make out what was being said by the chanting voices. And Trumble realised that it was desperately important that he should not give himself away, that he should not be discovered here in these damning circumstances at half-past two in the morning.

He felt sick and ill and his teeth began to chatter as the sense of what he heard began to penetrate his consciousness; the mumbling was repeated, a single voice then replied and the mumbling took up what the single voice was saying, amplifying it much as a congregation follows the lead of a priest. But this was like nothing Trumble had ever listened to in his life. Interested as he was in the occult and a dabbler on the fringe of things unseen, the ceremony taking place was so blasphemous and perverted that he trembled for his sanity.

All the strength went out of his limbs and he seemed to have fainted for a short while; when he came to himself again a different stage in the ceremony had been reached. Things were evidently rising to a climax; there was exultation and ecstasy in the voices and a black, savage anger. Trumble tried to blot out the words from his mind, but they slipped into his brain and burnt there like molten lead.

'Save Us, Lord Satan, we pray thee,' intoned the single voice.

'Save the Ancient One, O Lord Satan,' responded the congregation.

'Accept this, our Offering, with Thy blessing, Lord Satan,' said the single voice.

'The Offering, Lord Satan!' almost shrieked the worshippers.

'Accept this, our sacrifice, O Lord of the Serfs,' said the ringing voice.

'The sacrifice of the Ancient One, O Lord!' came the response.

'Bless us with Thy fertility, O Lord of the Flies,' the calm voice intoned.

'Accept this, our sacrifice, O Lord!' the mass of voices mumbled.

Overcome with shame and loathing, Trumble remained in a trembling heap, unable to move and quite powerless to blot out the sounds of the vile things he knew were happening only a few yards from his prostrate form. There was a long silence which turned his blood to ice and kept his ears straining for the unspeakable climax.

'Behold, the entrails of the Lamb, O Master!' said the single voice in ringing triumph.

'The Entrails, Lord Satan, Most Holy Master!' shouted the entire congregation.

There came a sound which Trumble sought in vain to blot from his consciousness; a great, welling cry which appeared to burst from the bowels of the earth, rising to a scream which indicated a human being at the utmost pitch of agony. It echoed and burst in Trumble's eardrums like the last paean of souls rotting in hell and the poet, shaking uncontrollably and almost vomiting with the extremity of his terror, felt the sound to be the aural equivalent of the torn viscera in the Bosch painting in the hall. Then the shriek cut off and was followed by a loathsome slopping noise which was as quickly drowned by the roaring approval of the congregation.

Even in his piteous state of nerves Trumble felt he must make a supreme effort; by a tremendous exertion of will he dragged himself several yards back in the direction of the study door. Trembling as though with ague, tottering like an old man, he at last clawed himself upright and gained the entrance. His hand was almost on the knob when a quick footstep sounded in the hall. Trumble fell to the floor behind an armchair and crouched with thudding heart. The door was opened, letting in a long shaft of light from the hall; fortunately, whoever it was left the door open, in order to pick his way through the darkened room. As he heard the footsteps ascend the spiral staircase, Trumble slipped through the opening, praying that his shadow on the floor would not be noticed by the ascending figure, which had its back to him.

Unfortunately, as he made for the staircase, reeling as though with fatigue, Trumble knocked against a table and made a loud clattering noise. With a whimper of terror he heard the footsteps rapidly descending the staircase. They were coming across the study floor. There was no time for Trumble to conceal himself. Gathering the frayed ends of his shrieking nerves he forced himself to walk towards the study door without concealment.

Joseph met him at the half-open door. The dark, hard face was expressionless in the dim light of the lamp. Trumble saw that he was wearing a dark black cloak, the collar of which was lined with red silk.

His legs were bare and he wore thonged sandals on his feet. He carried some sort of hood over his arm. Forcing himself to keep his voice calm, Trumble said, 'I heard a noise which woke me up. I was just coming down to see if everything was all right.'

'Everything is perfectly all right, sir,' said Joseph, but his eyes gazed at Trumble with bleak suspicion.

'I thought I heard voices,' said Trumble. He knew he had to justify his descent of the staircase and it would hardly do to let Joseph's explanation pass without some expostulation; Trumble had to steel himself to go on. He could not let the servant see that he was so easily satisfied; otherwise his suspicions might become aroused. And Trumble had much to do to prevent himself from falling when he imagined what might be the penalty if Dr Fabri realised that he had been in the study this morning and that he had heard . . . what he had heard.

'There is a meeting, sir,' said Joseph patiently, as though he were explaining a simple proposition to a child.

'That would account for the voices,' said Trumble, seeming satisfied with the servant's answer.

'The Society of the Sabbat, sir,' Joseph went on. 'The ladies and gentlemen you met earlier tonight. They are making a tape recording of certain occult rites. It is one of Dr Fabri's major interests. The recordings are very popular among Society members.'

'I see,' said Trumble, simulating relief. 'As long as all is in order. I'm sorry if I disturbed you. Is there anything I can do at all?'

He made as though to move towards the study door. Joseph did not appear to shift position but his tall form was suddenly blocking the way.

'Please return to bed, sir,' he said gravely.

'Well, thank you,' said Trumble, retreating to the foot of the staircase. 'I'd appreciate it if you didn't mention this to Dr Fabri. I felt there might be something wrong and I don't want him to think me an over-imaginative day-dreamer.'

Joseph allowed himself a faint glimmer of a smile. He had shut the study door behind him at the beginning of the conversation and Trumble could no longer hear the mumble of those hateful voices.

'I quite understand, sir,' said Joseph. He stood and watched as Trumble slowly ascended the staircase. When the poet had reached the landing he heard the noise of the key of the study door being turned in the lock. The corridor started to bend and warp in front of him as he made his way to his room. He somehow groped to the bed and then his legs gave way beneath him. He lay gasping for breath until he found the strength to crawl between the sheets.

Trumble felt so ill next morning that he sent a message to Dr Fabri, via Joseph. The servant brought food to his room and all day the secretary lay in a fevered stupor. He took dinner in bed and was relieved to hear from the servant that Dr Fabri excused himself from visiting his bedside; he sent his best wishes and hoped that Trumble would be feeling better in the morning. Indeed, by ten o'clock in the evening Trumble was so far recovered that he put on his dressing-gown and sat in the other room for a little while.

When he went through into the bathroom his face in the mirror was so strange that he had difficulty in recognising himself; apart from the stubble on his cheeks and his dishevelled hair, there was a glint in his eyes which was alien to him and his complexion was almost like chalk. Trumble had to admit that he had been badly frightened; but, looking back, realised at this distance in time that he might have been mistaken. While he had not believed Joseph's explanation regarding the recording last night, he now felt that it could have been possible.

If there were a Society of the Sabbat they may well have been doing a taped reconstruction of a Black Mass or Sabbat, but Trumble found this difficult to reconcile with the demoniac and horrifying quality of his experience the night before. Dr Fabri had not been to see him, neither had Joseph conveyed any message on the subject so it was just possible that the affair had a commonplace explanation; but even so, Trumble realised that he would have to go very carefully indeed during the next few days. Despite the depth of terror into which he had been plunged his curiosity had been aroused and he was determined to investigate further.

One thing which could not be explained away was the question posed by a simple exercise in mathematics; namely, how thirty substantial people of both sexes could have been accommodated in the small cabinet in which Trumble normally worked, crowded as it was with a desk, bookshelves and innumerable reference works. It was an insuperable problem, matched only by the equally weird spectacle of the shifting red lights in the garden. When Trumble felt equal to it he would devote some thought to the matter on the following day.

As it happened, things worked out more easily than he had supposed. Dr Fabri had gone away for a short period, Joseph informed him when he sat down for breakfast next morning. He did not know when he would be back, but he had left word for the secretary to carry on as usual. Joseph pointed out a pile of opened correspondence Dr Fabri had left by his plate and withdrew to his own enigmatic duties. Trumble sat long over his coffee and then gathered up the mail and made his way to the cabinet.

He could not repress a faint trembling in the muscles of his legs as he ascended the spiral staircase and the figures in the bronze Sabbat on the great door seemed to stare mockingly at him as he pulled it open. But once settled at his homely task of indexing the cuttings and cross-referencing his notes, Trumble's ragged nerves relaxed. The time passed, he worked steadily on and he was pleased to see by eleven o'clock that the pile of reference material in front of him was steadily diminishing. He paused in his efforts and then shuffled through the last cuttings, assessing the work remaining before lunch.

Then the clippings fluttered to the floor, his face turned pale and again there came an uncontrollable trembling in his limbs. Staring at him from the front page of a popular evening newspaper was a large photograph of a distinguished-looking man Trumble remembered only too well. The picture was captioned: 'The Late Ygor Zadek.' Over the top was a six-column headline which said: 'STAR 'CELLIST MURDERED IN ESSEX WOOD.'

With mounting horror, the secretary read how a farm worker had stumbled over the body of the world-famous 'cellist at the edge of Epping Forest. The report hinted that the corpse had been shockingly mutilated, evidently before death. The body had been dumped in the position it had been found after being transported there by car. The police were now concentrating on trying to trace the vehicle from the slender clues they had in their possession.

Sick at heart, Trumble put down the paper after examining the date-line; it was that day's early edition. The body had been found in the early hours of that morning. Trumble did not need to go into elaborate calculations to see that less than twenty-four hours had elapsed since he had last seen Zadek alive and well in Dr Fabri's house and the discovery of his disembowelled body that same morning. Trumble remembered the cry he had heard and again began to tremble uncontrollably.

To calm his racing thoughts he began to rearrange his desk, the trivial, commonplace actions gradually having the effect of calming his nerves and slowing down his churning mind. He bent down to pick up the clippings he had dropped to the floor; and then he saw that the grey carpeting which skirted the desk had been disturbed. A thin hair-line showed in the grey metal floor underneath.

He got up and went to the door; he listened intently but could hear nothing. He crossed to the study window and was reassured to see Joseph at the other end of the garden; he appeared to be trimming a rose bush. Trumble went back into the cabinet and thought long and deeply. He made up his mind. He closed the bronze door gently, isolating himself from the study and the house. The hum of the air-conditioning went reassuringly on. Then he got to his knees; unrolling the carpet he disclosed the smooth-fitting edges of a trapdoor.

Raising it by a metal flange let into its edge, Trumble saw a flight of steps leading below; they were modern in design, made of cedarwood and the treads were covered with rubber. Warm air came up to him. Trumble hesitated but a moment; then, leaving the trapdoor open, he pressed the switch set on the tread at the edge of the staircase and walked down into the cellar.

As neon tubes trembled into radiance in the high panelled ceiling, Trumble saw that the mystery was solved; here was the room for thirty people, a hundred people. The place was like a theatre; there must have been over two hundred leather tip-up seats. The chamber was decorated like a church and almost sybaritic in its luxury.

At the far end of the room were some dark blue curtains covered with cabalistic symbols. Let into the marble step in front of them was the legend, in gold lettering, which the terrible Aleister Crowley had made his motif, 'Do as Thou Wilt Shall be the Whole of the Law'.

Trumble walked down, mounted the marble steps and parted the curtains; the first thing he saw were two small, half-moon windows, high up in the wall, which must have been just above ground level. It was from these, evidently, that the red, flickering lights must have penetrated into the garden.

Trumble turned back to examine the area behind the curtains. There was a black marble altar with a curious dip and cavity let into it; behind the altar, in a niche towering up between the two windows, was an image which, fortunately for the secretary's sanity, was half-hidden in the shadow. The pendulous belly and the monstrous goathead made it perfectly obvious which form of worship was practised here. A copper bowl was lying on the altar, together with strange-looking instruments, including a bronze knife which had a long runnel let into the blade.

The knife and bowl were sticky and the bowl contained a residue of black viscous fluid which stank in Trumble's nostrils. He was overcome with nausea; turning, he reeled against the altar and putting out his hand to steady himself, felt it come away wet and scarlet. He saw that the whole of the top of the marble was awash with unspeakable foulness. He screamed then in the gloom of that charnel-house place and found himself running up the gangway between the seats, the breath sobbing in his throat.

He found some cloth near the foot of the ladder and wiped his hands clean; he shrank when he noticed that the cloth appeared to be a white robe like a surgeon's smock and that the front of it was already stained scarlet. The nausea rose again in his throat when he realised what lay underneath the quiet cabinet which he had used all these weeks as his office. He now understood the purpose of Dr Fabri's unholy ledgers and he knew, too, why the doctor had gone away for a few days. It was not hard to guess that one of his destinations would have been Essex. He had only taken Bassett beyond Guildford, but Trumble realised he would have to widen his area if he were to remain unsuspected.

His feet sped up the rungs of the ladder; he switched off the light, replaced the trapdoor, making sure that he left no stains on the metal and smoothed down the carpet over it. He inspected it anxiously, making sure that all was as it had been originally; his breath rasped unnaturally in his throat. When he got up to the desk he saw that someone had visited the cabinet in his absence; there was a new pile of correspondence on the green leather top. Trumble turned white and bit his lip. He glanced at his watch, saw that the midday post would just have been delivered. Joseph would know. He leaped for the door in a frenzy; it was quite immovable.

His hands were bleeding from beating against it when he realised the effort was quite useless; he calmed down then, noting that the key had been removed from the inside. He would never get out that way. He turned back to the inner cabinet, searching for a means of escape but the zinc walls were smooth and blank; there was not a join anywhere that he could discern. He would have to see what could be done in the underground chapel, though he dreaded descending again. Unless he could reason with Joseph. Perhaps the servant could hear him if he called out. A microphone within the cabinet, perhaps.

Trumble sweated and he swayed a little as he turned this way and that; the rumble of the air-conditioning went reassuringly on. But Trumble felt he could detect a faint hissing beyond this. Or was it his imagination? He licked his lips and plucked at his collar. Strangely enough, all fear was leaving him. He stared at the shelves and saw that a metal shutter had rolled back in the metal wall; there was a glass panel set into it.

On the other side stood his employer. Dr Fabri smiled encouragingly at him.

Trumble opened his mouth as if to say something, changed his mind and closed it again; he staggered as the gas hissed remorselessly into the small chamber, smoothly expunging the life from him. He understood many things as he fell against the desk. The Satanist had not forgotten the importance of the Poet. He had just time to note, entirely without surprise, before he went down to death, that the ledger in front of him was open.

And there, in the Archives of the Dead, as the latest entry, was his own name in Dr Fabri's impeccable, green-inked writing.

Mother of Serpents

Robert Bloch

———

9

Robert Bloch's name will forever be linked with that classic Alfred Hitchcock thriller, Psycho. *Bloch, who authored the screenplay and now devotes much of his time to writing scripts for Hollywood, is in many people's opinion the best horror story writer alive. Certainly, few other authors can match his incredibly vivid imagination and ability to conjure up the kind of terror which makes you look over your shoulder for hours after reading one of his stories. Prolific writer though Bloch is, one still has to search very thoroughly for material that is not already well known to enthusiasts, and tracking down this story about Voodoo (which even the author didn't have a copy of!) took considerable time. I hope you will agree after the trembling stops that the search was worth while.*

Voodooism is a queer thing. Forty years ago it was an unknown subject, save in certain esoteric circles. Today there is a surprising amount of information about it, due to research – and an even more surprising amount of misinformation.

Recent popular books on the subject are, for the most part, sheer romantic fancy; elaborated with the incomplete theorisings of ignoramuses.

Perhaps, though, this is for the best. For the truth about voodoo is such that no writer would care, or dare, to print it. Some of it is worse than their wildest fancies. I myself have seen certain things I do not dare to discuss. It would be useless to tell people anyway, for they would not believe me. And once again, this may be for the best. Knowledge can be a thousand times more terrifying than ignorance.

I know, though, for I have lived in Haiti, the dark island. I have learned much from legend, stumbled on many things through accident, and the bulk of my knowledge comes from the one really authentic source – the statements of the blacks. They're not talkative people, as a rule, those old natives of the back-hill country. It took patience and long familiarity with them before they unbent and told me their secrets.

That's why so many of the travel books are so palpably false – no writer who visits Haiti for six months or a year could possibly ingratiate himself into the confidence of those who know the facts. There are so few who really do know; so few who are not afraid to tell.

But I have learned. Let me tell you of the olden days; the old times, when Haiti rose to an empire, borne on a wave of blood.

It was many years ago, soon after the slaves had revolted. Toussaint l'Ouverture, Dessalines and King Christophe freed them from their French masters, freed them after uprisings and massacres and set up a kingdom founded on cruelty more fantastic than the despotism that reigned before.

There were no happy blacks in Haiti then. They had known too much of torture and death; the carefree life of their West Indian neighbours was utterly alien to these slaves and descendants of slaves. A strange mixture of races flourished: fierce tribesmen from Ashanti, Damballah, and the Guinea Coast; sullen Caribs; dusky offspring of renegade Frenchmen; bastard admixtures of Spanish, Negro, and Indian blood. Sly, treacherous half-breeds and mulattos ruled the coast, but there were even worse dwellers in the hills behind.

There were jungles in Haiti, impassable jungles, mountain-ringed and swamp-scourged forests filled with poisonous insects and pestilential fevers. White men dared not enter them, for they were worse than death. Blood-sucking plants, venomous reptiles, diseased orchids filled the forests, forests that hid horrors Africa had never known.

For that is where the real voodoo flourished, back there in the hills. Men lived there, it is said, descendants of escaped slaves, and outlaw factions that had been hunted from the coast. Furtive rumours told of isolated villages that practised cannibalism, mixed in with dark religious rites more dreadful and perverted than anything spawned in the Congo itself. Necrophilism, phallic worship, anthropomancy, and distorted versions of the Black Mass were commonplace. The shadow of *obeah* was everywhere. Human sacrifice was common, the offering up of roosters and goats an accepted thing. There were orgies around the voodoo altars, and blood was drunk in honour of *Baron Samede* and the old black gods brought from ancient lands.

Everybody knew about it. Each night the *ratta*-drums boomed out from the hills, and fires flared over the forests. Many known *papalois* and conjure-doctors resided on the edge of the coast itself, but they were never disturbed. Nearly all the 'civilised' blacks still believed in charms and philtres; even the churchgoers reverted to talismans and incantations in time of need. So-called 'educated' Negroes in Port-au-Prince society were admittedly emissaries from the barbarian tribes of the interior, and despite the outward show of civilisation the bloody priests still ruled behind the throne.

Of course there were scandals, mysterious disappearances, and occasional protests from emancipated citizens. But it was not wise to meddle with those who bowed to the Black Mother, or incur the anger of the terrible old men who dwelt in the shadow of the Snake.

Such was the status of sorcery when Haiti became a republic. People often wonder why there is still sorcery existent there to-day; more secretive, perhaps, but still surviving. They ask why the ghastly *zombies* are not destroyed, and why the government has not stepped in to stamp out the fiendish blood-cults that still lurk in the jungle gloom.

Perchance this tale will provide an answer; this old, secret tale of the new republic. Officials, remembering the story, are still afraid to interfere too strongly, and the laws that have been passed are very loosely enforced.

Because the Serpent Cult of Obeah will never die in Haiti – in Haiti, that fantastic island whose sinuous shoreline resembles the yawning jaws of a monstrous *snake*.

One of the earliest presidents of Haiti was an educated man. Although born on the island, he was schooled in France, and studied extensively while abroad. His accession to the highest office of the land found him an enlightened, sophisticated cosmopolite of the modern type. Of course he still liked to remove his shoes in the privacy of his office, but he never displayed his naked toes in an official capacity. Don't misunderstand – the man was no Emperor Jones; he was merely a polished ebony gentleman whose natural barbarity occasionally broke through its veneer of civilisation.

He was, in fact, a very shrewd man. He had to be in order to become president in those early days; only extremely shrewd men ever attained that dignity. Perhaps it would enlighten you a bit to say that in those times the term 'shrewd' was a polite Haitian synonym for 'crooked'. It is therefore easy to realise the president's character when you know that he was regarded as one of the most successful politicians the republic ever produced.

In his short reign he was opposed by very few enemies; and those that did work against him usually disappeared. The tall, coal-black man with the physical skull-conformation of a gorilla harboured a remarkably crafty brain beneath his beetling brow.

His ability was phenomenal. He had an insight into finance which profited him greatly; profited him, that is, in both his official and unofficial capacity. Whenever he saw fit to increase the taxes he increased the army as well, and sent it out to escort the state tax-collectors. His treaties with foreign countries were masterpieces of legal lawlessness. This black Machiavelli knew that he must work fast, since presidents had a peculiar way of dying in Haiti. They seemed peculiarly susceptible to disease – 'lead poisoning', as our modern gangster friends might say. So the president worked very fast indeed, and he did a masterful job.

This was truly remarkable, in view of his humble background. For his was a success saga in the good old Horatio Alger manner. His father was unknown. His mother was a conjure-woman in the hills, and though quite well known, she had been very poor. The president had been born in a log cabin; quite the classic setting for a future distinguished career. His early years had been most uneventful, until his adoption, at thirteen, by a benevolent Protestant minister. For a year he lived with this kind man, serving as houseboy in his home. Suddenly the poor minister died of an obscure ailment; this was most unfortunate, for he had been quite wealthy and his money was alleviating much of the suffering in this particular section. At any rate, this rich minister died, and the poor conjure-woman's son sailed to France for a university education.

As for the conjure-woman, she bought herself a new mule and said nothing. Her skill at herbs had given her son a chance in the world, and she was satisfied.

It was eight years before the boy returned. He had changed a great deal since his departure; he preferred the society of whites and the octoroon society people of Port-au-Prince. It is recorded that he rather ignored his old mother, too. His newly acquired fastidiousness made him painfully aware of the woman's ignorant simplicity. Besides, he was ambitious, and he did not care to publicise his relationship with such a notorious witch.

For she was quite famous in her way. Where she had come from and what her original history was, nobody knew. But for many years her hut in the mountains had been the rendezvous of strange worshippers and even stranger emissaries. The dark powers of *obeah* were evoked in her shadowy altar-place amidst the hills, and a furtive group of acolytes resided there with her. Her ritual fires always flared on moonless nights, and bullocks were given in bloody baptism to the Crawler of Midnight. For she was a Priestess of the Serpent.

The Snake-God, you know, is the real deity of the *obeah* cults. The blacks worshipped the Serpent in Dahomey and Senegal from time immemorial. They venerate the reptiles in a curious way, and there is some obscure linkage between the snake and the crescent moon. Curious, isn't it — this serpent superstition? The Garden of Eden had its tempter, you know, and the Bible tells of Moses and his staff of snakes. The Egyptians revered Set, and the ancient Hindus had a cobra god. It seems to be general throughout the world — the kindred hatred and reverence of serpents. Always they seem to be worshipped as creatures of evil. American Indians believed in Yig, and Aztec myths follow the pattern. And of course the Hopi ceremonial dances are of the same order.

But the African Serpent legends are particularly dreadful, and the Haitian adaptations of the sacrificial rites are worse.

At the time of which I speak some of the voodoo groups were believed to actually breed snakes; they smuggled the reptiles over from the Ivory Coast to use in their secret practices. There were tall tales current about twenty-foot pythons which swallowed infants offered up to them on the Black Altar, and about *sendings* of poisonous serpents which killed enemies of the voodoo-masters. It is a known fact that several anthropoid apes had been smuggled into the country by a peculiar cult that worshipped gorillas; so the serpent legends may have been equally true.

At any rate, the president's mother was a priestess, and equally as famous, in a way, as her distinguished son. He, just after his return, had slowly climbed to power. First he had been a tax-gatherer, then treasurer, and finally president. Several of his rivals died, and those who opposed him soon found it expedient to dissemble their hatred; for he was still a savage at heart, and savages like to torment their enemies. It was rumoured that he had constructed a secret torture chamber beneath the palace, and that its instruments were rusty, though not from disuse.

The breach between the young statesman and his mother began to widen just prior to his presidential incumbency. The immediate cause was his marriage to the daughter of a rich octoroon planter from the coast. Not only was the old woman humiliated because her son contaminated the family stock (she was pure Negro, and descendant of a Niger slave-king), but she was further indignant because she had not been invited to the wedding.

It was held in Port-au-Prince. The foreign consuls were there, and the cream of Haitian society was present. The lovely bride had been convent-bred, and her antecedents were held in the highest esteem. The groom wisely did not deign to desecrate the nuptial celebration by including his rather unsavoury parent.

She came, though, and watched the affair through the kitchen doorway. It was just as well that she did not make her presence known, as it would have embarrassed not only her son, but several others as well – official dignitaries who sometimes consulted her in their unofficial capacity.

What she saw of her son and his bride was not pleasing. The man was an affected dandy now, and his wife was a silly flirt. The atmosphere of the pomp and ostentation did not impress her; behind their debonair masks of polite sophistication she knew that most of those present were superstitious Negroes who would have run to her for charms or oracular advice the moment they were in trouble. Nevertheless, she took no action; she merely smiled rather bitterly and hobbled home. After all, she still loved her son.

The next affront, however, she could not overlook. This was

the inauguration of the new president. She was not invited to this affair either, yet she came. And this time she did not skulk in the shadows. After the oath of office was administered she marched boldly up to the new ruler of Haiti and accosted him before the very eyes of the German consul himself. She was a grotesque figure; an ungainly little harridan barely five feet tall, black, barefooted, and clad in rags.

Her son quite naturally ignored her presence. The withered crone licked her toothless gums in terrible silence. Then, quite calmly, she began to curse him – not in French, but in native *patois* of the hills. She called down the wrath of her bloody gods upon his ungrateful head, and threatened both him and his wife with vengeance for their smug ingratitude. The assembled guests were shocked.

So was the new president. However, he did not forget himself. Calmly he motioned to his guards, who led the now hysterical witch-woman away. He would deal with her later.

The next night when he saw fit to go into the dungeon and reason with his mother, she was gone. Disappeared, the guards told him, rolling their eyes mysteriously. He had the jailer shot, and went back to his official chambers.

He was a little worried about that curse business. You see, he knew what the woman was capable of. He did not like those threats against his wife, either. The next day he had some silver bullets moulded, like King Henry in the old days. He also bought an *ouanga* charm from a devil-doctor of his own acquaintance. Magic would fight magic.

That night a serpent came to him in dreams; a serpent with green eyes that whispered in the way of men and hissed at him with shrill and mocking laughter as he struck at it in his sleep. There was a reptilian odour in his bedroom the next morning, and a nauseous slime upon his pillow that gave forth a similar stench. And the president knew that only his charm had saved him.

That afternoon his wife missed one of her Paris frocks, and the president questioned his servants in his private torture chamber below. He learned some facts he dared not tell his bride, and thereafter he seemed very sad. He had seen his mother work with wax images before – little mannikins resembling men and women, dressed in parts of their stolen garments. Sometimes she stuck pins into them or roasted them over a slow fire. Always the real people sickened and died. This knowledge made the president quite unhappy, and he was still more overwrought when messengers returned and said that his mother was gone from her old hut in the hills.

Three days later his wife died, of a painful wound in her side which no doctors could explain. She was in agony until the end, and just before her passing it was rumoured that her body turned blue and bloated up to twice its normal size. Her features were eaten away as if with leprosy, and her swollen limbs looked like those of an elephantiasis victim. Loathsome tropical diseases abound in Haiti, but none of them kill in three days. . . .

After this the president went mad.

Like Cotton Mather of old, he started on a witch-hunting crusade. Soldiers and police were sent out to comb the countryside. Spies rode up to hovels on the mountain peaks, and armed patrols crouched in far-off fields where the living dead-men work, their glazed and glassy eyes staring ceaselessly at the moon. *Mamalois* were put to the question over slow fires, and possessors of forbidden books were roasted over flames fed by the very tomes they harboured. Blood-hounds yammered in the hills, and priests died on altars where they were wont to sacrifice. Only one order had been specially given: the president's mother was to be captured alive and unharmed.

Meanwhile he sat in the palace with the embers of slow insanity in his eyes – embers that flared into fiendish flame when the guards brought in the withered crone, who had been captured near that awful grove of idols in the swamp.

They took her downstairs, although she fought and clawed like a wildcat, and then the guards went away and left her son with her alone. Alone, in a torture chamber, with a mother who cursed him from the rack. Alone, with frantic fires in his eyes, and a great silver knife in his hand. . . .

The president spent many hours in his secret torture chamber during the next few days. He seldom was seen around the palace, and his servants were given orders that he must not be disturbed. On the fourth day he came up the hidden stairway for the last time, and the flickering madness in his eyes was gone.

Just what occurred in the dungeon below will never be rightly known. No doubt that is for the best. The president was a savage at heart, and to the brute, prolongation of pain always brings ecstasy. . . .

It is recorded, though, that the old witch-woman cursed her son with the Serpent's Curse in her dying breath, and that is the most terrible curse of all.

Some idea of what happened may be gained by the knowledge of the president's revenge; for he had a grim sense of humour, and a barbarian's idea of retribution. His wife had been killed by his mother, who fashioned a waxen image. He decided to do what would be exquisitely appropriate.

When he came up the stairs that last time, his servants saw that he bore with him a great candle, fashioned of corpse-fat. And since nobody ever saw his mother's body again, there were curious surmises as to where the corpse-fat was obtained. But then, the president's mind leaned toward grisly jests. . . .

The rest of the story is very simple. The president went directly to his chambers in the palace, where he placed the candle in a holder on his desk. He had neglected his work in the last few days, and there was much official business for him to transact. For a while he sat in silence, staring at the candle with a curious satisfied smile. Then he called for his papers and announced that he would attend to them immediately.

He worked all that night, with two guards stationed outside his door. Sitting at his desk, he pored over his task in the candle-light – the candlelight from the corpse-fat taper.

Evidently his mother's dying curse did not bother him at all. Once satisfied, his blood-lust abated, he discounted all possibility of revenge. Even he was not superstitious enough to believe that the sorceress could return from her grave. He was quite calm as he sat there, quite the civilised gentleman. The candle cast ominous shadows over the darkened room, but he did not notice – until it was too late. Then he looked up to see the corpse-fat candle wriggle into monstrous life.

His mother's curse. . . .

The candle – the corpse-fat candle – was *alive*! It was a sinuous, twisting thing, weaving in its holder with sinister purpose.

The flame-tipped end seemed to glow strongly into a sudden terrible semblance. The president, amazed, saw the fiery face – his mother's; a tiny wrinkled face of flame, with a corpse-fat body that darted out toward the man with hideous ease. The candle was lengthening as if the tallow were melting; lengthening, and reaching out towards him in a terrible way.

The president of Haiti screamed, but it was too late. The glowing flame on the end snuffed out, breaking the hypnotic spell that had held the man betranced. And at that moment the candle leapt, while the room faded into dreadful darkness. It was a ghastly darkness, filled with moans, and the sound of a thrashing body that grew fainter, and fainter. . . .

It was quite still by the time the guards had entered and turned up the lights once more. They knew about the corpse-fat candle and the witch-mother's curse. That is why they were the first to announce the president's death; the first to fire a bullet into his temple and claim he committed suicide.

They told the president's successor the story, and he gave orders that the crusade against voodoo be abandoned. It was better so, for the new man did not wish to die. The guards had explained why they shot the president and called it suicide, and his successor did not wish to risk the Serpent Curse.

For the president of Haiti had been strangled to death by his mother's corpse-fat candle – *a corpse-fat candle that was wound around his neck like a giant snake.*

Cerimarie

Arthur J Burks

—◆—

The author of this grisly tale of Voodoo describes himself as a 'double ghost writer'. For apart from the large number of supernatural and Occult stories that he turns out under his own name, Arthur J Burks is also one of America's top 'ghost' writers producing books for famous people. He spent a number of years just before World War II on Haiti — the setting of this story — and consequently came into frequent contact with Voodoo. On several ocasions he actually witnessed the terrible effects of the secret rites and this story resulted from one particularly revolting killing. Although Cerimarie *was a prize-winning short story when first published in America in 1924, this marks its first appearance in England.*

No OFFICER IN any of the American services in Haiti would have assigned Rodney Davis with such a mission as he had sought for himself. It was not the kind of job to give an entire battalion, let alone one man. Yet it was an undeniable fact that if ever the evil Voodoo Priest, Cerimarie Sam, was to be brought to the justice he so richly deserved it would most likely be accomplished by one brave man working unhindered and alone.

This still did not cause the commanding officer any less surprise when Davis sought an interview and asked that he be given the assignment. The CO had looked at him in complete amazement. Surely a man must be insane to ask for such a job. Cerimarie, if he existed in fact — which no white man knew for sure — was believed to be the greatest monster in all Haiti. A threat to the lives of every man, woman and child on the island. A trafficker in the most evil of all Black Arts. . . .

. . . But the CO knew how desperately his superiors wanted the menace of the priest ended. Nevertheless he couldn't help

wondering about Davis. No white man knew the inland trail
and jungle ways of Haiti as Cerimarie knew them, so how could
he hope to catch the native?

It was a reasonable question. But what the CO did not know
about was the raging fire for vengeance that burned in Davis. A
fire that had been fanned into life by the ghastly murder of little
Charlie Hepner, the man the soldiers called Music – the man
who had been Davis's special friend in the outfit.

For not only had Davis felt his comrade's death very deeply –
he had also been the one who had found him on that terrible
morning. . . .

Music had left the camp on a simple errand and planned to be
away for only an hour or two. No one had bothered overduly
about his absence until darkness had fallen. Then the battalion
– along with the anxious Rodney Davis – had turned out in
force and searched the surrounding jungle without success until
daylight.

Even when the men stopped for a quick breakfast, Davis continued to hunt feverishly. And it was his perseverance that eventually paid off. For he found Hepner – dead.

Death in itself is not so horrible to a soldier. In the field he
walks always by its side, growing calloused to the thought of
dying. But when death is attended with such gory details as
those which attended little Hepner, it is something else again.
Hepner's clothing had been stripped from his body and the little
Music had literally been skinned alive! From just above his
ankles the flesh had been cut to the bone and stripped off over
his feet – in the same way as a hunter skins the hide from a
rabbit's leg!

Davis's cry of agony as he recognised his little friend carried
back to the breakfasting men and something in it chilled every
last man of them to the bone. Even before they had reached the
scene, each man knew that he was soon to look upon some unspeakable horror. And not the least of the horrors was the appear-

ance of Davis himself. He had become in a few moments a graven marble image, cold as starshine, with eyes that saw but one thing, that recognised neither superior officer nor friend. A creature with but one aim in life and no hope beyond that aim. An automaton. A mechanical creature made to rend and destroy. . . .

. . . They sent him back to the capital city, where he spent six months in the study of Haitian patois. And, made mentally strong by the fires within him, he mastered the language – if it may be called a language. Then he sought his audience with the man at the top, made his request, was accepted, and sent forth, to become a pariah in Haiti, where all those outside uniform and without visible means of support are pariahs.

He had known that the slaying of Hepner, right on the very edge of the encampment in the hills, had been the work of Cerimarie Sam. For the detachment had had four or five native prisoners who had run to the scene and looked upon Hepner, and one of them had mentioned the name of the terrible priest before he could check himself. This had been enough.

The next morning the man who had spoken the dread name had been found dead outside the camp – his lips sewed together with hair from the tail of one of the detachments' horses. . . .

. . . Two months after his departure from the capital city of the Black Republic, Davis, every inch of his skin dyed ebony, lips thickened with injections of paraffin, and grimy from studied failure to bathe, entered a dim trail somewhere in that little known country lying inside the triangle formed by the capital city, Jacmel, and San Pierre. Something whispered to him that fulfilment was at hand. He met natives on the trail and avoided conversation with them with studied carelessness. Later in the day he encountered others of both sexes who travelled the same direction. It was much easier to join the pilgrimage than he had thought.

Almost too easy.

When the dim trail branched off into a dimmer trail and most of the people entered this, Davis managed to slip into the jungle on one side until darkness fell. Then he was another black shadow with those who went before and those who followed.

In a hollow surrounded by beetling hills he saw a great fire in an open place, beyond which was the odd shadow of some sort of building. He knew without being told what the building was. A shell of a place, covered with rude daubs, obscene in the extreme. Many people had gathered about the fire and the building. Restless men and women, beasts of prey more terrible because they were human beasts, slouched here and there, or sat on their haunches, sunken in apathy. They paid him suspiciously little attention as he crept in and joined the devotees.

There was a stir shortly, and an expectant craning of necks toward the dark opening in that building beyond the fire. Davis's nerves became as taut wire. Into the circle of light came an ebony woman with the form of a Venus and the face of a beast.

'Maman Loi! Maman Loi! Maman Loi!'

A weird moaning cry, thrice repeated. Greetings to the priestess of the serpent!

The woman began to dance, a slow movement of the body from the hips upward, not without a certain grace. The watchers moaned and touched their heads to the ground. The woman, weaving here and there like an upright serpent, undulated into the terrible spirit of the dance. Her bodily postures now expressed the lowest meanings of sensuality. The brain behind that black skull must have crawled with devilish vermin. Her movements were the acme of obscenity. The lust of the beast is clean because it is natural. The natural emotion of man is clean because it is sacred. But the lust expressed in the dance of the

Maman Loi was the lust of a man or woman for a beast — horrible, revolting, inexpressible in words. As she worked herself into a frenzy a sort of froth came to her lips; her eyes rolled until one could see the whites of them. She seemed to be possessed of serpents that crawled within her bosom, causing her to writhe with their writhing. In her frenzy, which the devotees began to share, she tore her thin clothing from her body, standing naked in the firelight and writhing still in the ghastly contortions of the dance. She fell to the ground at last, as if taken suddenly with epilepsy. When her bare feet fell into the fire she seemed not to notice.

Heads were raised and another wail went forth.

'Papa Loi! Papa Loi! Papa Loi!'

The priest came forth with the sacrifice! A goat without horns! A nude girl of sixteen or so, black as midnight, so stupefied with some sort of drug that she knew not where she went nor cared. Then Davis noticed several other things. The priest, his face hidden by a mask fashioned after a serpent's head, carried a red book in his hand. There was a round stone near the fire. The ground near the circle of devotees was covered with sawdust.

When the Papa Loi threw the girl upon the ground and opened the great vein in her neck, she made no sound. Only her eyes moved as do those of a stricken bull. The priest caught the blood in a vessel, dipped his fingers in it, and with the precise flicking movement of long practice made a cross of crimson in the sawdust. Three drops he let fall upon the holy stone, three drops he used to anoint the book.

There was a different timbre in the moaning of the devotees now. Louder, more malevolent, demanding that the ceremony proceed with greater speed. The priest, a butcher in the guise of a serpent, began his work. Davis saw revolting black lips become dyed with crimson, saw terrible trophies in the hands of the devotees, trophies that had once been part of a fellow being. When the trophies disappeared there was nothing but clean white bones and a circle of gorged beasts. Davis's head sank on to his chest in horror.

The ceremony proceeded to its inevitable conclusion as if there were no depth to the filth into which the devotees might plunge themselves. Men and women, one with the other, forced themselves far, far down below the level of the beasts – in the name of the most terrible religion.

Suddenly, almost instinctively, Davis looked up. The priest with the serpent's mask stood before him.

'I am Cerimarie Sam,' he said. 'Who are you?'

There was a threat in the voice that told Davis he had been found out. He looked around the circle before replying. He came to his feet with a leap that carried him atop the monster, this beast in human guise that murdered children; who had children by whatsoever woman he desired and attended none of them; who had even offered some of these children, on occasion, as sacrifices to the serpent. The devotees were too far gone in their beastliness to notice what took place.

It was only at dawn that they missed their high priest. And by then he had disappeared from among them. . . .

. . . Two weeks later Davis reported back to his commanding officer – who would have had him thrown out of the office as a dirty nigger had he not heard English words on the black man's lips.

After the greetings were over the CO asked:

'And what of Cerimarie Sam?'

'Very strange about him, sir,' replied Davis coldly, his eyes like points of fire. 'I found him all right. But someone had literally skinned him alive.'

The Witch

Shirley Jackson

———

II

Shirley Jackson has one distinction which none of the other contributors to this anthology can – or would probably want to – claim: she is said to be an 'amateur witch specialising in small scale black magic'. Married to literary critic Stanley Hyman, she leads an otherwise fairly quiet life in Vermont devoting most of her time to writing. Her major successes have been The Lottery *and* The Haunting of Hill House *which was made into a major film a few years ago. Her style is highly original as this story, which develops from a situation of complete normality into something quite horrifying, dramatically illustrates. Her spell will linger with you long after you have finished the story.*

THE COACH WAS so nearly empty that the little boy had a seat all to himself, and his mother sat across the aisle on the seat next to the little boy's sister, a baby with a piece of toast in one hand and a rattle in the other. She was strapped securely to the seat so she could sit up and look around, and whenever she began to slip slowly sideways the strap caught her and held her halfway until her mother turned around and straightened her again. The little boy was looking out of the window and eating a cookie, and the mother was reading quietly, answering the little boy's questions without looking up.

'We're on a river,' the little boy said. 'This is a river and we're on it.'

'Fine,' his mother said.

'We're on a bridge over a river,' the little boy said to himself.

The few other people in the coach were sitting at the other end of the car; if any of them had occasion to come down the aisle the little boy would look around and say, 'Hi', and the stranger would usually say, 'Hi', back and sometimes ask the little boy if he were enjoying the train ride, or even tell him he was a fine big fellow. These comments annoyed the little boy and he would turn irritably back to the window.

'There's a cow,' he would say, or, sighing, 'How far do we have to go?'

'Not much longer now,' his mother said, each time.

Once the baby, who was very quiet and busy with her rattle and her toast, which the mother would renew constantly, fell over too far sideways and banged her head. She began to cry, and for a minute there was noise and movement around the mother's seat. The little boy slid down from his own seat and ran across the aisle to pet his sister's feet and beg her not to cry, and finally the baby laughed and went back to her toast, and the little boy received a lollipop from his mother and went back to the window.

'I saw a witch,' he said to his mother after a minute. 'There was a big old ugly old bad old witch outside.'

'Fine,' his mother said.

'A big old ugly witch and I told her to go away and she went away,' the little boy went on, in a quiet narrative to himself, 'she came and she said, "I'm going to eat you up", and I said, "no, you're not", and I chased her away, the bad old mean witch.'

He stopped talking and looked up as the outside door of the coach opened and a man came in. He was an elderly man, with a pleasant face under white hair; his blue suit was only faintly touched by the disarray that comes from a long train trip. He was carrying a cigar, and when the little boy said 'Hi', the man gestured at him with the cigar and said, 'Hello yourself, son.' He stopped just beside the little boy's seat, and leaned against the back, looking down at the little boy, who craned his neck to look upward. 'What you looking for out that window?' the man asked.

'Witches,' the little boy said promptly. 'Bad old mean witches.' 'I see,' the man said. 'Find many?' 'My father smokes cigars,' the little boy said. 'All men smoke cigars,' the man said. 'Someday you'll smoke cigars, too.'

'I'm a man already,' the little boy said. 'How old are you?' the man asked. The little boy, at the eternal question, looked at the man suspiciously for a minute and then said, 'Twenty-six. Eight hunnerd and forty eighty.'

His mother lifted her head from the book. 'Four,' she said, smiling fondly at the little boy.

'Is that so?' the man said politely to the little boy. 'Twenty-six.' He nodded his head at the mother across the aisle. 'Is that your mother?'

The little boy leaned forward to look and then said, 'Yes, that's her.' 'What's your name?' the man asked. The little boy looked suspicious again. 'Mr Jesus,' he said. 'Johnny,' the little boy's mother said. She caught the little boy's eye and frowned deeply.

'That's my sister over there,' the little boy said to the man. 'She's twelve-and-a-half.' 'Do you love your sister?' the man asked. The little boy stared, and the man came around the side of the seat and sat down next to the little boy. 'Listen,' the man said, 'shall I tell you about my little sister?'

The mother, who had looked up anxiously when the man sat down next to her little boy, went peacefully back to her book.

'Tell me about your sister,' the little boy said. 'Was she a witch?'

'Maybe,' the man said.

The little boy laughed excitedly, and the man leaned back and puffed at his cigar. 'Once upon a time,' he began, 'I had a little sister, just like yours.' The little boy looked up at the man, nodding at every word. 'My little sister,' went on the man, 'was so pretty and so nice that I loved her more than anything else in the world. So shall I tell you what I did?'

The little boy nodded more vehemently, and the mother lifted her eyes from the book and smiled, listening.

'I bought her a rocking-horse and a doll and a million lolli-pops,' the man said, 'and then I took her and I put my hands around her neck and I pinched her and I pinched her until she was dead.'

The little boy gasped and the mother turned around, her smile fading. She opened her mouth, and then closed it again as the man went on, 'And then I took and I cut her head off and I took her head—' 'Did you cut her all in pieces?' the little boy asked breathlessly. 'I cut off her head and her hands and her feet and her hair and her nose,' said the man, 'and I hit her with a stick and I killed her.' 'Wait a minute,' the mother said, but the baby fell over sideways just at that minute and by the time the mother had set her up again the man was going on. 'And I took her head and I pulled out all her hair and—' 'Your little sister?' the little boy prompted eagerly. 'My little sister,' the man said firmly. 'And I put her head in a cage with a bear and the bear ate it all up.'

'Ate her head all up?' the little boy asked.

The mother put her book down and came across the aisle. She stood next to the man and said, 'Just what do you think you're doing?' The man looked up courteously and she said, 'Get out of here.'

'Did I frighten you?' the man said. He looked down at the little boy and nudged him with an elbow and he and the little boy laughed.

'This man cut up his little sister,' the little boy said to his mother.

'I can very easily call the conductor,' the mother said to the man.

'The conductor will eat my mommy,' the little boy said. 'We'll chop her head off.'

'And little sister's head too,' the man said. He stood up, and the mother stood back to let him get out of the seat. 'Don't ever come back in this car,' she said.

'My mommy will eat you,' the little boy said to the man. The man laughed, and the little boy laughed, and then the man said,

'Excuse me,' to the mother and went past her out of the car. When the door had closed behind him the little boy said, 'How much longer do we have to stay on this old train?'

'Not much longer,' the mother said. She stood looking at the little boy, wanting to say something, and finally she said, 'You sit still and be a good boy. You may have another lollipop.'

The little boy climbed down eagerly and followed his mother back to her seat. She took a lollipop from her bag in her pocket-book and gave it to him. 'What do you say?' she asked.

'Thank you,' the little boy said. 'Did that man really cut his little sister up in pieces?'

'He was just teasing,' the mother said, and added urgently, 'just teasing.'

'Prob'ly,' the little boy said. With his lollipop he went back to his own seat, and settled himself to look out the window again. 'Prob'ly he was a witch.'

Homecoming

Ray Bradbury

Ray Bradbury is probably today's most famous Science Fiction writer. Life magazine says of him, 'He has the ear of a poet and the soul of a moralist' and it has accorded him the rare honour – Ernest Hemingway is one of the few other authors to share it – of publishing his fiction in its usually news-only columns. Yet apart from his tales of the future and his film work (which takes most of his time now), Ray Bradbury is also a master of the horror story. His horror, however, is subtle, deceptive and creeps up on you when you are at your most unwary. His style, too, is quite unique and his conception incredibly bizarre. This story of Witchcraft is unlike any other you will ever read. And perhaps when you have finished you will think that is just as well!

'HERE THEY COME,' said Cecy, lying there flat in her bed.

'Where are they?' cried Timothy from the doorway.

'Some of them are over Europe, some over Asia, some of them over the Islands, some over South America!' said Cecy, her eyes closed, the lashes long, brown, and quivering.

Timothy came forward upon the bare plankings of the upstairs room. 'Who are they?'

'Uncle Einar and Uncle Fry, and there's Cousin William, and I see Frulda and Helgar and Aunt Morgiana and Cousin Vivian, and I see Uncle Johann! They're all coming fast!'

'Are they up in the sky?' cried Timothy, his little grey eyes flashing. Standing by the bed, he looked no more than his fourteen years. The wind blew outside, the house was dark and lit only by starlight.

'They're coming through the air and travelling along the ground, in many forms,' said Cecy, in her sleeping. She did not move on the bed; she thought inward on herself and told what she saw. 'I see a wolflike thing coming over a dark river – at the shallows — just above a waterfall, the starlight shining up his pelt. I see a brown oak leaf blowing far up in the sky. I see a small bat flying. I see many other things, running through the forest trees and slipping through the highest branches; and they're *all* coming this way!'

'Will they be here by tomorrow night?' Timothy clutched the bedclothes. The spider on his lapel swung like a black pendulum, excitedly dancing. He leaned over his sister. 'Will they all be here in time for the Homecoming?'

'Yes, yes, Timothy, yes,' sighed Cecy. She stiffened. 'Ask no more of me. Go away now. Let me travel in the places I like best.'

'Thanks, Cecy,' he said. Out in the hall, he ran to his room. He hurriedly made his bed. He had just awakened a few minutes ago, at sunset, and as the first stars had risen, he had gone to let his excitement about the party run with Cecy. Now she slept so quietly there was not a sound. The spider hung on a silvery lasso about Timothy's slender neck as he washed his face. 'Just think, Spid, tomorrow night is All-Hallows' Eve!'

He lifted his face and looked into the mirror. His was the only mirror allowed in the house. It was his mother's concession to his illness. Oh, if only he were not so afflicted! He opened his mouth, surveyed the poor, inadequate teeth nature had given him. No more than so many corn kernels — round, soft and pale in his jaws. Some of the high spirit died in him.

It was now totally dark and he lit a candle to see by. He felt exhausted. This past week the whole family had lived in the fashion of the old country. Sleeping by day, rousing at sunset to move about. There were blue hollows under his eyes. 'Spid, I'm no good,' he said, quietly, to the little creature. 'I can't even get used to sleeping days like the others.'

He took up the candleholder. Oh, to have strong teeth, with incisors like steel spikes. Or strong hands even, or a strong mind. Even to have the power to send one's mind out, free, as Cecy did.

226

But, no, he was the imperfect one, the sick one. He was even — he shivered and drew the candle flame closer — afraid of the dark. His brothers snorted at him. Bion and Leonard and Sam. They laughed at him because he slept in a bed. With Cecy it was different; her bed was part of her comfort for the composure necessary to send her mind abroad to hunt. But Timothy, did he sleep in the wonderful polished boxes like the others? He did not! Mother let him have his own room, his own bed, his own mirror. No wonder the family skirted him like a holy man's crucifix. If only the wings would sprout from his shoulder blades. He bared his back, stared at it. And sighed again. No chance. Never.

Downstairs were exciting and mysterious sounds, the slithering black crêpe going up in all the halls and on the ceilings and doors. The sputter of burning black tapers in the banistered stair well. Mother's voice, high and firm. Father's voice, echoing from the damp cellar. Bion walking from outside the old country house lugging vast two-gallon jugs.

'I've just got to go to the party, Spid,' said Timothy. The spider whirled at the end of its silk, and Timothy felt alone. He would polish cases, fetch toadstools and spiders, hang crêpe, but when the party started he'd be ignored. The less seen or said of the imperfect son the better.

All through the house below, Laura ran.

'The Homecoming!' she shouted gaily. 'The Homecoming!' Her footsteps everywhere at once.

Timothy passed Cecy's room again, and she was sleeping quietly. Once a month she went belowstairs. Always she stayed in bed. Lovely Cecy. He felt like asking her, 'Where are you now, Cecy? And in who? And what's happening? Are you beyond the hills? And what goes on there?' But he went on to Ellen's room instead.

Ellen sat at her desk, sorting out many kinds of blonde, red and black hair and the little scimitars of fingernail gathered from her manicurist job at the Mellin Village beauty parlour fifteen miles over. A sturdy mahogany case lay in one corner with her name on it.

'Go away,' she said, not even looking at him. 'I can't work with you gawking.'

'All-Hallows' Eve, Ellen; just think!' he said, trying to be friendly.

'Hunh!' She put some fingernail clippings in a small white sack, labelled them. 'What can it mean to you? What do you know of it? It'll scare the hell out of you. Go back to bed.'

His cheeks burned. 'I'm needed to polish and work and help serve.'

'If you don't go, you'll find a dozen raw oysters in your bed tomorrow,' said Ellen, matter-of-factly. 'Goodbye, Timothy.'

In his anger, rushing downstairs, he bumped into Laura.

'Watch where you're going!' she shrieked from clenched teeth.

She swept away. He ran to the open cellar door, smelled the channel of moist earthy air rising from below. 'Father?'

'It's about time,' Father shouted up the steps. 'Hurry down, or they'll be here before we're ready!'

Timothy hesitated only long enough to hear the million other sounds in the house. Brothers came and went like trains in a station, talking and arguing. If you stood in one spot long enough the entire household passed with their pale hands full of things. Leonard with his little black medical case, Samuel with his large, dusty ebony-bound book under his arm, bearing more black crêpe, and Bion excursioning to the car outside and bringing in many more gallons of liquid.

Father stopped polishing to give Timothy a rag and a scowl. He thumped the huge mahogany box. 'Come on, shine this up so we can start on another. Sleep your life away.'

While waxing the surface, Timothy looked inside.

'Uncle Einar's a big man, isn't he, Papa?'

'Unh.'

'How big is he?'

'The size of the box'll tell you.'

'I was only asking. Seven feet tall?'

'You talk a lot.'

About nine o'clock Timothy went out into the October weather. For two hours in the now-warm, now-cold wind he walked the meadows collecting toadstools and spiders. His heart began to beat with anticipation again. How many relatives had Mother said would come? Seventy? One hundred? He passed a farmhouse. If only you knew what was happening at our house, he said to the glowing windows. He climbed a hill and looked at the town, miles away, settling into sleep, the town hall clock high and round white in the distance. The town did not know, either. He brought home many jars of toadstools and spiders.

In the little chapel belowstairs a brief ceremony was celebrated. It was like all the other rituals over the years, with Father chanting the dark lines, Mother's beautiful white ivory hands moving in the reverse blessings, and all the children gathered except Cecy, who lay upstairs in bed. But Cecy was present. You saw her peering, now from Bion's eyes, now Samuel's, now Mother's, and you felt a movement and now she was in you, fleetingly and gone.

Timothy prayed to the Dark One with a tightened stomach. 'Please, please, help me grow up, help me be like my sisters and brothers. Don't let me be different. If only I could put the hair in the plastic images as Ellen does, or make people fall in love with me as Laura does with people, or read strange books as Sam does, or work in a respected job like Leonard and Bion do. Or even raise a family one day, as Mother and Father have done. . . .'

At midnight a storm hammered the house. Lightning struck

outside in amazing, snow-white bolts. There was a sound of an approaching, probing, sucking tornado, funnelling and nuzzling the moist night earth. Then the front door, blasted half off its hinges, hung stiff and discarded, and in trooped Grandmamma and Grandpapa, all the way from the old country!

From then on people arrived each hour. There was a flutter at the side window, a rap on the front porch, a knock at the back. There were fey noises from the cellar; autumn wind piped down the chimney throat, chanting. Mother filled the large crystal punch bowl with a scarlet fluid poured from the jugs Bion had carried home. Father swept from room to room lighting more tapers. Laura and Ellen hammered up more wolfsbane. And Timothy stood amidst this wild excitement, no expression to his face, his hands trembling at his sides, gazing now here, now there. Banging of doors, laughter, the sound of liquid pouring, darkness, sound of wind, the webbed thunder of wings, the padding of feet, the welcoming bursts of talk at the entrances, the transparent rattlings of casements, the shadows passing, coming, going, wavering.

'Well, well, and *this* must be Timothy!'

'What?'

A chilly hand took his hand. A long hairy face leaned down over him. 'A good lad, a fine lad,' said the stranger.

'Timothy,' said his mother. 'This is Uncle Jason.'

'Hello, Uncle Jason.'

'And over here——' Mother drifted Uncle Jason away. Uncle Jason peered back at Timothy over his caped shoulder, and winked.

Timothy stood alone.

From off a thousand miles in the candled darkness, he heard a high fluting voice; that was Ellen. 'And my brothers, they *are* clever. Can you guess their occupations, Aunt Morgiana?'

'I have no idea.'

'They operate the undertaking establishment in town.'

'What!' A gasp.

'Yes!' Shrill laughter. 'Isn't that priceless!'

Timothy stood very still.

A pause in the laughter. 'They bring home sustenance for Mama, Papa and all of us,' said Laura. 'Except, of course, Timothy. . . .'

An uneasy silence. Uncle Jason's voice demanded, 'Well? come now. What about Timothy?'

'Oh, Laura, your tongue,' said Mother.

Laura went on with it. Timothy shut his eyes. 'Timothy doesn't – well – doesn't *like* blood. He's delicate.'

'He'll learn,' said Mother. 'He'll learn,' she said very firmly. 'He's my son, and he'll learn. He's only fourteen.'

'But I was raised on the stuff,' said Uncle Jason, his voice passing from one room on into another. The wind played the trees outside like harps. A little rain spattered on the windows – 'raised on the stuff' passing away into faintness.

Timothy bit his lips and opened his eyes.

'Well, it was all my fault.' Mother was showing them into the kitchen now. 'I tried forcing him. You can't force children, you only make them sick, and then they never get a taste for things. Look at Bion, now, he was thirteen before he . . .'

'I understand,' murmured Uncle Jason. 'Timothy will come around.'

'I'm sure he will,' said Mother, defiantly.

Candle flames quivered as shadows crossed and recrossed the dozen musty rooms. Timothy was cold. He smelled the hot tallow in his nostrils and instinctively he grabbed at a candle and walked with it around and about the house, pretending to straighten the crêpe.

'*Timothy*,' someone whispered behind a patterned wall, hissing and sizzling and sighing the words, '*Timothy is afraid of the dark.*'

Leonard's voice. Hateful Leonard!

'I like the candle, that's all,' said Timothy in a reproachful whisper.

More lightning, more thunder. Cascades of roaring laughter. Bangings and clickings and shouts and rustles of clothing. Clammy fog swept through the front door. Out of the fog, settling his wings, stalked a tall man.

'Uncle Einar!'

Timothy propelled himself on his thin legs, straight through the fog, under the green webbing shadows. He threw himself across Einar's arms. Einar lifted him.

'You've wings, Timothy!' He tossed the boy light as thistles. 'Wings, Timothy: fly!' Faces wheeled under. Darkness rotated. The house blew away. Timothy felt breezelike. He flapped his arms. Einar's fingers caught and threw him once more to the ceiling. The ceiling rushed down like a charred wall. 'Fly, Timothy!' shouted Einar, loud and deep. 'Fly with wings! Wings!'

He felt an exquisite ecstasy in his shoulder blades, as if roots grew, burst to explode and blossom into new, moist membrane. He babbled wild stuff; again Einar hurled him high.

The autumn wind broke in a tide on the house, rain crashed down, shaking the beams, causing chandeliers to tilt their enraged candle lights. And the one hundred relatives peered out from every black, enchanted room, circling inward, all shapes and sizes, to where Einar balanced the child like a baton in the roaring spaces.

'Enough!' shouted Einar, at last.

Timothy, deposited on the floor timbers, exaltedly, exhaustedly fell against Uncle Einar, sobbing happily. 'Uncle, uncle, uncle!'

'Was it good, flying? Eh, Timothy?' said Uncle Einar, bending down, patting Timothy's head. 'Good, good.'

It was coming toward dawn. Most had arrived and were ready to bed down for the daylight, sleep motionlessly with no sound until the following sunset, when they would shout out of their mahogany boxes for the revelry.

Uncle Einar, followed by dozens of others, moved toward the cellar. Mother directed them downward to the crowded row on row of highly polished boxes. Einar, his wings like sea-green tarpaulins tented behind him, moved with a curious whistling down the passageway; where his wings touched they made a sound of drumheads gently beaten.

Upstairs, Timothy lay wearily thinking, trying to like the darkness. There was so much you could do in darkness that people couldn't criticise you for, because they never saw you. He *did* like the night, but it was a qualified liking: sometimes there was so much night he cried out in rebellion.

In the cellar, mahogany doors sealed downward, drawn in by pale hands. In corners, certain relatives circled three times to lie, heads on paws, eyelids shut. The sun rose. There was a sleeping.

Sunset. The revel exploded like a bat nest struck full, shrieking out, fluttering, spreading. Box doors banged wide. Steps rushed up from cellar damp. More late guests, kicking on front and back portals, were admitted.

It rained, and sodden visitors laid their capes, their water-pelleted hats, their sprinkled veils upon Timothy who bore them to a closet. The rooms were crowd-packed. The laughter of one cousin, shot from one room, angled off the wall of another, ricocheted, banked and returned to Timothy's ears from a fourth room, accurate and cynical.

A mouse ran across the floor.

'I know you, Niece Leibersrouter!' exclaimed Father around him but not to him. The dozens of towering people pressed in against him, elbowed him, ignored him.

Finally, he turned and slipped away up the stairs.

He called softly, 'Cecy. Where are you now, Cecy?'

She waited a long while before answering. 'In the Imperial Valley,' she murmured faintly. 'Beside the Salton Sea, near the

233

mud pots and the steam and the quiet. I'm inside a farmer's wife. I'm sitting on a front porch. I can make her move if I want, or do anything or think anything. The sun's going down.'

'What's it like, Cecy?'

'You can hear the mud pots hissing,' she said, slowly, as if speaking in a church. 'Little grey heads of steam push up the mud like bald men rising in the thick syrup, head first, out in the broiling channels. The grey heads rip like rubber fabric, collapse with noises like wet lips moving. And feathery plumes of steam escape from the ripped tissue. And there is a smell of deep sulphurous burning and old time. The dinosaur has been abroiling here ten million years.'

'Is he done yet, Cecy?'

The mouse spiralled three women's feet and vanished into a corner. Moments later a beautiful woman rose up out of nothing and stood in the corner, smiling her white smile at them all.

Something huddled against the flooded pane of the kitchen window. It sighed and wept and tapped continually, pressed against the glass, but Timothy could make nothing of it, he saw nothing. In imagination he was outside staring in. The rain was on him, the wind at him, and the taper-dotted darkness inside was inviting. Waltzes were being danced; tall thin figures pirouetted to outlandish music. Stars of light flickered off lifted bottles; small clods of earth crumbled from casques, and a spider fell and went silently legging over the floor.

Timothy shivered. He was inside the house again. Mother was calling him to run here, run there, help, serve, out to the kitchen now, fetch this, fetch that, bring the plates, heap the food – on and on – the party happened.

'Yes, he's done. Quite done.' Cecy's calm sleeper's lips turned up. The languid words fell slowly from her shaping mouth. 'Inside this woman's skull I am, looking out, watching the sea that does not move, and is so quiet it makes you afraid. I sit on the porch and wait for my husband to come home. Occasionally, a fish leaps, falls back, starlight edging it. The valley, the sea, the few cars, the wooden porch, my rocking chair, myself, the silence.'

'What now, Cecy?'

'I'm getting up from my rocking chair,' she said.

'Yes?'

'I'm walking off the porch, toward the mud pots. Planes fly over, like primordial birds. Then it is quiet, so quiet.'

'How long will you stay inside her, Cecy?'

'Until I've listened and looked and felt enough: until I've changed her life some way. I'm walking off the porch and along the wooden boards. My feet knock on the planks, tiredly, slowly.'

'And now?'

'Now the sulphur fumes are all around me. I stare at the bubbles as they break and smooth. A bird darts by my temple, shrieking. Suddenly I am in the bird and fly away! And as I fly inside my new small glass-bead eyes I see a woman below me, on a boardwalk, take one, two, three steps forward into the mud pots. I hear a sound as of a boulder plunged into molten depths. I keep flying; circle back. I see a white hand, like a spider, wriggle and disappear into the grey lava pool. The lava seals over. Now I'm flying home, swift, swift, swift!'

Something clapped hard against the window, Timothy started.

Cecy flicked her eyes wide, bright, full, happy, exhilarated.

'Now I'm *home*!' she said.

After a pause, Timothy ventured, 'The Homecoming's on. And everybody's here.'

'Then why are you upstairs?' She took his hand. 'Well, ask me.' She smiled slyly. 'Ask me what you came to ask.'

'I didn't come to ask anything,' he said. 'Well, almost nothing. Well – oh, Cecy!' It came from him in one long rapid flow. 'I want to do something at the party to make them look at me, something to make me good as them, something to make me belong, but there's nothing I can do and I feel funny and, well, I thought you might . . .'

'I might,' she said, closing her eyes, smiling inwardly. 'Stand up straight. Stand very still.' He obeyed. 'Now, shut your eyes and blank out your thought.'

He stood very straight and thought of nothing, or at least thought of thinking nothing.

She sighed. 'Shall we go downstairs now, Timothy?' Like a hand into a glove, Cecy was within him.

'Look, everybody!' Timothy held the glass of warm red liquid. He held up the glass so that the whole house turned to watch him. Aunts, uncles, cousins, brothers, sisters!

He drank it straight down.

He jerked a hand at his sister Laura. He held her gaze, whispering to her in a subtle voice that kept her silent, frozen. He felt tall as the trees as he walked to her. The party now slowed. It waited on all sides of him, watching. From all the room doors the faces peered. They were not laughing. Mother's face was astonished. Dad looked bewildered, but pleased and getting prouder every instant.

He nipped Laura, gently, over the neck vein. The candle flames swayed drunkenly. The wind climbed around on the roof outside. The relatives stared from all the doors. He popped toadstools into his mouth, swallowed, then beat his arms against his flanks and circled. 'Look, Uncle Einar! I can fly, at last!' Beat went his hands. Up and down pumped his feet. The faces flashed past him.

At the top of the stairs flapping, he heard his mother cry, 'Stop, Timothy!' far below. 'Hey!' shouted Timothy, and leaped off the top of the well, threshing.

Halfway down, the wings he thought he owned dissolved. He screamed. Uncle Einar caught him.

Timothy flailed whitely in the receiving arms. A voice burst out of his lips, unbidden. 'This is Cecy! This is Cecy! Come see me, all of you, upstairs, first room on the left!' Followed by a long trill of high laughter. Timothy tried to cut it off with his tongue.

Everybody was laughing. Einar set him down. Running through the crowding blackness as the relatives flowed upstairs toward Cecy's room to congratulate her, Timothy banged the front door open.

'Cecy, I hate you, I hate you!'

By the sycamore tree, in deep shadow, Timothy spewed out his dinner, sobbed bitterly and threshed in a pile of autumn leaves. Then he lay still. From his blouse pocket, from the protection of the matchbox he used for his retreat, the spider crawled forth. Spid walked along Timothy's arm. Spid explored up his neck to his ear and climbed in the ear to tickle it. Timothy shook his head. 'Don't, Spid. Don't.'

The feathery touch of a tentative feeler probing his eardrum set Timothy shivering. 'Don't Spid!' He sobbed somewhat less.

The spider travelled down his cheek, took a station under the boy's nose, looked up into the nostrils as if to seek the brain, and then clambered softly up over the rim of the nose to sit, to squat there peering at Timothy with green gem eyes until Timothy filled with ridiculous laughter. 'Go away, Spid!'

Timothy sat up, rustling the leaves. The land was very bright with the moon. In the house he could hear the faint ribaldry as Mirror, Mirror was played. Celebrants shouted dimly muffled, as they tried to identify those of themselves whose reflections did not, had not ever appeared in a glass.

'Timothy.' Uncle Einar's wings spread and twitched and came in with a sound like kettledrums. Timothy felt himself plucked up like a thimble and set upon Einar's shoulder. 'Don't feel badly, Nephew Timothy. Each to his own, each in his own way. How much better things are for you. How rich. The world's dead for us. We've seen so much of it, believe me. Life's best to those who live the least of it. It's worth more per ounce, Timothy, remember that.'

The rest of the black morning, from midnight on, Uncle Einar led him about the house, from room to room, weaving and singing. A horde of late arrivals set the entire hilarity off afresh. Great-great-great-great and a thousand more great-greats Grand mother was there, wrapped in Egyptian cerements. She said not a word, but lay straight as a burnt ironing board against the wall, her eye hollows cupping a distant, wise, silent glimmering. At the breakfast at four in the morning, one-thousand-odd greats Grandmamma was stiffly seated at the head of the longest table.

The numerous young cousins caroused at the crystal punch bowl. Their shiny olive-pit eyes, their conical, devilish faces and curly bronze hair hovered over the drinking table, their hard-soft, half-girl half-boy bodies wrestling against each other as they got unpleasantly, sullenly drunk. The wind got higher, the stars burned with fiery intensity, the noises redoubled, the dances quickened, the drinking became more positive. To Timothy there were thousands of things to hear and watch. The many darknesses roiled, bubbled, the many faces passed and repassed. . . .

'Listen!'

The party held its breath. Far away the town clock struck its chimes, saying six o'clock. The party was ending. In time to the rhythm of the striking clock, their one hundred voices began to sing songs that were four hundred years old, songs Timothy could not know. Arms twined, circling slowly, they sang, and somewhere in the cold distance of the morning the town clock finished out its chimes and quieted.

Timothy sang. He knew no words, no tune, yet the words and tune came round and high and good. And he gazed at the closed door at the top of the stairs.

'Thanks, Cecy,' he whispered. 'You're forgiven. Thanks.'

Then he just relaxed and let the words move, with Cecy's voice, free from his lips.

Goodbyes were said, there was a great rustling. Mother and Father stood at the door to shake hands and kiss each departing relative in turn. The sky beyond the open door coloured in the east. A cold wind entered. And Timothy felt himself seized and settled in one body after another, felt Cecy press him into Uncle Fry's head so he stared from the wrinkled leather face, then leaped in a flurry of leaves up over the house and awakening hills. . . .

Then, loping down a dirt path, he felt his red eyes burning, his fur pelt rimed with morning, as inside Cousin William he panted through a hollow and dissolved away. . . .

Like a pebble in Uncle Einar's mouth, Timothy flew in a webbed thunder, filling the sky. And then he was back, for all time, in his own body.

In the growing dawn, the last few were embracing and crying and thinking how the world was becoming less a place for them. There had been a time when they had met every year, but now decades passed with no reconciliation. 'Don't forget,' someone cried, 'we meet in Salem in 1970!'

Salem. Timothy's numbed mind turned the words over. Salem 1970. And there would be Uncle Fry and a thousand-times-great Grandmother in her withered cerements, and Mother and Father and Ellen and Laura and Cecy and all the rest. But would he be there? Could he be certain of staying alive until then?

With one last withering blast, away they all went, so many scarves, so many fluttery mammals, so many sere leaves, so many whining and clustering noises, so many midnights and insanities and dreams.

Mother shut the door. Laura picked up a broom. 'No,' said Mother. 'We'll clean tonight. Now we need sleep.' And the

Family vanished down cellar and upstairs. And Timothy moved in the crêpe-littered hall, his head down. Passing a party mirror, he saw the pale mortality of his face all cold and trembling.

'Timothy,' said Mother.

She came to touch her hand on his face. 'Son,' she said, 'we love you. Remember that. We all love you. No matter how different you are, no matter if you leave us one day.' She kissed his cheek. 'And if and when you die, your bones will lie undisturbed, we'll see to that. You'll lie at ease for ever, and I'll come visit every All-Hallows' Eve and tuck you in the more secure.'

The house was silent. Far away the wind went over a hill with its last cargo of dark bats, echoing, chittering.

Timothy walked up the steps, one by one, crying to himself all the way.

Never Bet the Devil Your Head

Edgar Allan Poe

———————

No collection of horror stories would be complete without a tale by the great master of the genre — the man on whom so many writers have modelled themselves, Edgar Allan Poe. Although Poe did not write a story directly concerned with either Witchcraft, Black Magic or Voodoo, he was constantly fascinated by malign and evil forces and employed them in his tales. The difficulty facing an anthologiser of Poe is to avoid republishing material which has already appeared countless times, and I count myself fortunate to have got a copy of this particularly rare story which has not been in print for over twenty-five years. If I say it features the Devil and is something of an object lesson to anyone who may think there is no danger in tampering with the power of the Evil One, I have probably said enough for enthusiasts to know they are in for something special. Never Bet The Devil Your Head is a masterpiece of black humour and was written by Poe as he neared the end of his monumentally talented but wretched and tormented life.

IT IS NOT my design to vituperate my deceased friend, Toby Dammit. He was a sad dog, it is true, and a dog's death it was that he died; but he himself was not to blame for his vices. They grew out of a personal defect in his mother. She did her best in the way of flogging him while an infant — for duties to her well-regulated mind were always pleasures, and babies, like tough steaks, or the modern Greek olive trees, are invariably the better for beating — but, poor woman! she had the misfortune to be left-handed, and a child flogged left-handedly had better be left unflogged. The world revolves from right to left. It will not do to whip a baby from left to right. If each blow in the proper direction drives an evil propensity out, it follows that every thump in an opposite one knocks its quota of wickedness in.

I was often present at Toby's chastisements and, even by the way in which he kicked, I could perceive that he was getting worse and worse every day. At last I saw through the tears in my eyes, that there was no hope for the villain at all; so, one day, when he had been cuffed until he grew so black in the face that one might have mistaken him for a little African, and no effect had been produced beyond that of making him wriggle himself into a fit, I could stand it no longer, but went down upon my knees forthwith, and, uplifting my voice, made prophecy of his ruin.

The fact is that his precocity in vice was awful. At five months of age he used to get into such passions that he was unable to articulate. At six months I caught him gnawing a pack of cards. At seven months, he was in the constant habit of catching and kissing the female babies. At eight months, he peremptorily refused to put his signature to the temperance pledge. Thus he went on increasing in iniquity, month after month, until, at the close of the first year, he not only insisted upon wearing moustaches, but had contracted a propensity for cursing and swearing, and for backing his assertions by bets.

Through this latter most ungentlemanly practice, the ruin which I had predicted to Toby Dammit overtook him at last. The fashion had 'grown with his growth, and strengthened with his strength', so that, when he came to be a man, he could scarcely utter a sentence without interlarding it with a proposition to gamble. Not that he actually laid wagers – no. I will do my friend the justice to say that he would as soon have laid eggs. With him the thing was a mere formula – nothing more. His expressions on this head had no meaning attached to them whatever. They were simple, if not altogether innocent expletives – imaginative phrases wherewith to round off a sentence. When he said, 'I'll bet you so and so', nobody ever thought of taking him up; but still I could not help thinking it my duty to put him down. The habit was an immoral one, and so I told him.

It was a vulgar one – this I begged him to believe. It was dis-countenanced by society – here I said nothing but the truth. It was forbidden by Act of Congress – here I had not the slightest intention of telling a lie. I remonstrated – but to no purpose. I demonstrated – in vain. I entreated – he smiled. I implored – he laughed. I preached – he sneered. I threatened – he swore. I kicked him – he called for the police. I pulled his nose – he blew it, and offered to bet the Devil his head that I would not venture to try that experiment again.

Poverty was another vice which the peculiar physical de-ficiency of Dammit's mother had entailed upon her son. He was detestably poor; and this was the reason, no doubt, that his expletive expressions about betting seldom took a pecuniary turn. I will not be bound to say that I ever heard him make use of such a figure of speech as 'I'll bet you a dollar'. It was usually 'I'll bet you what you please', or 'I'll bet you what you dare', or 'I'll bet you a trifle', or else, more significantly still, 'I'll bet the Devil my head'.

This latter form seemed to please him best: perhaps because it involved the least risk; for Dammit had become excessively parsimonious. Had any one taken him up, his head was small, and thus his loss would have been small, too. But these are my own reflections, and I am by no means sure that I am right in attributing them to him. At all events the phrase in question grew daily in favour, notwithstanding the gross impropriety of a man betting his brains like bank notes: – but this was a point which my friend's perversity of disposition would not permit him to comprehend. In the end, he abandoned all other forms of wager, and gave himself up to 'I'll bet the Devil my head', with a pertinacity and exclusiveness of devotion that displeased not less than it surprised me.

I am always displeased by circumstances for which I cannot account. Mysteries force a man to think, and so injure his health. The truth is, there was something in the air with which Mr

Dammit was wont to give utterance to his offensive expression – something in his manner of enunciation – which at first interested and afterwards made me very uneasy – something which, for want of a more definite term at present, I must be permitted to call queer. I began not to like it at all. Mr Dammit's soul was in a perilous state. I resolved to bring all my eloquence into play to save it. I vowed to serve him as St Patrick, in the Irish chronicle, is said to have served the toad, that is to say, 'awaken him to a sense of his situation'. I addressed myself to the task forthwith. Once more I betook myself to remonstrance. Again I collected my energies for a final attempt at expostulation.

When I had made an end of my lecture, Mr Dammit indulged himself in some very equivocal behaviour.

I can call to mind only the heads of his discourse. He would be obliged to me if I would hold my tongue. He wished none of my advice. He despised all my insinuations. He was old enough to take care of himself. Did I still think him Baby Dammit? Did I mean to say anything against his character? Did I intend to insult him? Was I a fool? Was my maternal parent aware, in a word, of my absence from the domiciliary residence? He would put this latter question to me as to a man of veracity, and he would bind himself to abide by my reply. Once more he would demand explicitly if my mother knew that I was out. My confusion, he said, betrayed me, and he would be willing to bet the Devil his head that she did not.

Mr Dammit did not pause for my rejoinder. Turning upon his heel, he left my presence with undignified precipitation. It was well for him that he did so. My feelings had been wounded. Even my anger had been aroused. For once I would have taken him upon his insulting wager. I would have won for the Arch-Enemy Mr Dammit's little head – for the fact is, my mamma was very well aware of my merely temporary absence from home.

But *Khoda shefa midehed* – Heaven gives relief – as the Mussulmen say when you tread upon their toes. It was in pursuance of my duty that I had been insulted, and I bore the insult like a man. It now seemed to me, however, that I had done all that could be required of me, in the case of this miserable individual, and I resolved to trouble him no longer with my counsel, but to leave him to his conscience and himself. But although I forbore to intrude with my advice, I could not bring myself to give up his society altogether. I even went so far as to humour some of his less reprehensible propensities; and there were times when I found myself lauding his wicked jokes, as epicures do mustard, with tears in my eyes: so profoundly did it grieve me to hear his evil talk.

One fine day, having strolled out together, arm in arm, our route led us in the direction of a river. There was a bridge, and we resolved to cross it. It was roofed over, by way of protection from the weather, and the archway having but few windows, was thus very uncomfortably dark. As we entered the passage, the contrast between the external glare, and the interior gloom, struck heavily upon my spirits. Not so upon those of the unhappy Dammit, who offered to bet the Devil his head that I was hipped. He seemed to be in an unusual good humour. He was excessively lively – so much so that I entertained I know not what of uneasy suspicion. It is not impossible that he was affected with the transcendentals. I am not well enough versed, however, in the diagnosis of this disease to speak with decision upon the point; and unhappily there were none of my friends of the 'Dial' present. I suggest the idea, nevertheless, because of a certain species of austere Merry-Andrewism which seemed to beset my poor friend, and caused him to make quite a Tom-fool of himself. Nothing would serve him but wriggling and skipping about under and over everything that came in his way; now shouting out, and now lisping out, all manner of odd little and big words, yet preserving the gravest face in the world all the time. I really could not make up my mind whether to kick or to pity him. At length, having passed nearly across the bridge, we approached the termination of the foot way, when our progress was impeded by a turnstile of some height. Through this I made my way quietly, pushing it around as usual. But this turn would not serve the turn of Mr Dammit. He insisted upon leaping the stile, and said he could cut a pigeon-wing over it in the air. Now this, conscientiously speaking, I did not think he could do. The best pigeon-winger over all kinds of style was my friend Mr Carlyle, and as I knew he could not do it, I would not believe that it could be done by Toby Dammit. I therefore told him, in so many words, that he was a braggadocio, and could not do what he said. For this, I had reason to be very sorry afterwards; for he straightway offered to bet the Devil his head that he could.

I was about to reply, notwithstanding my previous resolutions, with some remonstrance against his impiety, when I heard, close at my elbow, a slight cough, which sounded very much like the ejaculation 'ahem!' I started, and looked about me in surprise. My glance at length fell into a nook of the framework of the bridge, and upon the figure of a little lame old gentleman of venerable aspect. Nothing could be more reverend than his whole appearance; for he not only had on a full suit of black, but his shirt was perfectly clean and his collar turned very neatly down over a white cravat, while his hair was parted in front like a girl's. His hands were clasped pensively together over his stomach, and his two eyes were carefully rolled up into the top of his head.

Upon observing him more closely, I perceived that he wore a black silk apron over his small clothes; and this was a thing which I thought very odd. Before I had time to make any remark, however, upon so singular a circumstance, he interrupted me with a second 'ahem!'

To this observation I was not immediately prepared to reply. The fact is, remarks of this laconic nature are nearly unanswerable. I am not ashamed to say, therefore, that I turned to Mr Dammit for assistance.

'Dammit,' said I, 'what are you about? don't you hear? – the gentleman says "ahem!" ' I looked sternly at my friend while I thus addressed him; for to say the truth, I felt particularly puzzled, and when a man is particularly puzzled he must knit his brows and look savage, or else he is pretty sure to look like a fool.

'Dammit,' observed I – although this sounded very much like an oath, than which nothing was further from my thoughts – 'Dammit,' I suggested – 'the gentleman says "ahem!" '

'You don't say so?' gasped he at length, after turning more colours than a pirate runs up, one after the other, when chased by a man-o'-war. 'Are you quite sure he said that? Well, at all events, I am in for it now, and may as well put on a bold face upon the matter. Here goes then – ahem!'

At this the little old gentleman seemed pleased – God only knows why. He left his station at the nook of the bridge, limped forward with a gracious air, took Dammit by the hand and shook it cordially, looking all the while straight up in his face with an air of the most unadulterated benignity which it is possible for the mind of man to imagine.

'I am quite sure you will win it, Dammit,' said he with the frankest of all smiles, 'but we are obliged to have a trial, you know, for the sake of mere form.'

'Ahem!' replied my friend, taking off his coat with a deep sigh, tying a pocket-handkerchief around his waist, and producing an unaccountable alteration in his countenance by twisting up his eyes, and bringing down the corners of his mouth – 'ahem!' And 'ahem!' said he again, after a pause; and not another word more than 'ahem!' did I ever know him to say after that. 'Aha!' thought I, without expressing myself aloud – 'this is quite a remarkable silence on the part of Toby Dammit, and is no doubt a consequence of his verbosity upon a previous occasion. One extreme induces another. I wonder if he has forgotten the many unanswerable questions which he propounded to me so fluently on the day when I gave him my last lecture? At all events, he is cured of the transcendentals.'

The old gentleman now took Toby by the arm, and led him more into the shade of the bridge – a few paces back from the turnstile. 'My good fellow,' he said, 'I make it a point of conscience to allow you this much run. Wait here, till I take my place by the stile, so that I may see whether you go over it handsomely, and transcendentally, and don't omit any flourishes of the pigeon-wing. A mere form, you know. I will say, "one, two, three, and away." Mind you start at the word "away".' Here he took his position by the stile, paused a moment as if in profound reflection, then looked up and, I thought, smiled very slightly, then tightened the strings of his apron, then he took a long look at Dammit, and finally gave the word as agreed upon – 'One – two – three – and away!'

Punctually at the word 'away', my friend set off in a strong gallop. The stile was not very high, nor yet very low, but upon the whole I felt sure that he would clear it. And then what if he did not? – ah, that was the question – what if he did not? 'What right,' said I, 'had the old gentleman to make any other gentleman jump? Who is he? If he asks me to jump, I won't do it, that's flat, and I don't care who the devil he is.'

The bridge, as I say, was arched and covered in, in a very ridiculous manner, and there was a most uncomfortable echo about it at all times – an echo which I never before so particularly observed as when I uttered the four last words of my remark.

But what I said, or what I thought, or what I heard, occupied only an instant. In less than five seconds from his starting, my poor Toby had taken the leap. I saw him run nimbly, and spring grandly from the floor of the bridge, cutting the most awful flourishes with his legs as he went up. I saw him high in the air, pigeon-winging it to admiration just over the top of the stile; and of course I thought it an unusually singular thing that he did not continue to go over. But the whole leap was the affair of a moment, and, before I had a chance to make any profound reflections, down came Mr Dammit on the flat of his back, on the same side of the stile from which he had started. At the same instant I saw the old gentleman limping off at top speed, having caught and wrapped up in his apron something that fell heavily into it from the darkness of the arch just over the turnstile. I was completely astonished at what had happened and stood rooted to the spot for several moments. When I did collect my senses and hurried to my friend's aid I immediately wished I had not.

For his head had been completely severed from his body -- and no matter how much I searched I could find no trace of it whatsoever.

Acknowledgements

The editor is grateful to the following for permission to include copyright material in this collection:

The Executors of the Estate of H P Lovecraft, August Derleth and Scott Meredith Literary Agency for *The Peabody Heritage* by H P Lovecraft; the Executors of the Estate of W B Seabrook for *The Witch's Vengeance* by W B Seabrook; the Hutchinson Publishing Group and Dennis Wheatley for *The Snake* by Dennis Wheatley; Scott Meredith Literary Agency and August Derleth for *Prince Borgia's Mass* by August Derleth; Messrs A P Watt for *Secret Worship* by Algernon Blackwood; Basil Copper for his story *Archives of the Dead*; 'Weird Tales' and Robert Bloch for *Mother of Serpents* by Robert Bloch; Scott Meredith Literary Agency and Arthur J Burks for *Cerimarie* by Arthur J Burks; A M Heath & Co Ltd and Shirley Jackson for *The Witch* by Shirley Jackson; A D Peters & Co and Ray Bradbury for *Homecoming* by Ray Bradbury.

AN ENSIGN CRIME

Seek and Destroy
By RAY OWEN

WPS agent Steve Ray had pretty well convinced himself that the home ground assignment would produce little scope for exercising his talents. If his chief really wanted to put him on the shelf he might as well have sent him to South America to be run over by a bus and have done with him.

For a man who liked his tasks to be tough and his women to be at least warm if not willing, it was something of a let-down to find a girl he had lately bedded with suffering from a permanent chill in her Manhattan apartment. And when a chaser was provided in the shape of a threat to his own existence on a main thoroughfare, the overall complexion acquired a new hue for Ray, and the message came through in large letters – CUP.

His old enemies had followed him from Europe and were in the process of setting him up for a long drop.

25p

WORLD DISTRIBUTORS (Manchester) LTD

AN ENSIGN CRIME

The Killer's Conscience
By JARED INGERSOL

Homicide Inspector Ed Robbin had to start with
nothing more in the way of a clue than the faint and
alluring fragrance of perfume in the dead man's
apartment, when he was assigned to the murder of
financier Prentice Foster.
He located the wearer of that perfume, who was *not*
the murderer, and he also guessed who the killer was!
After that he had to get the physical as well as the
circumstantial evidence, piece by piece, before he
dared let the murderer know he was after him. It
wasn't an easy task, and there were many unpleasant
surprises in store before the killer was finally brought
to justice.

25p

WORLD DISTRIBUTORS (Manchester) LTD

AN ENSIGN CRIME

Hammerhead Reef
By KEITH CONWAY

Caloundra was just a sleepy Queensland resort
town where Jeff Curtin enjoyed the easy life abroad
his schooner. Until the blonde came.
Then all hell broke loose.
She nearly got Curtin killed the by savage shark
packs of Hammerhead Reef. A mystery sub. shot
up his boat and the Navy called him a liar when
he complained. His mate was murdered. The
beautiful Si-lim came out of nowhere, accompanied
by a giant gunman, and a twisted dwarf. A
megalomaniac sent him on a mind-bending, hurtling
nightmare through Outer Space.
There were illegal immigrants and a 100-mile long
island of sand where Curtin found himself an
unwilling contender in the sparring preliminaries to
World War III.
By the time it was over, he was glad to get back
to the killer shark packs for a little friendly
company.

25p

WORLD DISTRIBUTORS (Manchester) LTD

AN ENSIGN CRIME

They Call it Murder

By PETER CHAMBERS

Mark Preston was minding his own business in a
pleasant bar when Steiner called him. The
newspaperman wanted a few enquiries made, so
Preston obliged. Soon he was being threatened,
beaten up, and finally dragged out of bed as a
murder suspect.

Rourke of Homicide could smell a frame, and gave
Preston a chance to get at the truth before locking
him up. The trail led to some strange people, like
Tuck McGonigle, local representative for the
System. There was Skinny, the ferocious bartender,
and a man named Butterworth who controlled his
temper with bright orange pills. Luckily, there were
also the dames, Luscious Clementina Daws, the
most unlikely secretary Preston ever encountered.
There was curvy Sheila Bishop, whose psychedelic
apartment hurt his eyes.

Preston disliked jail and was glad to be bailed out.
Had he known what for, he'd probably have stayed
inside.

25p

WORLD DISTRIBUTORS (Manchester) LTD